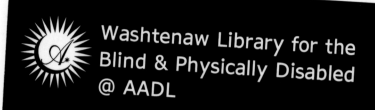 Washtenaw Library for the Blind & Physically Disabled @ AADL

If you are only able to read large print, you may qualify for WLBPD @ AADL services, including receiving audio and large print books by mail at no charge.

For more information:

Email • wlbpd@aadl.org
Phone • (734) 327-4224
Website • wlbpd.aadl.org

Sheila Radley has written several crime novels, the first of which, *Death and the Maiden*, was shortlisted for the Crime Writers' Association John Creasey Award. She lives in Norfolk.

NEW BLOOD FROM OLD BONES

Tudor England, 1530: The town of Castleacre, Norfolk, ancestral home of the Ackland family, is dependent upon the great Cluniac Priory that overshadows it. When Will Ackland, younger son of an impoverished gentleman, returns home after years abroad he finds his evil-tempered brother Gilbert cursing the Prior's new bailiff for his exactions. Then a corpse is discovered, not only stabbed but mutilated beyond recognition. Is it the Prior's bailiff? If so, Gilbert is the chief suspect. But Will discovers that the bailiff had other enemies, and he begins to unravel a tangle of concealed passion that leaves more than one man dead.

Books by Sheila Radley
Published by The House of Ulverscroft:

THE CHIEF INSPECTOR'S DAUGHTER
BLOOD ON THE HAPPY HIGHWAY
FATE WORSE THAN DEATH
WHO SAW HIM DIE?
THIS WAY OUT
CROSS MY HEART AND HOPE TO DIE
FAIR GAME

SHEILA RADLEY

NEW BLOOD
FROM
OLD BONES

A Tudor Mystery

Complete and Unabridged

ULVERSCROFT
Leicester

First published in Great Britain in 1998 by
Constable & Company Limited
London

First Large Print Edition
published 2000
by arrangement with
Constable & Company Limited
London

British Library CIP Data

Radley, Sheila, *1928 –*
New blood from old bones.—Large print ed.—
Ulverscroft large print series: mystery
1. Great Britain—History—Henry VIII,
1509 – 1547 —Fiction
2. Detective and mystery stories
3. Large type books
I. Title
823.9'14 [F]

ISBN 0–7089–4199–0

Published by
F. A. Thorpe (Publishing) Ltd.
Anstey, Leicestershire

Set by Words & Graphics Ltd.
Anstey, Leicestershire
Printed and bound in Great Britain by
T. J. International Ltd., Padstow, Cornwall

This book is printed on acid-free paper

To our friends Kay, Alan and Kim,
with special thanks to Kim,
who drew the map

Author's Note

Castle Acre, a Norfolk village with the ruins of a Norman castle on one side, and Cluniac priory on the other, has provided the setting for this book. But I have taken liberties with it's history and topography, and the resulting Castleacre is a place of fiction.

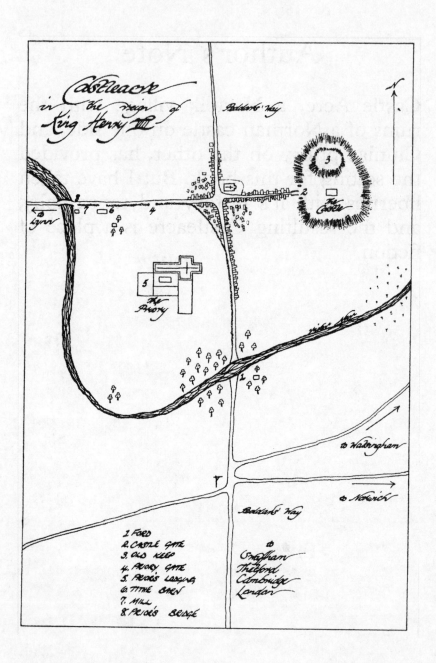

Castleacre in the reign of King Henry VIII

Palmers' Way

N

→ to Lynn

8

7 6 4

2

3 The Castle

5 The Priory

to the hill

1

to Wadingham →

to Norwich →

Palmers' Way

1. FORD
2. CASTLE GATE
3. OLD KEEP
4. PRIORY GATE
5. PRIOR'S LODGING
6. TITHE BARN
7. MILL
8. PRIOR'S BRIDGE

to
Swaffham
Thetford
Cambridge
London

1

On a yellow day in September in the year 1530, when fields were in stubble after harvest and crab-apples hung deceitfully ripe from hedgerows along the dusty way, Will Ackland came riding home from the foreign wars.

It had taken him a long time to make this homecoming. The high-spirited young man who had left his law books and his new wife to volunteer for the sport of war had been changed by the experience. Pain and fear of death had matured him, and so had grief. Now, at the age of thirty-one, he was lean and quietly spoken, with a dry wit and watchful grey-green eyes under thick dark brows.

Like other folk on the road — pilgrims and pedlars, vagabonds, messengers, carters, rent-collectors, packhorse carriers, drovers with their cattle, wayfarers of every rank, and those who went silently about the King's business — he was stained by the sweat and dust of travel. His sturdy young servant, who rode laggardly behind him, had more than his share of the grime but none of Will's patience.

'Shall we never be at Castleacre?' complained Ned Pye. 'I've seen more than enough of your dull Norfolk already,' he added, knowing he was safely out of reach of a box on the ear.

His master paid no heed. Ned had been in his service from the age of eighteen, in the King's army and out of it, and Will allowed him an occasional sauciness. He had good reason to be thankful for Ned's loyalty and strength.

Will Ackland had lain wounded in a Normandy priory, likely to die from loss of blood, when King Henry VIII's second French war ended in dishonour. Instead of enforcing his claim to the French throne, the King had been obliged by lack of funds to sue for peace without having gained one yard of land beyond Calais. But the deep arrow wounds in Will's thigh took so long to heal that it was many weeks before he and Ned could return to England.

There, in Dover, he had found letters from Castleacre awaiting him with tragic news. While he was away, his wife Anne had died giving birth to their child. Believing in his anguish that there was nothing for him in England, Will had immediately taken ship again for France.

At Calais he had fallen in with an esquire

he had known in London, where they were students of the law at Gray's Inn. The esquire was now on his way to Paris in the service of a royal envoy, an English nobleman. With one of his attendants sick of a fever, and finding that Will spoke fluent French after his stay in the priory, the nobleman had offered him a place in his service.

In the following years Will Ackland and his servant had travelled between the English court and those of France, the Emperor and the Pope. It was those years of being in silent attendance when great men conferred, serving his noble master by assessing what lay concealed behind the smooth words of foreign ministers of state, that had taught Will patience and watchfulness. But after four years he had had enough of it.

Though he had kept his distance from Castleacre, letters from his sister who had charge of the child told him how Anne's daughter grew. And now that his grief for his wife had lessened to a permanent ache, sharpening whenever something recalled her to his mind — just as the pain of his wounds, though far less grievous than bereavement, still flared up every now and then — he no longer thought ill of the child for having taken her mother's life.

Elizabeth, that was his daughter's name.

Betsy, they called her. Suddenly anxious to see her, he had given up the salary and perquisites of service, taken sail for England, bought horses at Dover and set out for home. Even so, he had spent two weeks over the ride to Norfolk, lingering in London and in Cambridge while he accustomed himself to being his own man again.

Behind him, as they rode the last few miles, Ned Pye was still grumbling.

A bold young man, with plump cheeks and thatch the colour of new straw, Ned had been sorry to relinquish their former way of life. He had enjoyed travelling to foreign cities, boasting to foreign women, riding sound horses and eating and drinking well at his master's master's expense. On the other hand, being London-born, he would have settled happily enough in that city. But the countryside appealed to him not at all, and he had spent much of the journey singing a tuneless lament for everything he was leaving behind.

'What is it *now*?' demanded Will, out of patience at last, turning in his saddle as he heard Ned trying to stir his unwilling horse to a canter.

'Even in Norfolk they know a nag when they see one!' complained his servant as he came near. 'That woman selling fruit at the wayside — ' He tried to bite a pear he had snatched from her basket, found it rock-hard and hurled it away indignantly. 'She mocked me for riding such a poor mount.'

'She mocked you for not knowing a keeping pear from an eater, more like,' said Will. They were about to overtake a husbandman and his wife, both tottering under the weight of the laden panniers that hung from their shoulder yokes. 'If the horse isn't good enough for you, you must journey on foot. And if it's London you hanker for, you have my leave to turn round and trudge back.'

Ned's eyes rounded at the affront. 'There's small thanks for the man who carried you off the battlefield on his shoulders!'

'You've had my thanks these four years. If you'd sought a rich man's gratitude you should have saved a knight, not a poor student.'

'If only I had,' mourned Ned with a gusty sigh. 'But my tender heart always gets the better of my head . . . Promise me, though, Master Will, that I shall have a good horse when we reach the castle?'

'Ah, the castle,' said Will dryly. 'There'll be a choice of horses for you there — and fountains flowing with wine, and dancing girls, and roasted swan for your dinner too.

Have done, you knave, and ride with reverence, for we're now in Norfolk's holy land.'

They were riding north on an ancient road, the Peddars' Way, that was said to have been made by the old Romans. Straight as a rule for the most part, it ran direct through the town of Castleacre on its way to the sea coast at the Wash. And hereabouts, near the valley of the river Nar, there were so many religious houses — abbeys, priories, nunneries, friaries, as well as chantries and parish churches — that the volume of prayer, so it was said, was enough to keep the saints in permanent attendance upon Norfolk. The strongest sound of the countryside was the call of their bells, echoing and re-echoing far and near.

Hereabouts too, there was a converging of the roads that led pilgrims from all parts of the kingdom towards the great shrine of Our Lady at Walsingham. The Cluniac priory of Castleacre, one of the largest and finest and best-endowed in the entire eastern part of England, provided both a rest for pilgrims before the last day's journey to Walsingham, and a place of pilgrimage on its own account.

On that September day the great bells of

the priory were drawing pilgrims to the shrine of St Matthew at Castleacre. At the forthcoming feast of St Matthew, those crowding into the priory church to repent of their sins and ask for the prayers of the monks could obtain a special indulgence, a remission of the suffering they feared to endure as souls in purgatory after they died.

The priory church, with its richly glazed windows and intricately sculpted stone, had long been a place of great splendour. Gifts of money or valuables had been made not only by penitents, but by those who came to invoke the aid of the saints, or to return thanks for favours received. The wealthy had also made bequests, often of land or property, in return for the saying of masses for the salvation of their souls. In the light of countless votive candles, the many carved and painted images of the saints shone all over with jewels and gold and silver.

The church possessed many saintly relics, but none was more venerated than the relic of St Matthew. Resting within a magnificent shrine, in a glass-sided reliquary adorned with rubies and sapphires, lay two of the bones of the apostle's hand.

This relic had miraculous powers of healing. For two hundred years and more, as chronicled in the reign of King Henry VI by one of the monks of Castleacre, many of the pilgrims who flocked to pray at the shrine had been cured of grievous ailments. But it was on the feast day of St Matthew that pilgrims could hope to witness an even greater miracle.

Then, on the twenty-first day of September each year, at the ringing of the great bell, the reliquary would be lifted down from its glittering shrine. It would be held high by the monks and borne in solemn procession behind the cross, with plainchant, censers, banners and candles, and with the prior and sub-prior wearing their most magnificent priestly copes.

The procession would pass first through every part of the church except the nave, and then out round the cloister, before returning through the great west door. Having passed slowly through the nave, they would halt before the rood screen before re-entering the choir to begin High Mass. And the pilgrims who had squeezed into the crowded nave would press forward, open-mouthed with awe, craning through candlelight and clouds of incense to see for themselves whether the miracle had indeed recurred, and the dry bones of the saint were once again bedewed with blood.

★ ★ ★

Will Ackland reined in his horse. They had crested Bartholomew's Hills, a downland sheep pasture a mile to the south of Castleacre, and the shallow valley of the Nar was spread before them.

He pointed out to Ned Pye the great stone tower, clamouring with the sound of bells, that rose from the valley floor. The top of the tower, rearing high above the trees that marked the course of the river, was shaped to a massive red-tiled point in the style of France, where the Cluniac order had originated.

'There's the priory church of Castleacre. The town lies above and to the east of it, beyond the trees, and the castle to the east of that.'

'I see no castle,' said Ned, disappointed.

'You will when we reach the river. You'll find it much smaller than the priory,' Will warned, but his servant seemed disinclined to believe it.

They rode on, to the place where pilgrims from other parts of England joined the Peddars' Way before continuing to Castleacre or Walsingham. At the crossroads stood a gibbet as a warning to thieves and would-be murderers. Its upright post leaned forward, habituated to a dangling weight on the extended arm, though the thing that swayed there now was light enough, nothing but rags and bones abandoned even by carrion crows. All the travellers skirted it, and crossed themselves as they did so.

Those who were going to Castleacre for St Matthew's feast now filled the road. Some solitary pilgrims strode along in seasoned walking boots, with staves in their hands and scallop shell badges in their hats to signify that they had made the great pilgrimage to the Spanish shrine of St James at Compostella. Of the others, some went penitently barefoot for at least the last mile. Those who sought healing leaned for support on their friends, or were carried on litters. But most of the pilgrims rode in cheerful company, including a group of nuns perched on muleback with their priest and their steward in attendance.

Some distance behind the nuns, but gaining on them, an archdeacon came cantering on a fine horse, accompanied by his chaplain and clerks. Servants rode before him to clear the way, but people were glad enough to move when they recognised his stern face, and the black gown, silver cross and close-fitting black cap that marked his office.

None wanted to offend him, for the

archdeacon travelled the diocese to enquire into the state of each parish church, and the conduct of both clergy and people. Those who offended against church law would be summoned to attend the archdeacon's court, which had power to excommunicate them for heresy, and to fine or imprison for other offences. The church's law touched every part of life, and those who kept well within the common law might still fear being reported to the archdeacon. As a Castleacre blacksmith had once complained to Will, with so many ways to offend — speaking ill of the priest, absence from the church, disturbance within it, failure to pay tithe, bastardy, adultery, fornication — any red-blooded parishioner was hard put to keep out of trouble.

But many travellers were coming to Castleacre with little but profit on their minds. Mingling with the pilgrims were country people laden with extra supplies of vegetables and fruit, butter and cheese. Pedlars and chapmen came from afar with trinkets and pins and bobbins and ribbons, bringing a wealth of news both true and false. Strolling bands of players came to provide entertainment, as did minstrel troupes, and a man with a performing ape, and another leading a dancing bear. And mingling with the crowds, heedless of the stocks in the market place and the gibbet on Bartholomew's Hills, there were sure to be vagabonds, beggars and thieves.

Progress was slow as the crowds moved down the long slope towards the ford, where the Peddars' Way crossed the river to the south of the town. Just before the ford, the road rose over a bank topped by an oak tree. From this bank, as Will remembered from his boyhood, there was a good view of the town and the castle, held in the shallow embrace of the river as it flowed below them and on past the priory to the port of Bishop's Lynn.

Will drew his horse to one side, under the branches of the oak from which he and his schoolfellows had used to spy on travellers coming to the town. Then, as now, those on horseback splashed through the water and those on foot crossed by the upstream stepping stones. The scene was entirely familiar — and yet different, as all homecoming travellers discover when they notice an empty skyline where trees once stood, or find a view blocked by a growing thicket, or see a new roof where there was none before.

The river, though, was just as he remembered it. He breathed pleasurably deep as he watched the weed waving in the clear, fast-flowing chalk stream and smelled the peppery freshness of watercress. He and his friends had often spied on the servant girls who came down from the town to wash linen, and sometimes themselves, at the stepping stones. It was in the deep pool above the stones that he had learned to swim. And further downriver, near the priory, he had once spent an idle afternoon in competition with some of the monks, seeing who would be first to tickle a trout.

Will turned his head as Ned Pye rode up the bank to join him. 'There is the whole of Castleacre,' he announced, with a grand gesture that swept from the riverside priory, itself the size of a small town, up across rising fields to the town proper, overtopped by the tower of the parish church, and so to the walls of his ancestral home. But he spoke with a twitch of amusement, for his servant had always been over-impressed by the knowledge that the Acklands lived in a castle.

Ned's face lengthened with dismay.

'*That* is your castle? But it's ruined!'

'Destroyed two hundred and fifty years ago,' said Will. He laughed at his servant's gloom. 'Why do we need a fortress? We have no enemies to fight, nor noble friends to impress.'

He looked with some affection at the remaining stone walls that had once sur-rounded a castle keep, built on the far side of the valley in the time of the Norman kings to control the crossing of the Nar. The outer walls had been breached in the barons' wars, and had crumbled thereafter from age and disuse. In the reign of King Henry VII the old keep had been used by the Acklands as a quarry, when they had built themselves a dwelling house within the outer walls.

'One of my ancestors sided with a baron who was defeated,' Will explained. 'All his lands, except for the remains of the castle, were seized by the victor and given to the priory. Our family still farmed the land — as my brother Gilbert has done since our father's death — but we are merely impoverished gentlemen, and tenants of the priory.'

Ned Pye shook his head, bemused, as he tried to adjust his ambitions to his master's situation. 'Then — in truth — your family can provide you with nothing?'

'Nothing at all. No money, no land, no property,' said Will. 'I've told you before — I am a penniless younger brother, as you have cause to know from the quality of your horse.'

Ned nodded ruefully. 'I never believed the fountains flowing with wine, nor yet the dancing girls and the roasted swan. But I was sure a castle could provide me with a better mount than this . . . '

'Even if it could, I would never give you a good horse,' said his master. 'Your hands are too hard.'

'Not too hard to tend your wounds until I got you to the French priory!'

'True. And I shall never forget it, with you to remind me so often. Well, you have leave to drink at my expense at an alehouse in the town while we're here — so long as you're sober enough to bring my boots and shaving water every morning.'

'Ha!' snorted Ned Pye. 'I knew there would be a catch in your offer.' He looked with disparagement towards the thatched roofs and gables that climbed higgledy-piggledy up the slope of the valley from the ford and clustered round the parish church. 'By the Mass,' he said, 'I never saw such a poor little town as yours. When can we go back to London?'

'In a week's time. I must return for my final year of studies before I qualify as a barrister,' said Will. 'While I'm here, making the acquaintance of my daughter, you must occupy yourself — but without disgracing my family, if you please. You'll find entertainment enough in the town during St Matthew's feast.'

Will guided his horse down the bank to join the crowds approaching the ford. Ned

Pye followed, grumbling. 'Entertainment?' Will heard him scoff. 'Two poxy jesters and a moth-eaten old bear . . . '

The bear was indeed a poor creature, shambling along some yards ahead of them with its toes turned in. It was docile enough, but muzzled with iron and no doubt clipped about the claws. The thick-set bearward held it on a heavy chain attached to a stake, while his boy followed carrying their pack, and the drum and pipe to which the wretched creature would be made to perform a shuffling dance.

But the water of the river seemed to revive the bear. It stopped to drink deep, then raised its great head and sniffed the air. Suddenly, regardless of people, horses and mules in the way, it plunged downstream, jerking the bearward off his feet though he still hung on to its chain.

There was a great commotion, a shouting and a splashing as folk stumbled out of the animal's path. Nuns scattered like mounted magpies. The archdeacon's fine horse reared, nearly unseating him. The bearward's boy waded after his floundering master, drumming to call the creature to order.

The bear, however, was intent upon reaching a barrier formed halfway across the river by a fallen bough. Debris had built up

16

against the bough, formed of branches and weed and oddments dropped by travellers as they crossed the ford. The largest of these oddments looked like a ragged bundle of cloth, partially floating in the water and rocking a little as the bear splashed towards it.

By this time the bearward had regained his feet, though up to his haunches in the river. Cursing and belabouring the animal with his stake, he began to haul it away as it attempted to snout through its muzzle at the water-logged bundle. The boy joined him, waist-deep, and together they heaved on its chain.

The crowds, including Will and his servant, had perforce to move on, pushed across the ford by those following behind. Besides, all were weary after their travels and intent upon reaching the end of their journey.

But Will Ackland's curiosity had been roused. He made a point of watching as his horse splashed past, and saw the man and the boy dragging the reluctant bear out of the water. And he noticed that as they regained dry ground, the bearward glanced back fearfully at the half-submerged bundle of rags and crossed himself.

2

The gaze of every wayfarer, after crossing the ford, was drawn to the great grey bulk of the priory. With its splendid bell-resounding church — bigger by far than the parish church up on the ridge — and all the other stone buildings that rose above the high walls that encircled its precinct, it dominated the shallow valley.

Its domination was almost complete, for the priory owned most of the land hereabouts and land elsewhere besides. Like every other religious house it offered hospitality to travellers as well as to pilgrims. But its gatehouse stood on the north side of the outer wall and everyone bound for the priory had first to journey up through the town, to the great profit of the people of Castleacre.

Travellers of high rank, clerics, and nuns on pilgrimage, would all ride without pause to the priory where they could be sure of good food and drink and comfortable beds in the guest houses. Poor pilgrims and wayfarers would also go straight to the priory, where they would be sheltered overnight and given food at the almonry. But for those with money in their pockets, the town itself was the immediate goal.

Over three centuries, as the fame of Castleacre priory had grown, alehouse keepers and tradesmen had moved their premises further and further down towards the ford to capture incoming customers. Seeing the town so near, and scenting food in the smoke from its fires, weary travellers had always hurried eagerly into its embrace. And the street called Southgate had never disappointed them, for shoes could be mended here, horses could be shod, hot pottage and meat pasties could be eaten and — above all — thirsts could be quenched.

'By the Mass,' croaked Ned Pye hopefully above the noise, as he and his master edged through the crowds in the narrow street, their horses delicately avoiding the outstretched legs of the drinkers who filled the benches outside every alehouse, 'I'm as dry as a gammon of bacon hung on a chimney . . .'

Will Ackland ignored him, for he was intent on stopping the first honest Castleacre man he saw and sending him, with a groat for his trouble, to give a message to the parish constable. Then he rode on, with Ned croaking indignantly behind him. Presently the street widened to form the sloping market place, just below the church, where an inn at the sign of the Woolpack provided refreshment and beds for dealers in the cloth trade. From there, Will turned east along Castlegate. Ahead of them, at the end of this street, stood what was left of the Acklands' castle.

It looked more imposing from the town than it did from the river. The old Normans had built it well, and though the outer walls were now in some places no higher than a house, they were set on the edge of a great earthwork that rose out of a wide, scrub-grown ditch. Castlegate street ran directly to the edge of the ditch, which was crossed by a stone bridge. On the far side of the bridge was a high gatehouse, set in the outer wall.

Even Ned Pye seemed to find the gatehouse still impressive, with its twin round towers on either side joined by a stone vaulting that supported an upper chamber. But the massive oak gates in the entrance arch stood permanently wide, broken by a battering ram more than two centuries before.

'Give you good day, Jacob!' shouted Will as they clattered through the archway. The old yardman, who had been watching for him these three days past, cried a toothless welcome, and barking dogs rushed out to escort them in.

The gate led to the lower ward of the

castle, an open place of several acres where men-at-arms would once have lived and fought. Now, to Ned's wry disapproval, it was nothing more than a walled farmstead, busily domestic in the mellow sunshine of the September afternoon. From their right, as they rode in, the regular thump of flails from the direction of the barn — built, like the stables, the cowshed and the hogsty, against the inside of the old wall — told that corn was being threshed. But Ned was heartened by what was happening to the left of the gate, convenient for the kitchen of the Acklands' dwelling, where serving women were busy about the well and dairy, and appetising smells emerged with the smoke from bakehouse and brewhouse.

A paved way led across from the gate to the dwelling, still known in the town as 'the castle' though it was no greater in size than a manor house. But it was solidly built from the stones of the Norman keep whose scant remains stood behind and above it on a high scrub-covered mound.

The house had a steeply pitched tiled roof, a massive central chimney stack, mullioned windows and a gabled two-storey porch. It faced south, towards a garden of herbs. For the rest, there was a large vegetable patch, grazing for the house-cows, beehives, a round dove-house built of stone, and an orchard patrolled by a gaggle of geese, all within the embrace of the old outer walls.

As the men rode up to the house, scattering fowls, a tall gentlewoman appeared at the front door. Her hair was covered by her linen under-cap, but Ned knew her by her dark eyebrows and the level gaze of her eyes as his master's elder sister, Dame Margaret Morston. She had been widowed young, and had returned to take charge of domestic affairs at the castle after their mother's death. Will had spoken of her affectionately as 'Meg'.

But there was no suggestion, as she stood waiting for them with folded hands and a stern expression, of any return of affection on her part.

'*William Ackland*' — she accused her brother, as though he were still an unruly boy half her height — 'where have you *been* all this while?'

Ned shot an astonished look at his master, and was relieved to see that he disregarded his sister's scolding. Indeed, he had a great grin on his face.

'Meg!' cried Will, swinging out of the saddle and going to her with hands outstretched, for he knew that her greeting was nothing more than a tease, a reminder of her fruitless attempts to discipline him when he was a boy. Her frown had already changed to a welcoming smile. Plucking up her gown she ran to embrace him, heedless of the dirt of travel that caked his short coat, hose and riding boots.

'Oh,' she exclaimed with relief, 'I am thankful to have you safe home!'

'And I to see you again.' He kissed her on both cheeks, and added with due humility, 'I ask your pardon, sister, for staying away so long.'

'And so you should!' Dame Meg retorted with spirit. Standing back to look at him, her hands on his upper arms, she went through the motion — immovably big as he was — of giving him a good shake, just as she used to do when he vexed her in their youth. 'So you should ask pardon, for you've been needed here. Even more so these last months.'

Will returned her searching gaze. Though still a handsome woman, she looked older than her thirty-six years. There were lines of worry on her face, and her brown eyes, once so lively, were dulled.

'What's amiss?' he asked. And then, with a rush of anxiety: 'Is my daughter well?'

'As always, thank God. She's a fine, healthy child. She was chasing butterflies in the garden when Jacob told us you were coming, and her nurse hurried her indoors to dress in

23

your honour. You'll see her soon enough. But now' — she turned to smile at the sturdy young man who was holding the horses — 'this must be the famous Ned Pye, to whom we're indebted for saving your life in the wars!'

'The same,' agreed Will, beckoning him forward. 'You'll find Ned an honest rogue. You may trust him with your money, but never with a modest maid or a good horse for he'd soon ruin both.'

Ned swept his cap from his yellow hair and made her an elaborate bow in the fashion he had seen in Italy. 'I am your servant, madam.' Then, grinning, he added, 'If truth is being told, even Master Will has a fault or two. But' — virtuously — 'my lips are sealed.'

'Ha!' said Dame Meg, amused by his impudence. 'I'd have you know there's nothing you could tell me of my brother that would astonish me. But you are most welcome here, Ned Pye. Leave the horses with Jacob and go to the kitchen, there's food and drink waiting for you. Come, Will.'

She led her brother through the porch and into the screens passage, at the far end of which rose the stair-turret. On the left, some of the indoor servants clustered in welcome under the archway that led from the kitchens and buttery, the older women competing to relieve him of his riding coat. The absence of any young serving women, and the shrieks and giggles Will could hear from the kitchen quarters, suggested that Ned was already making their acquaintance.

The door on the right of the passage led to the hall, with its heavily beamed ceiling, into which sunlight came slanting through the hazy window glass. A bough smouldered on its bed of ash in the great chimney place. In front of it, an old hound and a tangle of cats slumbered together on the rushes. The hall was exactly as Will remembered it, with the long table and plain stools and benches — all the furnishing there was in his mother's time — greatly improved by the addition of his sister's possessions.

Dame Meg had no children. After the death of her late husband, a prosperous elderly merchant of Lynn, she had brought her household goods with her to Castleacre. Until she chose to re-marry, or to move elsewhere, the Acklands had the benefit of her fine Flanders tapestry with its scenes of hawking and hunting, her painted wall-hangings, and all her beds, chairs, chests, cupboards, cushions, linen and silver plate.

'How many suitors have you now?' Will teased her as they passed through the hall and into the parlour. His wounded leg was stiff and aching after the long ride, but he tried to conceal the weakness from his sister. 'Is Reginald Bixley still hopeful?'

'So it seems,' said Meg carelessly. 'And others not worth naming, who come to woo me for my land and properties. It's an enviable state, to be a prosperous widow, and I sha'n't surrender it lightly. My father made me marry a man I could not love, and I'll never marry another unless my heart is in it.'

'Well said,' approved her brother. In truth, he knew more than one lively young man who had married a rich widow to give himself a start in the world, and pleased her well enough into the bargain. But having himself married for love, he wanted no less for his sister.

The best of her belongings had gone to the furnishing of the parlour. Meg sat down in her big cushioned chair, placed in the window to give her a good light for sewing, and resumed the making of a child's linen shift. Will sat near, stretching his leg when he thought she was not looking. A servant brought wine for Dame Meg, and ale from the brewhouse to quench Will's thirst. As soon as they were alone, he repeated his question.

'What's amiss, Meg? Is it Gilbert? Or poor Alice?'

Since their brother's marriage, shortly after Will's own, they had always referred privately to his wife as 'poor Alice'. The daughter of a yeoman farmer, her attraction for Gilbert Ackland had been her dowry of twelve good ewes and the annual services of her father's best ram. For the yeoman, the attraction of the match lay in the fact that his daughter would be marrying into the ranks of the gentry.

For Alice herself, though, Gilbert's brother and sister had seen little advantage. She was by nature pale and timid, and as fearful of her overbearing husband as she had been of her father. By right, since Gilbert at thirty-three was the elder brother and head of the Ackland family, Alice had become mistress of the castle on her marriage. But when Meg had proposed to move to a house she owned at Lynn, so as to leave the new mistress in charge, poor Alice had begged her tearfully to continue as before.

Meg sighed as she sewed. 'I am sorry for all her misfortunes. But' — her frown gathered — 'Gib's conduct worries me far more. He was always hot-headed, you know that well enough. Of late, though, he's been so beyond reason that I dread to think how it will end.'

They were interrupted by a tap at the door, and now a wholesome-looking country girl entered and made a bob. 'Shall I bring in Mistress Betsy?' she asked.

Dame Meg drew breath. 'A moment, Agnes.' Then, quickly and almost with apology to Will: 'Knowing nothing about children, I have brought her up as our mother did us . . . '

'And I'm thankful for your care of her, Meg,' he assured her. 'I am greatly in your debt. But if my fondness can ever repay, you are richer by far than your husband left you.'

'Have done, Will Ackland!' she protested, pink-cheeked. 'Now, are you ready to meet your daughter?'

He rose to his feet, his stomach tightening with unease. He had looked forward to this moment throughout the journey from France. Now it had come he felt as nervous as when, a tongue-tied youth, he first went to Anne to tell her of his love.

What was he going to say to her child? He knew no children — what did a man say to them? Would Betsy be able to love him as a father, even though he had seen nothing of her all these years?

But his unease was outdone by that of his daughter. She entered the room reluctantly, a tiny maid in a stiff new gown, her white-capped head hanging shyly, one hand clinging for dear life to her nurse's skirts.

Meg cleared her throat. 'Come, Betsy,' she said in an echo of the formal voice their mother had always used, sounding stern for fear of spoiling the child by showing affection to her, 'greet your father as you have been taught.'

Agnes, without doubt the provider of affection, gently pushed her towards Will. But Betsy would go no more than a few steps before plucking at her gown to raise it from the floor, and making a wobbly curtsey.

'I hope I see you well, sir,' she babbled dutifully, without raising her head. Then she ran, breathless, to her nurse and hid her face.

'My feet are well, I thank you,' he answered wryly, 'for that is all you'll see of me unless you look up. Or I of you.' He held out his hands. 'Come, sweet Betsy . . . '

'Sit down, Will,' said his sister in her own voice. 'You're too tall for the child.'

He folded his length on to a stool, and tried again to coax her to him. His daughter would not budge, but this time she favoured him with a glance.

He had hoped that she would be the image of her mother, but she was not, and he was disappointed. Her skin was fair, and so was the hair that flowed from under her cap on to her shoulders — but it was not the lovely gold of Anne's, and nor were her eyes the colour of

29

bluebells that pool the woodland floor in springtime.

But she was a pretty child, for all that. And there was something about the shape of her brow and the turn of her head, some fleetingly familiar look, that told him she was undoubtedly Anne's daughter.

'Did you catch any butterflies in the garden?' he asked her, smiling.

Betsy shook her head and said nothing, but she returned a cautious smile. Taking this for encouragement, Will continued.

'Do you have any little cousins for company?' Though Meg's letters had told him all the news of the town and county, she had scarce made mention of their brother's family. When Gilbert had married he had boasted of his intention to breed sons, but Will had heard nothing of them.

Betsy seemed unable to understand her father's question, and her thumb stole into her mouth for comfort. Meg gave him a swift answer.

'Alice has no children as yet,' she said. And then, in their mother's voice: 'Take your thumb from your mouth, Betsy, or your nurse will have to bind it.'

Downcast again, the child immediately did as she was told. Happily, Will remembered that he had brought a gift for her. Saying so, he pretended to search his doublet and his pouch, with a good deal of muttering on the lines of *Now where did I put it?* while his daughter watched wide-eyed.

'Ah, here it is!' He held out a small purse of soft leather, with something hard inside. 'Shall you open it?'

He had chosen the gift in Italy, spending more than he could well afford by way of apology for his neglect. Betsy stole forward to take it from him, her mouth rounding with astonishment as she discovered the cross of ivory, delicately carved and studded with seed pearls and corals, hanging from a fine gold chain. She smiled at him without reserve and, prompted by Dame Meg, whispered her thanks. Then she ran to show the gift, eagerly to her nurse and shyly to her aunt.

'Come,' said Will, 'I shall fasten it for you,' and his daughter came at once and stood between his knees. She smelled so fresh and sweet, and her huge grey eyes searched his face with such wonder, that his fingers shook as he closed the chain round her tender neck. Overwhelmed by an impulse of love, he seized her in his arms and stood up, hugging her to him and pressing his lips against her cheek.

His daughter's response was not what he had hoped. The small body went rigid, the hands tried to push him away, the pink mouth opened in a wail of fright. Agnes rushed forward to rescue and carry off her tearful charge, and Will was left foolishly empty-handed, regretting his ardent haste.

'I was too sudden for her. She will like me better when she knows me,' he said, trying to hide his disappointment.

'She will like you better when you've shaved and put on clean linen,' said his sister dryly.

Will clapped a hand to his bristling chin.

'I' faith, I had forgot! Well, I can shave my beard sooner than I can change this foul shirt, for the linen I brought with me is all the same. When we came through London, Ned took my shirts to his mother at Blackfriars by the Thames, and I swear she washed them at Puddle Wharf for they came back smelling of mud.'

'Then I'll gladly find you one of Gib's shirts, for all our sakes. It will be over-large for you, and patched too. But at least it has been washed in sweet water from the Nar.'

'Not always so sweet,' Will remembered. 'When we crossed the river,' he told her — making nothing of it, for death is the common end of life — 'there was a dead body floating downstream of the ford.'

Meg could not take the news so lightly. Her

face went suddenly white, and her eyes widened with what looked almost like fear.

'*Whose body?*' she whispered hoarsely.

Her anxiety took Will by surprise. 'Who knows, with so many folk on the road?' He sought to reassure her: 'All I saw were rags. Some vagabond, no doubt, drowned from infirmity or too much ale.'

'In rags, you say . . . ?' Meg recovered her colour and nodded with what seemed to be relief. 'Well, well,' she murmured, crossing herself. 'Whoever it is, poor wretch, God ha' mercy on his soul.'

33

3

Washed and shaven, and clean-shirted by courtesy of his brother — though without Gilbert's knowledge, for Gib had always disliked him for being fleeter of foot and quicker to draw a bow, as well as for his aptitude for learning — Will rejoined his sister in the parlour.

He had brought with him a small roll of cloth containing his gift to her. Laying aside her sewing, she unrolled the cloth and discovered with evident pleasure a piece of the finest Flemish lace, exquisitely worked.

'I thought it would make you a cap and cuffs — or a collar, perhaps, as is the fashion in France,' he suggested. 'I brought another piece for poor Alice.'

They could hear slow steps in the passage outside and presently his brother's wife came into the room, leaning back for balance for she was heavy with child. Her pale protruding eyes, set wide in an unhappy face, gave her the look of a frightened hare.

'Alice!' said Will kindly, taking her hand and kissing her on the cheek before leading her to a chair. 'You're just in time for my gift-giving. Here is what I brought you from Antwerp.'

'For me?' She looked amazed, unaccustomed to receiving gifts from anyone. He urged her to unroll the cloth, and she did it slowly, gasping with delight as she saw the beauty of the lace.

'Oh, Will!' she said, her cheeks flushing pink. She looked up at him. 'Oh, Will . . .' she repeated in a different, despairing tone, and he saw that the shine in her eyes was caused by tears.

'I brought just the same for Meg,' he said, off-handed with unease. Then, hoping to stop her weeping: 'I'm very happy for you, Alice, to see you in this condition. And if the child is not a son, I'm sure Gib will be as pleased with a daughter as I am.'

To his astonishment, Alice gave a great sob and stumbled, anguished, from the room. Meg frowned at him, rose hurriedly and followed her.

'What did I do wrong this time?' Will asked when his sister returned, bemused by his new-found aptitude for reducing the females of his family to tears.

Meg sighed. 'It was not your fault, you were not to know. Poor Alice cannot bear Gilbert a child. She miscarried three times, and though she gave birth to a son last year he lived but a few hours. Since then, she has walked to Walsingham to pray for help at the shrine of Our Lady. We all had such hope for the child she now carries — but it no longer moves in her womb. We fear it will be still-born.'

Will slapped his head in dismay. 'By the Mass, I would not for the world have added to her distress! No wonder Gib is unreasonable.'

'No,' said Meg firmly, 'there's more to it than that. Gib cares little enough for his wife, and the lack of a child cannot cause such anger in a man. I tell you, Will, he's so far beyond reason that I fear he may be mad. Were it not for poor Alice, I would have taken Betsy and left the castle months ago.'

'Is my daughter safe here?' he demanded, alarmed.

'Agnes keeps her out of his way, never fear. Well, you must judge him for yourself at supper. But say nothing to provoke him, I beg you, and do not rise to his provocation, for I dread the consequence of any quarrel. He can be violent in his anger . . .'

Meg broke off, for there was a commotion outside in the yard. One of the carts was returning from the fields, with a heavy rumbling of wheels, the guiding shouts of the carter and the clop of great hooves on stone.

Now there came the clatter of a ridden horse, and the resounding bellow of a man's voice raised in fury.

There was a quick tap on the parlour door. It opened without pause and the anxious face of a young serving woman appeared round it. 'Madam, the master is home!' she gabbled, and disappeared as quickly as she had come.

Dame Meg raised her eyebrows at her brother. 'So we hear,' she said, putting aside her sewing.

The front door banged open and a roaring noise resounded through the house as Gilbert Ackland flung anger at anyone who crossed his path. 'I must fetch poor Alice,' said Meg. 'He never speaks to her at meals, but he demands her presence. Go in and try to quieten him, Will — but for all our sakes, do not quarrel.'

Will returned to the hall and found its peacefulness gone with the sunlight. Spurred on by the uproar from the passage the servants scurried about, covering the long table with a linen cloth, setting out knives, spoons, pewter plates and Dame Meg's second-best horn drinking cups with the silver rims, and bringing bread and salt, a large cheese and a dish of green walnuts. Basins of warm water and towels were set out for hand-washing. A gangling boy lit tallow candles against the gloom of early evening, and hastily kicked the log on the hearth into flame. Woken from their slumbers by a shower of sparks, the old hound and the cats vacated the front of the fire of their own accord and slunk off elsewhere, out of the way of trouble.

Trouble appeared almost immediately, in the person of Gilbert Ackland. His massive presence, as he strode into the hall with a couple of baleful hounds at heel, overshadowed the room like a thundercloud.

'Ale!' he shouted as he came. 'God's death, must a man die of thirst before he is served? Ale, do you hear!' And the boy cried a desperate 'Anon, anon, sir,' as he ran to the buttery.

Gilbert took up a glowering stand in front of the chimney place, his doublet stained, his legs in their darned hose as solid as tree trunks, his boots clogged with mire. He was shorter than his younger brother, but thickly black-bearded and with the neck and shoulders of an ox.

The boy hurried back with a flagon, and his master seized it in both hands and drank deep. Will had been waiting quietly in the shadows, but now he moved forward. As Gilbert lowered the flagon to take breath, Will walked up to him with an outstretched hand.

'Brother,' he said. 'I hope I see you well?'

Gilbert ignored his hand, and looked him over darkly. 'Not as well as you, brother!' he said with a sneer. 'Coming here in your foreign finery to mock me . . .'

'Neither foreign nor fine,' Will assured him, with truth for he had left the best of his clothes, with his books, at the room he was to share at Gray's Inn when he returned to his studies. 'I'll wager,' he added, opening his doublet to show proof, 'that my shirt is no better than your own.'

Gilbert snorted, unwilling to forgo his grievance. 'No doubt you have brought a retinue, to be housed and fed at my expense?'

'A servant and two horses,' said Will calmly, refusing to be provoked. 'And never fear, I shall pay all the cost of our visit.'

'Now you speak of paying! What of your daughter, hey? You leave the child in my charge for four whole years, without contributing so much as a groat ——'

'Not so, Gilbert!' said his sister firmly as she brought his downcast wife into the hall. 'You know full well that Betsy is in my charge, at her mother's dying wish. And that Will has set aside the income from her mother's dowry for her support.'

She helped Alice to her place as the titular mistress of the house, the chair at the foot of the table. Meg herself remained standing with her hands on the back of the chair, one of her own pieces of furniture.

'But you are master here, Gib,' she went on, humouring him. 'It shall be as you wish. If Will's child is to leave, then so be it. You must remember, though,' she added, 'that if Betsy goes I shall go too — and take all my goods with me. I think you will miss our contribution to the comfort and expenses of your household.'

Gilbert shuffled the rushes with his boots. 'Not so hasty, Meg,' he muttered. 'I did but tease my brother . . . '

'Then have done. Will, say the grace for us.'

He bent his head. '*Benedictus benedicat, per Jesum Christum Dominum nostrum, Amen.*'

'Amen. Now sit down both of you, and let us eat our supper.'

Still glowering, Gilbert took his place at the head of the table. Will sat opposite Meg, and greeted Alice in a tone that he hoped would make amends for his earlier clumsiness. She was pale except for a swollen redness about her lowered eyelids, and she made no reply apart from a quiver of a smile. Her husband took no more notice of her than he did of the flies that pestered round the food.

The church enjoined that on the eve of a

40

Sunday or a saint's day, everyone should fast by abstaining from eating meat. But Gilbert took little heed of church law and insisted on being served his favourite dish, a hot mutton pie, with boiled cabbage well sprinkled with vinegar and pepper. The other dishes were a pottage of herbs, baked cod, a salad of endive cut small and salted, apples roasted with honey and cloves, and almond tarts.

Alice ate almost nothing, and drank only a few sips of watered wine. Every now and then she pressed her napkin to her mouth while her thin shoulders were shaken by a suppressed sob. Gilbert sat under a dark cloud of anger, silent only because he was stuffing his cheeks with food.

Meg glanced across the table at her younger brother and shrugged her helplessness. Then, drawing breath, she asked, 'What news from London, Will?'

From the concern in her voice, this was no idle question. He could guess what news she wanted, for it was spoken of openly, and with anger, in London. But he had learned more on his travels than it was wise to reveal, except in secrecy; for who knew who might hear?

'Touching what?' he asked lightly.

'Why, her grace Queen Katherine! We have heard it said that the King intends to put her

41

aside — to divorce her. Can this be true?'

'I fear so.'

Meg drew herself up, flushed with indignation. 'Then I think it foul shame.'

'Have a care what you say on matters touching the King,' cautioned Will. 'It's safest never to speak against him.'

Meg rejected caution. 'I would say so to King Henry himself, if he were here!' she retorted, her eyes flashing. 'I think it foul shame, to put aside a gracious and charitable lady who has been a good wife to him these twenty years. Will, he *cannot*. Why should he want it?'

'King Henry needs an heir, that is why.'

'He already has one — the Princess Mary, his daughter by Queen Katherine.'

'A female heir must have a future husband,' Will pointed out. 'If the Princess were to marry an English nobleman, the country would be rent by division and civil strife, as it was before Henry Tudor won the crown. And should she marry a foreign prince, we risk the domination of his country. The King needs a male heir to secure the safety of the realm.'

His sister stared at him, hot with indignation. 'Then you are in favour of King Henry putting aside his wife, and taking another in order to get a boy? Shame on you, Will Ackland!'

'No,' said Will. 'You asked me why the King proposes it, and I have told you. But I like it no more than you do.'

'*You* do not like it?' Gilbert Ackland raised his face from his food and spluttered contempt through his greasy beard. 'What's it to you, brother? I am King Henry's man in this. I say he is right *as a man* to put away his wife if she cannot bear him an heir. God's blood, if a man can have no satisfaction from his wife, then he's entitled to seek it from another!'

★ ★ ★

The sight of Alice's white cheeks, glistening in the candlelight as her tears coursed dumbly down, stirred Will to anger. Glaring at Gilbert, he clenched his fists and was about to spring up when he received a sharp kick on the shin, a reminder from Meg not to allow himself to be provoked.

'Come, Alice,' she said, rising from the table serenely as befitted a widowed gentlewoman. 'Let us go to the parlour and see how we shall make use of Will's lace.'

As he waited for them to leave, Will let out his pent-up breath and unclenched his fists. Five years ago — or at any earlier time in his life — he would have given his brother a bloody nose for less than this. Though Gib always had weight and strength on his side in their many brawls, Will had had the advantage of greater agility, a longer reach and a cooler head.

He was confident that he could still out-ride and out-shoot his brother, but he knew that his wounds had made him less agile. Besides, as the father of a young daughter, and very nearly a barrister, he should be past brawling. There was nothing he could gain for his sister-in-law by striking her husband, much as Gib deserved it. Better by far to take Meg's advice, keep the peace, and find out what — apart from Alice's inability to give him a child — was rousing Gilbert to such fury.

Will released his own anger by going to the fireplace and giving the log a great kick with his good leg, sending up a spurt of flame. Then he sat down again at the table, wiped his knife on a hunk of bread, and cut into the cheese.

'How was the harvest, brother?' he asked.

It is the prerogative of every farmer to grumble about the harvest, and Gilbert did so. This year, as every year, he had sweated and struggled to produce enough, after paying his outgoings and taxes, not only to subsist on until the next harvest but to give him a profitable surplus besides. And this year — as every year since he had taken over the farm on his father's death — his hope of anything beyond bare subsistence had been thwarted. Taxes were burden enough, but what weighed him down intolerably were the demands of the priory.

As landlord, the priory was entitled to rent for the land that Gilbert farmed. But before paying his rent he had to pay his tithe, and that also went to the priory.

The tithe — the annual levy on parishioners of one tenth of their income, payable in cash or kind, which according to church law was intended to provide the living of the Castleacre parish priest — had for the past two centuries been appropriated by the priory. As for rent, the priory demanded part of it in kind. Together, the two demands reduced the grain in Gilbert's barns and the stock in his fields to subsistence levels.

'*The priory...*' he snarled, thumping the table with his fist. 'God's death, the Acklands were once landlords of this valley. Now we are mere tenants of a religious house!'

Will tried to calm him.

'Gib, it has been thus these two hundred years and more,' he said, reaching for the dish of walnuts. 'Our family has never had money since, save for our grandfather's marriage to the widow who paid for the building of this house. Our late father, God rest his soul, paid his tithe and his rent as you do — but without complaint, as I remember.'

'He loved the priory, that is why,' snapped Gilbert. 'I do *not*.'

'Our upbringing was different,' Will reminded him. 'We were not educated by the monks, as he was. He loved the priory for its great processions, and the sound of plainchant.'

'And for the sight of its great treasures, the gold and the silver and the jewels! Our father loved the priory better than he loved his children. He thought it *right*,' said Gilbert between clenched teeth, 'that the rents and tithes we sweat to pay should be used to beautify the priory church. Aye, and to build the prior a fine new lodging, too! Body of God' — he swept aside the dish with the remains of the mutton pie and sent it clanging to the floor, where the meat was seized upon by the dogs — 'how it angers me!'

Will split open a green walnut with his knife, and began to prise out the twisted kernel with long fingers that were soon stained by the juice.

'From what I've heard on my travels,' he said evenly, 'religious houses oppress their tenants no more than any other great landlord. Would you rather your payments were used to build a nobleman's palace, and to adorn the ladies of his family?'

Gilbert did not answer, but stabbed moodily at a wooden trencher with the sharp point of his knife.

'As for Prior Nicholas himself,' Will went on, 'our father always spoke of him as a just landlord. What has changed him, since you became tenant here?'

'It's naught to do with the prior,' said Gilbert scornfully. 'He is too lordly to concern himself with such matters. My enemy is the whole priory — and their bailiff who collects the rent and tithe.'

Will was surprised. 'I remember the prior's bailiff as a jovial man. He would visit the castle once a year to assess us for the tithe, but all he did was to sit in the buttery drinking ale and talking of old times. Whatever my father sent to the priory as tithe, that he accepted.'

'Ha! That was the old bailiff, who had respect for the Ackland name. There has been a new bailiff these three years, Walter Bostock. He exacts from me every last grain of corn he considers due. Aye, and he enjoys doing it!'

Gilbert pushed himself up from the table

47

and strode about the room mouthing his rage, his face in the flickering light as grotesque as any gargoyle's.

'I see Walter Bostock everywhere, not only riding round the land but within the castle itself. I am a freeholder, here within these walls, and the landlord's bailiff has no right to enter my gates. But Bostock comes to pry in my barns by right of collecting tithe, and I cannot deny him. He watches and counts and makes a note of all I produce. He knows every strip of corn, every field of hay, every horse, beast, sheep, hog and fowl. He knows of every creature born, every ounce of honey made by the bees, every jugful of milk and ale. Nothing escapes him.

'And then there are death payments. Walter Bostock came here ten days ago and threatened me with the law. He said he had seen in an old account book that we had made no payment on my father's death. He demanded it there and then: not only my best beast, to go to the priory which is my landlord, but also my second best beast, to go to the priory which steals what is due to the parish church!'

Gilbert came back to the table in a rush, eyes gleaming through his tangle of hair and beard.

'Now do you understand me, brother?' he

hissed. 'God's blood, how could any man endure what I have suffered from the prior's bailiff!'

And saying so, he snatched up his knife and plunged it deep in the cheese, up to the hilt.

4

The sky next morning was a sharper blue, for the wind lay with its feet towards the morning. An overnight breath of frost had put a chill in the bright air, and all of Castleacre — the castle, the town, the priory — was sprinkled with the first falling of yellow leaves.

It was the feast day of St Matthew and the bells of all the churches filled the valley with their ringing. Every parishioner had an obligation to attend Mass at the parish church on saints' days and Sundays, and Will accompanied Meg and poor Alice, with their servants. Gilbert, risking his absence being reported by the churchwardens to the archdeacon, had ridden out early, no one knew where. As for Ned Pye, he had scant regard for the church and belonged to no parish. Short of sleep after a night of activity in the town, he had returned to his straw pallet and pulled his blanket over his ears to muffle the noise of the bells.

Alice walked slowly, and the nave was already crowded with parishioners by the time they arrived, the infirm on the benches by the wall and everyone else standing. In comparison with the priory church, the parish church was small and poorly endowed, but even so the interior blazed with candlelit colour. All of it — the roof timbers, the great crucifix above the rood screen between chancel and nave, the sculpted stone, the plastered walls, the carved ends of the benches — was brightly painted, not only with religious subjects but with every part of God's Creation, in a lively confusion of birds and beasts and flowers and stars.

There were saints by the score: large and small, fashioned in stone and wood, painted singly or depicted in vivid scenes from their lives. Every parishioner was intent on lighting a candle and praying to one or other of them, as well as lighting a candle in honour of St Matthew.

Alice wanted, with good reason, to address her prayers to Our Lady. Will and Meg escorted their sister-in-law to the alabaster statue and stood close to protect her from the crush. The statue glittered with the many golden and jewelled offerings that had been made over the centuries, some of them by the Ackland family, most recently by Alice herself. Despite her past disappointments, and her fears for the child she carried, she remained steadfast in her devotion. Her face as she prayed shone with the fervour of her belief that through Our Lady's intercession, the child might yet be born alive.

Will was doubtful of such a miracle. But as he took Alice's arm and made a way through the crowds so that she could reach a bench, he reflected that she was still a young woman — unlike King Henry's Queen — and there was every hope that she would bear a living child in the future. Sorry as he was for his sister-in-law, his private prayers while the priest celebrated the Mass beyond the rood screen were not for her, but for his dead wife Anne.

He returned to the castle in a mood of sadness and remorse, and was not disposed to be indulgent with Ned Pye. Finding his servant still snoring, Will tipped him off his pallet on to the floor and threw a pan of cold water over his head.

'Hell's jaws!' spluttered Ned, aggrieved. He sat up and spat out a mouthful of water. 'I'm wet as a herring.'

'Pickled as, more like. Shave yourself, and put on a clean shirt, for my godfather is expecting us to call on him.'

When Ned was fit to be seen, they walked together — Will for the second time that morning — along the cobbles of Castlegate. This was the oldest street in the town, where the weavers lived. Its tall narrow houses, built of timbers infilled with wattle and daub, and thatched with reed from the riverside, were huddled so close that they seemed to prop each other up.

On any other weekday the women would have been spinning within their open doors, and the street would have been loud with the repeated clack-clack of shuttles thrown across looms. But the church enjoined the laity to observe each feast day, after Mass, as a holy day during which they did no work, and most of them needed no second bidding.

Will's intention had been to introduce his servant to the townsfolk they met as they walked along Castlegate. But Ned had always been a useful man on their travels, making it his immediate business wherever they rested to find out who was who and what was what, and it seemed from his various greetings that he had been introducing himself already.

'How now, my liking?' he called up to the daughter of a house who leaned from an overhanging window as they passed. 'Shall we meet in the market place?' She favoured him with a smile and a twirling of her long hair through her fingers, but before anything more could be said she was pulled sternly away by her mother, who glared down at him and slammed the shutter to.

'One of your conquests from last night?' asked Will.

'Never clapped eyes on her 'til this moment,' said Ned cheerfully. 'But it's useful to have a few spare strings to my bow.'

'Ah — you're reconciled to a stay in Castleacre, then?'

'That I am not! Half a day will exhaust its poor pleasures, and those I would gladly forgo. Give me the word, Master Will, and I'll be packed and saddled for London before you can pull on your riding boots.'

'Not so fast. There's disquiet in my family, and I must attend to that first. You know of it, no doubt?'

'I know your brother is at the root of it,' said Ned bluntly. 'All the servants, indoors and out, go in fear of him.'

'And what do they say is the cause of his anger?'

'Why, everything to do with the priory. Most of all the prior's bailiff.'

'So I learned from Gilbert himself. Saddle the horses directly after dinner, Ned. We'll go in search of the bailiff, and see for ourselves whether he's more unreasonable than my brother.'

Castleacre was now a-buzz with happy anticipation. The two men followed a rising hubbub until they reached the middle of the town, where the market place sloped down from the parish church. Most of the shops fronted this place, as did the Woolpack inn and several alehouses with which Ned seemed already familiar. Early in the day as it was, all of them were busy.

The pilgrims were still at their devotions in the priory church, but holiday-makers from throughout the valley had come crowding to Castleacre, intent on enjoying themselves. In the market place, hucksters were crying their wares and jugglers competed to provide entertainment, trying to keep in the air whatever they could seize — apples, onions, turnips, eggs — from the baskets of wondering countryfolk. An ape on the end of a chain leaped gibbering on folk's shoulders, causing shrieks and laughter. Children and dogs dodged about. Outlandishly costumed players gestured and shouted, one musician turned a hurdy-gurdy while others blew mightily on horns and bag-pipes, bawdy songs were sung and dances were danced. And as Will pushed a way through the crowds he came again upon the mangy bear, standing upright in its chains to perform a sad shuffle. He gave it a nod of acknowledgement, at the same time tossing a few pence into the cap of the bearward's boy for the valour of his unheard piping.

With Ned lagging, for he had interests of his own, Will made for Northgate. This street left the market place at its highest point, beside the church tower, and very soon narrowed to become the continuation of the Peddars' Way. It led on towards the sea coast, from where it was said the old Romans had crossed the Wash by ferry on their way to Lincoln.

For all its shortness, Northgate was a street of importance. To one side, behind the church, stood the ancient timber-and-flint gildhall. On the opposite side of the street were the almshouses, and the grammar school where Will and Gib had been sent to learn Latin. And in this street stood the finest house in the town, that of Will's godfather, an old friend of his late father.

Lawrence Throssell was a man of law, having practised as a barrister at Westminster and Norwich. Three times a widower, and now nearing sixty, he had finally returned to Castleacre to undertake the office of a justice of the peace, and to enjoy his garden.

Will was deeply indebted to his godfather. Lawrence Throssell had provided funds to enable him to follow in his own footsteps, and Will felt rightly abashed that he had abandoned his lengthy studies a year before their completion to chase off to the wars.

There was, though, a greater cause for Will's unease as he neared his godfather's house. It was not merely his studies that he had left to go to war, but his new wife. When he married Anne, she was Lawrence Throssell's only surviving child. Now, he expected a justly harsh reception from her childless father.

'Is my chin still bleeding where I nicked it with my knife when I shaved?' Will demanded of his servant, voicing trivialities to conceal his anxiety. 'Are you sure my coat is clean?'

'Have done, Master Will,' said Ned Pye, giving his shoulder a clap that served both to convey encouragement and to remove some dust he had omitted to brush off. 'You'll pass muster. I'll see you safe inside, and after that I have business of my own to attend to. If you need me afore dinner, you'll find me at the sign of the Green Man.'

They had come to the house built by Lawrence Throssell's father, who had made his fortune in the cloth trade in the reign of King Henry VII. The house was built of timbers infilled with brick, the same size as the Acklands' but much finer in construction and detail, with two chimney stacks on the tiled roof, each stack supporting a cluster of chimneys, and each chimney differently built in a twisting pattern of bricks. Its garden was at the back, and its many-paned windows looked out directly on Northgate street.

Preparing himself for the difficult meeting with Anne's father, Will drew a deep breath before knocking on the heavy door. It was opened by a serving man, who made way immediately for a small, upright gentleman with a wisp of grey beard, wearing a skull cap and a long gown of fine worsted cloth.

'Godfather — ' said Will, making him the reverence that was his due.

'William,' returned Lawrence Throssell, standing on tip-toe to embrace his godson. His voice was small and his movements bird-like in their quickness. 'I thank God you are safe home.'

His welcome held warmth, but at a distance. He did not smile wholeheartedly until he turned to Will's servant. 'And you, sirrah — you must be Ned Pye who saved my godson's life! Come, let me greet you.'

Ned came forward, red-faced, wiping his hands down the back of his jerkin.

"Twas no more than any good servant would have done,' he mumbled, enveloping the small hand Justice Throssell held out to him. 'In truth, Master Will was as valiant a soldier as any on the battlefield, and I am proud to serve him.' Then he leaned forward and added in a loud whisper, 'But I dare not tell him so, or he would dock my wages.'

Lawrence Throssell gave a chirrup of a laugh. 'I see you are as big a knave as he wrote to tell me. Take this for my thanks, Ned Pye,' he added, handing him a well-filled purse, 'And God keep you.'

Ned's eyes rounded as he felt the weight of the purse. 'I thank you, sir! And I would have you know that your town of Castleacre is as fine as any I have seen in England. Aye, and in Europe, too! I was saying so to Master Will only this morning . . . ' And with a great grin at both of them he strode off jauntily towards the market place.

His godfather's embrace had not reassured Will, for the old gentleman was too courteous to show displeasure in front of a servant. Despite his seeming fragility, Lawrence Throssell was stern in judgement. The matter between them would have to be resolved. It could not be ignored, on either side, in a pretence of forgetting.

But the presence throughout the house of the justice's own servants, peering round doorways to bob and smile sadly at the husband of their late young mistress Anne, hindered private conversation. As they went through the oak-panelled hall, Will could do no more than make enquiry after his godfather's health.

'I hope I see you well, sir?'

'Tolerably well, I thank God, though the east wind that blows up the valley vexes my bones.'

'Ah yes,' Will offered a sympathetic pleasantry: 'The lazy Norfolk wind, that never troubles to go round but blows straight through you. My grandfather used to complain of it.'

They had entered the parlour at the back of the house, and a servant followed bringing wine. He was about to pour it, but Lawrence Throssell dismissed him and left the wine unpoured. Still standing he turned, straight-faced, to Will. The room was warm, with a flickering log in the hearth and sunlight coming through the windows, but a distinct coolness lay between them.

'Sir,' said Will, pulling off his cap and gripping it in his fingers. He felt as uneasy as when he had come here, with nothing but his eventual prospects as a lawyer to commend him, to ask Anne's father for her hand in marriage. The fine room, with its linenfold panelling round the walls, and the entwined initials of Lawrence Throssell's parents carved among foliage on the bressumer above the deep chimney place, was sadly familiar. 'I beg you to hear what I have to say.'

Stiffly straight, his hands clasped, Master

Justice Throssell prepared to listen — as he would to any defendant brought before him. Though he was smaller than his godson by a head, there was no doubting his authority.

'Well, William Ackland?'

'Sir — ' repeated Will, his voice firm but deeply sincere. 'I caused you much grief by leaving your daughter — my wife — to go to the wars. Truly, I know not how to ask your forgiveness. But I beg you to believe this: it was not for want of love for Anne that I left, nor for want of love for you that I failed to return before now. And though my grief for her untimely death cannot outweigh a loving father's, yet it has caused me more pain than you could ever wish on me.'

Lawrence Throssell's eyes had clouded. His first words were low with sadness. 'I never wished pain on you, Will.'

Then his eyes cleared to a piercing blue and his voice grew stern. 'But I was angry with you. Many a carefree student leaves his books to go to the wars, and that I could forgive. But for a new-married man to leave his wife when she was with child — that was the work of a common rogue!'

Will nodded wretchedly, having scourged himself with the same accusation often enough. 'I do not deny it, sir.'

In truth he had an argument in his own

defence, with which he had sometimes tried to comfort himself. Too proud to put it forward now, he waited for the expected dismissal from his godfather's house.

But Lawrence Throssell's demeanour had changed. His shoulders had lost their stiffness, and his face took on a wry smile.

'It was Anne herself who saved you from my wrath. She told me she had agreed to your leaving. You were too spirited, she said, to stay buried in your law books when other young men were fired with the excitement of war. Loving you as she did, she would not persuade you to stay — for fear, she said, that you might regret it as you grew old.'

Will felt reprieved, but no less guilty. 'True, she consented to my going. But I was wrong to press for it, with Anne in her condition. I was a young fool, and had no thought of being wounded, nor of being away from her beyond a month or two. As for regret — God knows I have lived with that ever since.'

'Ah, William — '

Lawrence Throssell came close and reached up to embrace him again, this time with wholehearted warmth. 'We have both suffered enough over our sweet Anne — let us not spoil our friendship any longer.'

The old gentleman bustled about, filling

two glasses. 'Come, sit with me and drink a little malmsey wine. I' faith, we had all feared you dead in battle. Knowing you to be alive, and engaged abroad in the service of the Crown, was relief enough. And besides' — his eyes brightened — 'in your absence I have had the joy of visits from my granddaughter. She is a fine child.'

Will smiled at once. 'Indeed she is,' he said proudly, 'and more like her mother than like me, I thank God!' Then he paused. 'I do desire, sir, to see the place where Anne is buried.'

'We shall go there before noon. And afterwards you shall join me at dinner — I have ordered your favourite dish of trout, fresh from the Nar.'

Recalling his most recent sighting of the river, Will accepted with some caution. 'I'll dine with you gladly, godfather. But as for eating fish new-caught from those waters . . . '

Lawrence Throssell chuckled. 'You need not fear for your stomach — I gave orders that the trout should be caught well upstream of where the dead body lay! It was you who found it, so the constable sent me word.'

'Not I, but a dancing bear. I merely sent to tell of it. Did the constable recognise the body — or was it some vagabond, drunk or dead of disease, as I thought from the rags?'

'It was neither accident nor a natural death,' said the justice. 'The man was murdered, it seems. As to who he is, the constable knows not — and I thank God for that. I have feared these past few months that murder would be done in Castleacre.'

'My sister Meg seemed to fear it too,' Will agreed, 'when I told her of the dead body. I talked last night with my brother, and I know what you both feared — that it was the prior's bailiff who lay dead, and by Gilbert's hand.'

'True, true.' His godfather sighed. 'Your brother has brought dishonour on the Ackland name. He drinks too much, ill-treats his men, and abuses anyone who crosses his path. It's well known that he has uttered threats against Walter Bostock, the bailiff. If Bostock were done to death, the whole town would name Gilbert his murderer without benefit of trial.'

'Then I am thankful it was a man in rags who died,' said Will. 'A quarrel between vagabonds, do you suppose?'

Justice Throssell frowned. 'From what my servants have heard, there may be more to it than that. I have sent word to the constable

64

to meet me at the mortuary at noon, so that I may view the body before burial.'

The old gentleman hesitated, his authority less sure. 'Go with me, Will, I pray you, and lend me your eyes, for mine are no longer as sharp as once they were.'

5

Will had brought his godfather the gift of an Italian pen knife, a fine blade with a handle of carved ivory. Having admired it and given his thanks, Lawrence Throssell called for his cloak against the late September breeze. Then the two set out for the place of Anne's burial, Will shortening his stride to suit the old gentleman's trotting pace.

As soon as they left the house in Northgate street they could hear music and the buzz of enjoyment from the centre of the town. The solemnities at the priory church would have been completed by now. The great processional service of the Festal Mass would be over, and the bloodstained bones of St Matthew would have been returned to their shrine. The pilgrims, in high spirits after witnessing the holy miracle, would be flocking to the market place in search of earthly pleasures, food and drink and entertainment and gaudy things to buy. But Will and his godfather were going no further than the parish church, and they entered quietly by a small north door.

Lawrence's late father, John Throssell the

66

clothier, had been a devout man and a good citizen. He had bequeathed money to build and endow the free grammar school for the education of poor boys of the town, and also to build and endow almshouses for twelve poor old men and women. But during his lifetime he had spent much of his wealth on the parish church, enlarging it with a new chancel and a south porch, building the lofty tower, and filling the great east window with a richness of stained glass.

In the year 1495, John Throssell had built a chantry chapel at the east end of the north aisle. Here, in a plain marble tomb chest, he had laid to rest the mortal remains of his parents to await God's judgement day. And he had given an endowment of land, to provide in perpetuity for a chantry priest to say a daily Mass for the souls of his parents, and in the fullness of time for his own soul and those of his descendants.

Using the chantry priest's door — when he was not at prayer in the chapel the priest taught the youngest of the grammar school children to read — the men entered a small outer chamber. From there, first crossing themselves with holy water from the stoup by the inner door, they entered the stone-vaulted chantry chapel.

It was divided from the chancel of the

church by an open archway. The glass of the east window above the altar-cross was plain, the better to show the paintings of the saints on the plaster walls, their vivid colours shining in the light of the candles that burned before them. One wall showed the folly of earthly vanity, with three kings sumptuously attired yet skeletal beneath their jewelled crowns. And every part of the chapel's plaster without a painting was decorated with the green of leaf-tendrils and the red of Tudor roses.

Will was familiar enough with the chapel, and with the older memorials. What he had come to see was the brass plate in memory of his dead wife, and her father quietly withdrew to let him see it alone.

The engraved brasses of John Throssell's parents were set on top of their tomb chest. Later brasses — including John's own, with his wife, and that of his granddaughter Anne — were set in the stone-flagged floor. All of them faced east, as did the bodies beneath, to await resurrection.

Will knew from his travels that the plates were not in fact brass but latten, an alloy, cast in Flanders and shipped to London for engraving. He knew, too, that the engravers could not be expected to produce a likeness of their subject. They had no means of knowing Anne's appearance, and all they could provide was the figure of a lady of similar years, dressed according to her rank and the fashion of the time. Will was prepared for disappointment. Even so, he found himself staring down at the brass in dismay.

The stiff figure standing with her hands together in prayer, with a fully dressed infant praying at her feet, was older than Anne by ten years. She was a wealthy London gentlewoman, dressed far too elaborately for Norfolk. Her face and nose were long and melancholy, quite unlike those of his sweet, smiling Anne.

Will shook his head, unmoved except by regret for a wasted memorial. It gave him no sense of Anne's presence. But then he began to read the words engraved beneath the figure.

Here lyeth buried ANNE ACKLAND, wyf of WILLm ACKLAND gent. of Castleacre, dau. of LAWRENCE THROSSELL, Justice of the Peace in the County of Norfolk. She dyed ye 18 of May Ao Dni 1526 aet. suae 20

His eyes had become unaccountably dim, and he went down on one knee the better to see what he was reading.

IN YOUTHFUL YEERES I WAS
BEREFT OF BRETH.
THE DEVINE POWER, OF ME DID
SO DEVISE
THAT I IN GRAVE SHOULD LIE A
LINGERING SLEEPE
TILL SOUND OF TRUMP DOE
SUMMON ME TO RISE

Will felt a thickening in his throat. To see the facts engraved on cold metal was to re-live his anguish. *That Anne should have been bereft of breath at the age of twenty — and on the eighteenth of May, the sweet o' the year...*

But that was four years ago, and much had happened since then. He swallowed, dashed the back of his hand across his eyes, and slowly got to his feet. Then he lit a candle, said a prayer for the repose of her soul, and went outside to join his waiting godfather.

Lawrence Throssell took his arm for a moment. 'Is the memorial well done?' he asked, looking anxiously up at him.

Will cleared his throat, and gave the older man the reassurance he sought. 'I thank you, yes — it is well done.'

They walked round the tower of the church and came to the south side. Here in the sun, with the noise and colour of the market place before them, Will lifted his head and breathed more easily.

'Tell me,' enquired his godfather, spying up at him shrewdly, 'have you any thought of marrying again?'

'No, I have not!'

'Come — you are too young a man to forgo it.'

Will paused. 'I do not deny some dalliance, in France and Italy,' he said. 'But as for marriage — I could not marry where I cannot love, and I cannot love except with heart and mind, as it was with Anne.'

'Well, well.' Lawrence Throssell smiled benevolently. 'I have married thrice, and loved all three women in good measure. I would have you know, son-in-law, that when you desire to marry again, you will have my blessing. And now we will say no more on't.'

★ ★ ★

The church bell had already rung the noonday hour and there was no sign of the constable. They returned to the northern side of the church, where the low, stone-built mortuary stood among the grave-mounds, shadowed by a great yew tree.

In the far corner of the churchyard a new grave was in process of being dug. No one was in sight, but earth was being heaved up by the spadeful as though some great mole was working in the depths. And from the depths, between heavings, came a cheerful whistling.

'Are you there, master sexton?' called Justice Throssell.

There was a scrambling from below and presently an earthy countenance, as hairy as a mole's, peered at them over the mound of excavated soil.

'Good morrow, sirs!' cried Hob Pulfer merrily. An empty flagon, lying on the grass beside his mattock and cast-off jerkin, no doubt accounted for his good humour.

'A fine day to be out in the air! Eh, master?' he added, addressing a skull he had brought up with him from the grave, and then tossing it to one side for reburial. Other bones he had left half-embedded in the soil, for the churchyard had been well used over the centuries and there was no ground that had not already been occupied more than once.

'Are you come to see the murdered corse, sir?' he asked Justice Throssell. He grinned, his stump-toothed mouth as dark as the grave he was digging. 'I warrant you'll find him a mystery!'

'You do not know him?'

'Nay! And nor would his own mother. Not

only was he stabbed, sir, he was beaten about the head. But I know *this* about him — 'The sexton tapped his nose with one earth-caked finger. 'Whoever killed him,' he said, nodding sagely, 'wanted him well dead.'

6

The sexton's son, another Hob, as squat as his father and almost as hairy, came hurrying round the church tower from the direction of the market place. He was carrying a filled flagon, which he tried to hide behind his back as soon as he saw Justice Throssell.

'Give you good day, sirs,' he mumbled. And to his father: 'The constable's now coming.'

'Then we are required to attend the corse,' said the sexton importantly. 'Lend me a hand out of here, boy — and do not spill the ale, for I have need of a draught of it. Master Justice Throssell knows full well that grave-digging's a thirsty business.'

Will and his godfather were already on their way towards the mortuary, whose narrow window-slit revealed the flickering light of a candle.

'I shall have the corpse brought outside,' the justice was saying. 'Nothing will be served by our peering at it by candlelight. I must convince myself of the constable's belief that it's a stranger's.'

'Is John Perry still constable?' asked Will.

'He died of the pox last year. Thomas

Gosnold of Southacre had already served as juryman, and I gave him the appointment. Such a substantial yeoman farmer will not be likely to take bribes, nor perjure himself, for fear of God and the honour of his descendants. And if public order is threatened, Thomas has servants of his own to quell unrest.'

'A substantial man indeed,' Will agreed. 'Thomas Gosnold has by far the biggest acreage of any of the priory's tenants. His flock of sheep is five times the size of my brother's.'

'True — and there's the rub. He's always occupied about his farm, and an unpaid office is burdensome. Thomas is as honest a constable as I have known, and yet he will do no more than he has to. It will suit him well if the murdered man is a stranger, for then there is naught we can do but give him a Christian burial.'

A heavy horseman had come cantering up to the northern gate of the churchyard. Dismounting hurriedly, and flinging his reins to one of the boys who had run behind in the hope of earning a penny, Thomas Gosnold strode between the graves to join the justice of the peace.

'Your pardon for my lateness, sir,' he cried as he approached, wiping the sweat from his brow with the sleeve of his workaday jerkin to emphasise his haste. He was some ten years older than Will, every inch as tall but as solid as a barn door, with bristling reddish hair and beard, and small blue eyes in a heavy, florid face.

'And Master Will Ackland!' he continued with guarded courtesy. 'I am glad to see you safe home from your travels — but I had not thought to see you here, sir.'

Will held out his hand in greeting. 'I do but keep company with my godfather, master constable,' he said.

'Aye . . . but — '

Justice Throssell intervened, an edge of sharpness in his voice. 'I have bidden my godson to dinner,' he said, 'and we are already late. Shall we proceed? Have the sexton bring the corpse into daylight, master constable, so that we may view it more clearly.'

'No need for that, sir! The dead man was naught but a vagabond. Candlelight will show you he's beyond recognition.'

Justice Throssell, half the constable's size, looked up at him sternly. 'Outside, if you please.'

'Sir — ' The constable still hesitated. He glanced from one to the other.

'I fear the corpse will quite destroy your

76

appetites. 'Tis my duty to show it to you, Master Justice Throssell — but Master Will has no need to endure the sight.'

'*Endure* it? I have been a soldier,' Will reminded him, impatient on his godfather's behalf, 'and have seen many a bloody corpse on the battlefield. And caused some of the deaths, too. Have done, master constable, and proceed as Justice Throssell bade you.'

Frowning, Thomas Gosnold clamped his lips and beckoned to the sexton and his son. The three of them entered the mortuary and presently emerged, the two Hobs hefting between them a humped board covered by a piece of coarse woolen cloth that would later serve as a shroud. The constable followed carrying a pair of trestles. There was some muttering from all three of them as they endeavoured to set the trestles squarely on the uneven ground, and the weighted board on the trestles, but at last it was precariously achieved.

The constable plucked up one corner of the cloth. ''Tis as I warned you, sir,' he said, almost with relish. And then he threw back enough of it to reveal the head of the corpse.

The noonday sun, mellow as it was, lit up an injury as violent as any Will had seen. The murderer had used some heavy object to batter his victim's face, and as the constable

77

had told them it was beyond recognition.

The sight was not a bloody one, for the corpse had long been immersed in the river and all the blood had drained. What was left, mingled with silt and strands of water-weed, was a pulp of grey-white flesh, splintered bone and smashed teeth, together with a single fearsomely displaced eyeball. The whole was topped by a ragged slime of hair.

Justice Throssell drew in his breath sharply, and they all crossed themselves. Then, his high voice steady, he told the sexton to remove the cloth entirely.

The man was of short-to-middling height and sparely built, and the few sodden garments that clung about his body seemed to be too large for him. His feet were bare, and he wore only a shirt and a pair of hose, both ragged. Now that the corpse was uncovered, flies were beginning to buzz about and gather on it.

'Have you not had the body stripped, master constable?' said Justice Throssell.

'Nay, sir — for fear o' the pox.'

'But the sexton told me the man had been stabbed. How did you know that, Hob Pulfer?'

Taken aback, the sexton opened and closed his hair-fringed mouth, then opened it again. 'Why, sir — the constable told me!'

Thomas Gosnold shot him a frown. 'I did but turn back the vagabond's shirt, sir.'

'And found no disease? Then be so good, master sexton, you and your son, as to strip the corpse completely. Vagabond or no, he's a Christian soul and must be accounted for as best we can. If we're able to tell nothing from his face, we may do so from his body.'

Will stood silent, watching as the lolling corpse was bared to their view. The most notable feature was on the hairless chest, a gaping white mouth where a knife thrust had penetrated. It was near to the heart, though perhaps not near enough to have killed him immediately.

He appeared to be a man of forty or fifty, with no noteworthy scars or blemishes to distinguish him. One thing, though, was clear to Will. He said nothing, out of courtesy to his godfather, for he did not want to usurp the older man's authority. But Justice Throssell, for all his shortness of sight, had made the same observation.

'This is no vagabond, master constable! He has no sores, nor signs of rough living, and he was well fed. Did you not notice that when you saw his wound?'

Thomas Gosnold made haste to justify himself. ''Twas dusk, sir, before I had time to view the corpse. The rags seemed proof that he was a vagabond.'

'Not proof enough, as you can see. What say you now, concerning the rags?'

'Why, sir — ' The constable hesitated, his eyes bulging with the effort of thought. Then his brow lightened. 'Why, he was a penitent on pilgrimage! His sins were so grievous to God that he dressed in rags and walked barefoot as part of his penance. There's many such on the road. And murder is done easily enough, as we all know — a jostling, a harsh word, then tempers flare and knives are out.

'Aye' — the constable warmed to his imagining — 'there you have it, sir! The man was a penitent, come from a distance on pilgrimage and set upon by some vagabond at the ford. The knife wound did not kill him, and so he was battered to death. We cannot know who he is. Let us ask the priest to give him a Christian burial, and have done.'

Justice Throssell fingered the grey wisp of his beard. 'What do you say, Master Will Ackland?'

'Shall we see t'other side of the corpse, sir?' suggested Will. 'We may learn something more from that.'

At a nod from the justice the two Hobs turned the corpse over, retrieving the limbs as they flopped awry. And immediately there was a stirring of interest, and of some alarm, for what was now revealed was a large splash of roughened crimson skin on the man's left buttock.

'Save us, Holy Mother of God,' cried the sexton, crossing himself as did his son. ''A's been touched by the Devil!'

'Not so,' Will said quickly. 'There was a companion of mine in the wars, who died of his wounds. He had just such a hidden birthmark, known to none until his body was stripped for burial. And he was as good a Christian man as any I've known, and died as godly a death. There's naught to fear — as Master Justice Throssell and the constable will tell you.'

The constable had looked uneasy, as though he would gladly have crossed himself too, but he had taken his cue from the justice. Now he squared his shoulders and cleared his throat. 'Aye, aye,' he agreed.

'Indeed. And now we have some means of recognition after all,' said Justice Throssell with satisfaction. 'Not public recognition, I grant you — but enough for a wife's proof, if her husband is missing.'

'He could have walked fifty mile or more!' protested the constable. 'We cannot search Norfolk and Suffolk for missing husbands!'

'Nor do I suggest it. But we cannot bury

the corpse unknown, master constable, until we are sure he is not from this parish.'

The justice turned to Hob the elder. 'Now, master sexton. You are the expert here, for you have been burying our corpses these twenty years and more. How long has this man been dead?'

Hob puffed out his chest, well pleased with the recognition of his craft. 'Aye, sir,' he beamed, showing the brown stumps of his teeth. 'Sexton for twenty-three year, and 'prentice to my father afore that, as young Hob is to me. Now, as to this corse . . . '

He moved importantly round the trestle, waving away the flies, prodding and sniffing at the body, and nodding his head wisely. ''Tis a matter of how long a's been in the water, for water will hasten the bloating. Now, some corses I have buried — '

'Your judgement, if you please,' interrupted Justice Throssell.

'Aye, well, sir — ' Knowing better than to vex him by any further delay the sexton pronounced, ticking off the time on his earthy fingers: 'Three days, by my reckoning. A' did not die today — nor yesterday when the corse was found — but the day afore that.'

The justice glanced at Will, who nodded a qualified agreement. The man had been dead long enough for rigor mortis to come and go, yet not so long that corruption had begun to advance. Three days was probably right, by his battlefield reckoning — though he could not be sure, for the running water might have affected duration of the rigor.

'Then to your duty, master constable!' piped Justice Throssell. 'Put word about the parish instantly for the name of any man of this age and stature, missing these three days past or thereabouts. And give me no more talk of burying until your duty's done.'

★   ★   ★

Lawrence Throssell's table was much better appointed than that at the castle, with linen of finer quality, slender drinking glasses, silver spoons, and a handsome silver salt as a centrepiece. The servants were more attentive in offering basins of warm water and towels for them to wash their hands. The food was of better quality too, for Lawrence had an uneasy stomach and insisted that his cook must use grease sparingly. The dish of fresh trout was griddled, and served with spinach and a salad of watercress very lightly salted. There was also shredded cheese with sugar and sage, fine wheaten bread, choice apples and sweet chestnuts.

The justice said the *Benedictus* and then urged his guest to fall to. But Will ate little, not so much because the corpse had spoiled his appetite but because he had a great deal on his mind.

'You found the truth of what I told you about the constable?' said his godfather. He had sent away the servants, and he himself filled their glasses with good white Rhenish wine.

'I did,' agreed Will, adding justly: 'Though it can be understood, for farming is a busy enough life without the distraction of holding office. But Thomas Gosnold sees only what he wants to see — and hopes you will see nothing more. Why else should he object to your viewing the corpse in daylight?'

'Or to your keen-eyed presence, William. What did you see that I missed?'

'Only the feet, and then only because I was standing near. I wanted the corpse turned over so that I could see their soles. The constable must have seen them too, but their condition did not suit his argument. That dead man was no penitent on barefoot pilgrimage! He was used to wearing well-fitting boots — and to riding rather than walking, for his feet were not broken nor even roughened by hard use.'

Lawrence Throssell looked up from his fish, his eyes shrewd.

'Then what is your opinion of the murdered man?'

'Why, that he was not wearing those rags when he was stabbed. There was no cut in the shirt that matched the knife thrust to his chest, therefore the rags must have been put on him after. As for his head — '

'Good, good,' interrupted the Justice. 'I was sure you would notice what I failed to see. But I saw his head well enough. In all my years I have never known the victim of a quarrel between strangers to be beaten so savagely.'

'You confirm what I thought, sir. Why should a stranger, having already stabbed a man in a quarrel, go to the extreme of destroying his features? Why should he exchange his victim's clothes for rags? The only reason, to my mind, is that the murderer wanted to prevent recognition of the dead man. And that must mean — as you suggested — that the victim does indeed belong to this parish.'

Justice Throssell was nodding his head with satisfaction, but Will was sombre.

'Not only that, I fear,' he said, pushing his

plate aside. He had knifed the succulent pink flesh of the trout from its backbone, but he had no heart to eat.

'The conclusion I have come to will distress my family, as it does me, but it has to be said. The murderer, too, must be a man of this parish. Why else should he fear recognition of his victim? He must know that if the body could be recognised, he would instantly be accused of the deed. And that points to one man, whose threats to kill — as you told me this morning — are known throughout the town.'

Lawrence Throssell frowned in solemn agreement and abandoned his own dinner.

'If the body is Walter Bostock's, it bodes ill for your brother . . . But for all I know,' he counselled hopefully, 'the prior's bailiff is alive and well.'

'Please God he is. But my sister Meg described him when we talked of him last night. She said he was some ten years older than Gib, and a good deal smaller in stature — as is the corpse.'

Will rose from the table. 'By your leave, godfather. It was my intention to seek out the bailiff this afternoon, but now there's some urgency in the matter. I'll bring news as soon as I can.'

'Do so, William.' Lawrence Throssell rose

86

too, tugging uneasily at his beard. 'You will know Walter Bostock if you see him,' he said, 'for his features are distinctive. He's easily recognised by his two front teeth set wide apart, and his broken nose.'

7

Will emerged from his godfather's house to find a cluster of serving women near the well on the opposite side of Northgate, gathered round a yellow-haired young man who had charge of two horses. From the laughter and the stirring of excitement about him, it seemed that Ned Pye was holding court.

Recognising Master Will Ackland, two gossips on the fringe of the group gave him a hasty good day, pretended they had taken no interest in the cause of the commotion, and went about their business. The serving women scattered, giggling, their pails half-filled with the water they had fetched as an excuse to leave their work.

Ned was clearly pleased with himself, though he claimed not to be. 'These simple Norfolk women,' he scoffed as he handed his master the reins of his horse. 'They'll marvel at any tale of travel I tell 'em.'

'Not so,' Will informed him. 'They're less easily gulled than you think, for I heard a gossip declare that Rome itself could not be finer than Swaffham on a market day. Here, catch!'

He tossed Ned one of the choice apples that his godfather had pressed on him as he left. Both horses — Ned's ageing bay mare, Will's black stallion with a white blaze — instantly pushed forward, snuffling eagerly. Their mouths reached out with velvet insistence, and the men had no option but to share their fruit.

'There's much to tell,' Will began as they all stood crunching. 'But some of it you've no doubt heard in the town?'

'Heard and seen,' Ned agreed. 'I made an early acquaintance of the sexton, and saw the corpse for myself. I've heard since that the constable seeks to know if any man of the parish is missing.'

'And what's your opinion of the injuries to the face?'

'That's easily said. Whoever killed him had cause to hate him.'

'So it seems.' Will paused for a moment, absently convincing his horse that the palm of his hand was empty. 'More force was used, for longer, than mere concealment warranted. There must have been a passion in those blows, a kind of madness . . . '

He frowned, reluctant to say more. His servant said nothing at all as they both mounted, but he had begun to whistle elaborately. It seemed that his suspicions were much the same as his master's.

'You are too hasty, Ned Pye,' said Will sternly, mindful of his godfather's advice. 'Be convinced — as I am — that we shall find the prior's bailiff alive, and my brother guilty of nothing more than gross ill-humour.'

Their way took them the short distance down Northgate to the market place, over which there now hung an air of exhaustion. After a busy feast-day morning of drinking, buying, gawping and laughing, of selling and entertaining, of eating and more drinking, most people — parishioners, countryfolk and pilgrims alike — were slumped in a comfortable half-stupor in the warmth of the sun. The dancing bear lay sprawled too, looking like nothing more than a discarded heap of mangy fur, except that it twitched and snuffled in its muzzled sleep.

Picking their way among the snorers, Will and his servant crossed the market place and took the street to the west, Priorygate. There were few houses here, and then only on its northern side, for it was bordered to the south by the great flint wall surrounding the priory precinct, halfway along which was the gatehouse.

A midday dole of food was given out at the almonry, every day of the year, to poor travellers and pilgrims, and to any who could not support themselves on account of age, misfortune or infirmity. Today it had been given out later than usual because of the morning's great ceremonies, and the poor had waited long for their food. But to celebrate the feast of St Matthew, all those who pressed forward to receive the dole had been given not only a lump of cheese and a loaf of coarse rye bread, but a herring as well.

As Will and Ned Pye rode along the street, the poor were beginning to emerge from the precinct. Hungry, ragged, old and not so old, foul-smelling, crippled, blind, they came jostling out through the gatehouse clutching their dole. Those who lived in the town scurried with the bounty as fast as they could to their hovels. The rest of them fell-to by the wayside, tearing ravenously at the food and quarrelling over fallen fragments.

'Lord!' observed Ned Pye with scorn, 'here's a feast indeed! I trust the monks, with their solemn vows of poverty, are enjoying a herring apiece for their dinner too. Not to mention the prior and his guests . . . He must live in a poor lodging, if this humble gatehouse is anything to judge by!'

His master was too preoccupied to reply. Ned stopped to stare at the imposing two-storey building, with its great central archway, through which a good road led down across grassland to the grandeur of the priory. The gatehouse had been built within the past thirty years, of red bricks ornamented with lozenges of blue, and dressed with stone. A row of carved shields on the north face bore the arms of the priory's royal and noble benefactors. In all, it was larger and much finer than the Acklands' gatehouse would ever have been, even at the height of the castle's power.

'A simple place, i' faith . . . ' concluded Ned. But his master had ridden on, past the gatehouse and down the long slope that led to the bridge over the river, and Ned had to gallop after him.

From the gatehouse on, there was no one on the road at all. Ordinarily there would be many comings and goings, for the road served the tithe barn, the mill, and the warehouses fronting the wharf, but these were all owned by the priory and were out of use in honour of St Matthew's day.

'This is the quickest way to Lynn,' Will told Ned Pye when his servant caught him up, 'either by road or by river. Thanks,' he pointed out, 'to the priory which did all the building.'

'Thanks?' said Ned. 'I've heard few thanks in the town! What with tolls to pay for the use of the bridge, and charges for grinding corn at the mill and loading merchandise at the wharf, there's many a Castleacre man holds a grudge against the priory.'

'Oh, aye,' said Will, dismissive for once of his countrymen. 'They always grumble against the priory, but any other landowner would irk them just as much. They can't see what great prosperity the monks have brought to Castleacre over the centuries. If we, the Acklands, still owned all the land here, we could never have built the bridge, nor the mill, nor the wharf. Without the wealth of the priory, and the crowds of pilgrims it brings, this would be a poor little town.'

Ned did more of his meaningful whistling, but his master ignored him.

They had come to a place where the great wall curved back, making room for carts to turn. Within the wall and overshadowing it stood the tithe barn, fully as long and as high as the nave of the parish church.

Access from the road to the barn was through a wide gateway in the wall, but today the iron-bound oaken gates were closed and barred. The bailiff's dwelling could still be reached by going through a postern. Will led the way, ducking as he rode through, and then on past one end of the tithe barn, scattering fowls that were pecking up spilled grain. The barn towered above them, with its stone walls, its massively downsweeping thatched roof, and its three gabled entrance bays, each of them tall enough to allow a high-laden cart to be driven through.

'Hah!' snorted Ned Pye. 'Here's another grumble against the priory. Small wonder, when every man sees a tenth of his produce swallowed up in that great maw!'

Will rode on. Anxious to assure himself of his brother's innocence, he galloped along the narrow path that led across rough pasture to the bailiff's house. Backed by a clump of oak trees, it stood on the valley's slope from where it overlooked the tithe barn, and was distantly overlooked in its turn by the great tower of the priory.

The prior's bailiff could consider himself a yeoman by virtue of his occupation. His thatched house was surrounded by a domestic farmstead, with herbs and vegetables, fruit trees and small livestock. The whole was bounded by a hedge of furze bushes, which did the double duty of keeping out the priory's cattle and providing prickly branches on which — as now — linen could be spread out to dry.

Will had not expected the bailiff himself to be at home. He had thought to hear of his whereabouts from his wife, a child or a servant. But seeing the door of the house shut on so warm an afternoon, and hearing no answer to Ned's shout of *Ho within!* as they approached, Will feared that the entire household must have gone to celebrate the feast day.

He was about to ride on towards the priory and seek information there, when he saw a tall, well-made woman emerge from the trees behind the house, herding pigs that had been foraging for acorns. She drove them through a gap in the furze, closed it again with a hurdle of wattles, and then came across the farmstead with the pigs oinking after her.

Evidently she was unmarried, for her dark hair flowed free from under her linen cap and hung about her shoulders. Her skirts were hoist well above her ankles for easier working, and her feet were bare.

'Where can I find your master, my good woman?' called Will.

She waited until she was near before she spoke, raising her hand to shade her eyes from the sun.

'I am Sibbel Bostock. What master should I have,' she asked with spirit, 'save my husband, the prior's bailiff?'

Will's error reddened his cheek. He would not knowingly have insulted her — but yeomen's wives, in his experience, usually took good care not to be mistaken for unmarried women of lesser rank.

'Your pardon, mistress,' he said with a stiff inclination of his head. He waited for a reply to his question, but she was busy driving the pigs into their hurdled enclosure and gave him no answer. She was somewhere between him and his sister in age, her eyes and mouth large, her skin as brown as that of any husbandman's wife. The disarray of her hair was caused by its thickness, for her cap could not contain it, and as she moved it twined about the column of her throat.

Will persisted, with some vexation. 'I am brother to Gilbert Ackland,' he told her, 'and I have business with your husband. Be so good as to tell me where I may find him.'

She left the pigs immediately and came closer, looking up at him with eyes that were almost black, yet bright as if newly burnished. Her colouring, more Italian than English, was not to Will's liking. True, he had once found dark eyes attractive; but they had been in a younger face and under a hotter sun than this.

'Then you must be Master Will Ackland, home from your travels,' said the bailiff's wife with eager respect. 'Will it please you to dismount and refresh yourself? I have some good elderberry wine of last year's making.'

He refused with the briefest courtesy. 'I

thank you, no. My business is urgent. I must know where the bailiff is.'

She shook her head. 'You will not find him in Castleacre, sir. He is gone away.'

'Gone?' Will's fears redoubled. His horse, responding to the tension its rider communicated, shifted its hooves and tossed its head. 'How long has the bailiff been away?' he demanded, shortening the reins. 'Which way did he go?'

'Why, he set out yesterday at dawn to ride to Bromholm. He goes there each year, to make the Michaelmas reckoning.'

Will slackened his grip on the reins. 'Ah . . . ' he said with guarded relief. 'Bromholm priory, that was once a daughter house of Castleacre, and still holds land on this priory's behalf. Tell me, Mistress Bostock: when your husband set out yesterday, did he travel alone?'

'Aye, so far as I know.'

'And when do you expect him back?'

'He's usually away a se'ennight.' The bailiff's wife placed a hand on Will's stirrup leather, and tilted back her head to look directly up at him with her bright dark eyes. 'Is there aught I can do for you, sir, in his absence? Shall you leave a message against his return?'

'It can wait,' said Will, turning his horse

away. He wished her an abrupt farewell, and cantered back the way he had come.

But Ned Pye was never one to miss an opportunity. Pausing beside the bailiff's wife, he bent down from his saddle to gaze boldly into her eyes.

'My master,' he said in his most beguiling voice, 'has too much on his mind to recognise a good offer. For my part, I would gladly come another time to taste your elderberry wine.'

Sibbel Bostock gave him short shrift.

'Be off with you, Jackanapes!' she retorted, with a flash of contempt and a box on the ear that left his head ringing. And though Ned essayed a jaunty whistle as he caught up with his master at the tithe barn, pride deterred him from making any mention of her.

'So the bailiff is alive, after all,' he said as they rode back to the town together. 'If he set out early yesterday, he cannot be the man who was murdered at the ford, for the corpse is older than that. A man killed yesterday at dawn,' he said, drawing on his battlefield experience, 'would ha' been stiff when we saw him this morning. All's well, Master Will — you need have no further concern for your brother.'

'Would it were so,' said Will. 'There's reason for hope, I grant you. But that corpse has lain for some time in fast-running water, losing all its blood. Tell me, from your knowledge — would it have begun to rot sooner than a blood-filled corpse on dry land, or later?'

Ned scratched his head. 'Mass,' he admitted, 'I cannot tell.'

'No more can I. And if there's doubt as to the day when the man was killed, we cannot know that the corpse is *not* the bailiff's. What I need, to be sure of my brother's innocence, is eye-witness proof that Walter Bostock is alive.'

Ned guessed what he would be required to do next. He was not displeased, for he saw advantage in it.

'It's a long ride to Bromholm,' he asserted, though he had no knowledge of the place.

'The priory is near Bacton, on the sea coast north of Yarmouth, forty-odd mile east of here. You can reach it in less than a day and a half, if you ride hard.'

'*Ride hard?* On this sorry old nag, already worn out by the journey from Dover?' Ned grimaced and shook his head. 'No, Master Will — if you want me there and back in haste, I must needs have a good horse.'

'And so you shall,' promised his master. 'As soon as we reach the Woolpack inn, we'll choose you a horse from the stables there.'

99

Ned was gratified, but wary of such an easy victory. 'A young horse, mind, sound in wind and limb?'

'The very best the innkeeper can provide. If you leave by the Walsingham road, and then turn east along the valley of the Nar, you'll reach North Elmham by nightfall. Tomorrow, ride east through Reepham, Aylsham and North Walsham, changing your horse as need be.'

Ned looked accusingly at his master. '*Change* my horse?'

'So I said.' Will gave him a twitch of a grin. 'I never promised to buy you one. You'll journey faster if you hire fresh horses as you go.'

'I might have known,' grumbled Ned Pye. 'Servants,' he continued in an injured voice, 'must always suffer the whims of their masters . . .'

They were approaching the market place, where noise was rising again. The holiday-makers and entertainers must have climbed back to their feet, however unsteadily, the keepers of shops and alehouses were no doubt redoubling their efforts to profit from the crowds, and enjoyment was likely to continue with dancing and singing and dicing and drinking far into the night.

'And what message,' Ned continued with

vexation as their horses began to push through the outer fringes of the crowd, 'am I to give the bailiff if I find him?'

'None at all,' said Will briskly. 'Ask one of the lay-brothers to point him out to you, and satisfy yourself that you've seen him. You'll know him by his broken nose, and a gap between his two front teeth.'

'And if he's not been seen there — ?'

'As soon as you're sure, either way, return with the news as fast as you can. You'll find the road between North Walsham and Bromholm crowded, though, for the priory there is famous as a place of pilgrimage.'

Their horses were now surrounded by the newly fed poor, all pushing towards the market place. Some were beggars and vagabonds, intent on taking advantage of unwary holiday-makers. Others were poor pilgrims, on their way home or to other shrines, and lingering in Castleacre to enjoy the free entertainment. Most of them were now in good spirits, and helped the horses along with cries and slaps.

'Bromholm, did you say, master?' quavered an aged pilgrim eagerly, gazing up at Will rheumy-eyed from where he trudged between their two horses. 'I ha' been on pilgrimage to Bromholm! I ha' prayed before their wondrous true relic of the Holy Cross!'

101

'Pah!' said Ned Pye, feeling thoroughly disagreeable. 'When a man has travelled half over Europe, as I have, he knows that if all the supposed relics of the Holy Cross in all the churches of Christendom were put together, there'd be a forest of crosses! Aye, and if all the supposed bones of the saints were mended, they'd have more arms and legs than they knew what to do with. And as for new blood appearing on the bones — '

'Have done, Ned Pye!' said his master in a voice of thunder. The old pilgrim was standing stock still, heedless of the jostling of those behind him, staring up at Ned with a fallen jaw and eyes that were fast losing the last of their light.

Will bent from his saddle and gripped the man's shoulder for a moment. 'Go on in faith, friend,' he reassured him. And then, with his disgruntled servant riding ahead and shouting *Way, way!*, he forced a passage through the crowded market place to reach the stables at the Woolpack inn.

8

Master Justice Throssell was heartened by the news his godson brought. Inviting him to his parlour again, he poured two glasses of the Rhenish wine.

'I'll send word to the constable that the prior's bailiff, though absent, is accounted for. But you are right to be cautious, Will. We must know for sure that Walter Bostock is alive before we can be confident of your brother's innocence.'

'Is there news of any other missing men? I heard the enquiry spoken of at the inn.'

'It seems that it has caused a stir. My own servants have been about this business, as have the constable's, though they're hampered by the feast-day crowds.'

The justice's sparse beard twitched with amusement. 'Two absentees from home have already been declared. Mistress Pardew, wife to poor wandering Tom, swears the corpse must be her husband's though his age is greater than mine, and he has but one arm. And the wife of Jack Broach the thatcher claimed he was missing, in the hope that he would be caught in fornication and brought by the churchwardens before the arch-deacon. But it seems that the constable's servants knew full well where to find him.'

Will laughed, remembering Jack Broach. 'Sleeping out of the way of his wife in the barn behind the Green Man, I have no doubt, and drunk as a rat into the bargain! Well, these tales will serve to take attention from my brother. As to the corpse . . . ?'

'He must be buried by dusk tomorrow,' said Justice Throssell, 'for he'll keep no longer. Should anyone seek to claim him later, he can be identified by knowledge of his birthmark.

'But enough of Castleacre!' Unequal in size as he was to his great chair, Lawrence Throssell eased himself eagerly forward. 'I long to hear the news you have gathered on your travels. How does England stand now with France? And with the emperor?'

The old gentleman bombarded Will with questions, but did not stay to listen to his answers. He seemed to have something of more immediate importance on his mind, and presently he burst out with it.

'And what of King Henry and His Holiness the Pope? What of the King's great matter — the annulment of his marriage, which only the Pope can authorise? I know what occurred last year, when Cardinal Wolsey and another Papal legate sat in London to judge the King's case. I heard tell of Queen Katherine's dignity as she rejected the tribunal, saying she could have no fair trial in England. But what now, Will? Is the case going to Rome, as she wishes?'

Will shook his head. 'The Pope prevaricates, as always. Though he's supreme head of the church, he fears to offend any of the great rulers of Europe. He wishes to please our King, and yet he dare not give way to his urging, for the Queen has the support of her nephew the Emperor. Meanwhile, King Henry gives his attention to little else. During the past three years, I've travelled to and from Rome with royal envoys five times, on this matter alone. The king grows increasingly angry that his wishes are frustrated.'

'Ha! Because,' said Justice Throssell, outraged, 'he desires to marry one of the Queen's maids of honour! I heard so from one of my fellow justices, who was at Westminster earlier in the year.' He brooded, swirling the pale wine in his glass. 'I have heard it said that Her Grace would resolve the matter by renouncing the world and retiring to a nunnery.'

'It's said so,' agreed Will. 'But not by the Queen. That course has been urged on her many times, not only by the King but by the

Pope himself. But Queen Katherine will never do so, for all that she's a very devout lady. She holds herself to be King Henry's true and lawful wife, and mother of his rightful heir, the Princess Mary.'

'And so I do believe,' asserted Lawrence Throssell loyally. 'And so does every man of sound mind in Norfolk. Aye, and throughout the kingdom, I have no doubt. There was such rejoicing, twenty years ago, when they were married — and evidence enough of their happiness . . .'

The old gentleman sighed. 'Well, well. The King can obtain an annulment only if he shows that their marriage was invalid, and he has no good case for that.'

'Good case or not,' said Will, 'King Henry has convinced himself of its truth. He cites the Bible for authority. Though the Queen has borne him sons, none lived beyond a few weeks. He says this is God's judgement on him for unlawfully marrying his brother's widow.'

Justice Throssell snuffled with indignation. 'The King has no ground for that argument! When he married Prince Arthur's widow, it was with special dispensation from the Pope.'

'So I understand. But now he states that his conscience is so greatly troubled by this matter that nothing will resolve it but an

106

annulment of the marriage.'

'Hmm,' said the justice darkly. He sighed again, then creaked to his feet. 'My bones tell me 'tis pity to waste the sun, when winter lasts so long. Let us walk in the garden for a while.'

Enclosed as it was by a high brick wall, his garden was warm and mellow, the colours turning as the season turned. No livestock were kept here, apart from bees and doves, and there was no disorder, only carefully tended herbs, flowering plants and fruiting trees. The damask roses that were the old gentleman's pride were over, but their fruits glowed scarlet in the sun.

The two men walked together along the swept paths, Will pacing slowly, Lawrence Throssell pausing every now and then in mid-trot to cup in his hand a ripening quince or a medlar, absently drawing it to his godson's attention without interrupting their talk.

'And how does the Queen reply to the King's argument that their marriage was invalid?' he asked.

'Her Grace's defence never wavers. She told the tribunal, on oath, that she never had conjugal relations with Prince Arthur, and that she was a virgin at the time of her marriage to King Henry. She challenged the

King to deny that, but he would not answer.'

'No, for he knows it to be true, as I and many others have always believed. I recall,' said Justice Throssell, 'that I was a young lawyer at Westminster at the time of the marriage of Prince Arthur, the Prince of Wales, to the Princess Katherine of Aragon. I saw them both.

'The bride was just sixteen years old, small for her age, but of a pleasing appearance. We had all expected her to be dark, being Spanish, and her fairness surprised us — but then, she has English Plantagenet blood in her veins. Prince Arthur was a year younger, and half a head shorter still — he was puny, a child in appearance. He had always been frail and sickly, quite unlike his younger brother Prince Henry. No one who saw them, as I did, ever believed that their marriage had been consummated. There was sadness, but no surprise, when Arthur died not five months later.'

'And that,' said Will, 'was, what, nearly thirty year ago? I heard tell of it when I was in London last year, at the time of the tribunal. Courtiers who had been in attendance on the night of that marriage gave evidence at the tribunal on behalf of the King. They tried to prove that Katherine could not have been a virgin when she married King Henry.

'One of them swore that Prince Arthur had called from the marriage bed for ale, early next morning, saying he was dry for he had been in the midst of Spain that night. But if the prince did indeed say so, was it any more than the boast of a weakling boy? I think the King's conscience need no more trouble him on that account than it has done these twenty years past.'

'My opinion chimes with yours, Will,' agreed his godfather. 'The King may cite his conscience as reason for divorce, but here's the truth on't: he is a lusty gentleman, and the Queen — his elder by six years — is now past child-bearing. To get a male heir he must needs marry a younger woman, and he's already made his choice.'

The old gentleman paused, shaking his head with regret. 'That it should be Nan Bullen' — he pronounced the name Boleyn in the Norfolk way — 'a girl born at Blickling in this county, who has betrayed her mistress the Queen and thrust herself into his favour . . . But there' — he shook his head again — 'she had example from her elder sister Mary, who was the King's whore before her.'

'True,' said Will. 'But there's a difference. The King merely dallied with Mary Boleyn, as he did earlier with Bessie Blount who bore his bastard son, Henry Fitzroy. He's deeply enamoured of Anne Boleyn, and has been so these four years.'

'I heard it said that she did not let him have his way with her,' conceded Lawrence Throssell somewhat grudgingly. 'She could not do so, and keep his favour, unless he loved her. But does she hold him off still?'

Will laughed. 'I am not in her confidence, godfather, nor that of King Henry! It's rumoured that she allows him many liberties — but it would be a rash man who enquired more closely. Anne Boleyn is a clever young woman, bold and strong-willed, and she intends to be Queen. She behaves so at court already, and is kissed openly by the King despite Queen Katherine's presence.'

Justice Throssell exclaimed his disapproval at some length. 'She must be a great beauty, to captivate him in this way,' he concluded.

'Not so,' said Will. 'Her mouth is too large and her eyes are too black, for she's as dark-hued as our Spanish Queen is fair. And yet . . . '

He paused for a moment. The image that had come fleetingly into his mind was not that of Anne Boleyn but of Sibbel Bostock, wife to the prior's bailiff, an older woman but of similar appearance.

'Yet it is said that she captivates the King with the brilliance of her eyes and the liveliness of her spirit. He seems bewitched by her, and can deny her nothing.'

Lawrence Throssell's brow had creased with anxiety. 'Then how will this great matter be resolved? These are not private troubles. Here is a contest between the supreme spiritual authority of Rome, and the governance of this realm. What is to happen, if the Pope will not grant King Henry a divorce?'

Will stopped in his walk, and turned to look at his godfather. 'The King is known to be terrible in his anger,' he said soberly. 'When his patience is exhausted, I think he will let no one — not even His Holiness the Pope — stand in his way.'

★ ★ ★

Anxious for further discussion, Lawrence Throssell tried to persuade his godson to linger. But Will was eager to return to the castle and see his daughter again.

There was none of the usual farmstead noise and bustle within the castle walls for most of the servants had gone to enjoy the holiday. As soon as he rode through the gatehouse he spied Betsy's little white-capped head bobbing about on the far side of the herb garden, but she did not notice his arrival. Dismounting, he walked towards her

111

and took her — without intention — by surprise. One of the many cats, harboured in the castle against vermin, came loping out from behind an overgrown lavender bush and Betsy ran laughing after it.

Glad to see her happiness, Will bent and held out his hands to catch her. But the child was so dismayed by the reappearance of the tall stranger who was said to be her father that she stopped in mid-run, as though caught in wrong-doing. And there for a moment she remained frozen, her eyes big with alarm, her mouth silently open, her small hands splayed like starfish.

Trying to put her at her ease, he went down on his haunches to match her height. But the nearness of his face alarmed Betsy more, and she herself promptly squatted, her gown crumpled on the ground, her head low, one plump finger absorbedly making lines in the dust.

'"Tis allowed to laugh and run,' he assured her. 'I like to see you do it. Your Aunt Meg,' he added, in some desperation to obtain a response, 'always laughed and ran when *she* was a girl.'

Betsy responded immediately. She said nothing, but raised her head and looked at him in total disbelief, clearly convinced that her aunt could never have been a child.

Perplexed, Will cast about for some topic of mutual interest. His eye fell on one of the cats, a battle-scarred black hunter now dozing in retirement under a bush of marjoram.

'There's an old friend of mine,' he said. 'I called him Jasper. Is that his name still?'

Betsy nodded. Emboldened by the stranger's acquaintance with the animal, she rose to her feet. 'Jasper will scratch if you touch him,' she said, evidently passing on a warning she had been given.

'So he will, for he's now old and disagreeable. But what of that pretty greystriped Cyprus cat — who is she?'

His daughter beamed, her pink-cheeked face now confidently on a level with his. 'Tabitha,' she said.

'A most suitable name,' Will agreed. Then, 'Aha! What young vagabond have we here?'

He reached out and scooped up a passing kitten, its fur the colour of apricots, and held it up on the palm of his hand. The little creature, its round eyes still a pale blue, peered at him apprehensively.

'Now I have you, sirrah!' Will made his voice gruff. 'Tell me your name at once, and what business you have in this parish, or I'll report you to the constable!'

Her shyness quite forgotten, Betsy stood chuckling at her father's knee. ''Tis Watkin,'

113

she said. 'He's not a vagabond, he lives here! He'll be a mouser when he's grown.'

'*When he's grown*, hey? A fine excuse for idleness!' said Will sternly. He addressed his captive again: 'The constable will charge you, sirrah, with being a sturdy beggar, for though you are able-bodied you make no attempt to earn. The magistrate will have you set in the stocks for it, there to remain for three days and nights on a diet of bread and water. What say you to that?'

The kitten mewed a protest. Betsy, beside herself with laughter, hugged her father's knee. But their pastime was interrupted by a hurried and anxious Dame Meg Morston.

'There you are, Will! Go to your nurse, child.'

He nodded confirmation to his daughter. 'Go, Betsy,' he said, pouring the kitten off his hand into her arms. Then he stood up with a grimace, for his wounded leg had stiffened while he crouched.

'What is it, Meg?'

'Why didn't you tell me?' scolded his sister. 'One of the servants is back from the town, with news that the body you found is that of a Castleacre man! Is it — is it the prior's bailiff?'

Her eyes were apprehensive, and Will sought to reassure her. There would be time enough for anxiety if Ned Pye were to return without having found the man.

He put his hands on her shoulders and rallied her with a small shake. 'Come, Meg! When did you ever believe the rumours that Castleacre folk call 'news'? In truth, the body from the river is beyond recognition. He could have travelled here from anywhere. He'll be buried unknown, when Justice Throssell is assured that every man of this parish can be accounted for. As for Walter Bostock, his wife tells me that he's over at Bromholm priory for the Michaelmas reckoning.'

Relief smoothed Meg's forehead. 'Thank God — I truly feared that Gilbert's madness had driven him to murder. Oh, but he's in a difficult humour, Will. He said no word at dinner, save to snarl because most of the servants were absent. Now he's gone up to the old keep, where he'll sometimes brood among the ruins for hours on end.'

'I'll go and speak with him,' said her brother, though remembering Gib's stoked-up outburst of anger the night before, he was privately doubtful of doing any good.

'No, leave him,' urged Meg. 'I fear he will turn to violence.'

'Better that he should turn it on me, then.'

'Well, go to him if you must. But keep Ned Pye somewhere near,' she cautioned, 'for your own safety.'

'Ned's up to mischief elsewhere,' said Will, concealing his servant's destination from her. 'There's too little scope for his talents in Castleacre, and I sent him away for a few days. But have no fear — I'll deal with Gib if need be.'

'No doubt you will!' Her voice teased him, but clearly she meant it when she added, 'If you're not back for supper I'll send men to find you, armed with cudgels.'

9

The lower ward of the castle, where the house and farmstead were, was already in evening shadow. But the old keep stood high on the upper ward, an earthwork behind the house, and its ruined walls — as uneven as rotten teeth — caught the last rays of the sun.

When they were boys, Will and Gib had spent many warlike hours up there, fighting the barons' wars over again. As the elder, Gib had always claimed the right to be first holder of the keep, and that had suited Will, the more active and inventive of the two. Between them, they had demolished whole armies of imaginary archers and knights as they fought for possession of the keep. But every battle had ended in fierce single combat among the ruins, and both of them bore faded scars to remind them of their rivalry.

The earthwork of the upper ward stood as high as the chimneys of the house, and its sides were as steep as the roof. It was overgrown with birch trees, now in yellowing leaf, and bushes glistening with berries, except where a wide scar ran straight from top to bottom. This was where the stones that had been taken from the old keep in Will's grandfather's day had been slid down to the lower ward for the building of the house. The process had gouged away the thin soil, making the scar as white and in places as steep as Dover cliff, for wind and weather had worn it to bare, slippery chalk.

Climbing this cliff was one of the challenges Will had enjoyed in his youth. He had known better, though, than to take such an exposed route when his brother was holding the keep, for that would have been to invite defeat. Instead, he had found several different ways up through the maze of goat paths that traversed the scrub, so that he could always take Gilbert by surprise.

Since then, the goats had been banished to the outer ditch of the castle, and the scrub had grown and tangled beyond recognition. Gilbert had no doubt made a winding path up to the keep, but it was not immediately obvious and Will did not intend to skulk about in search of it. On this delicate errand — wanting to hear what Gib would say about the murder, but without antagonising him — he preferred to make an open approach. And besides, he relished the challenge of climbing the mound again.

Casting off his cap and doublet he stood, as in youth, in shirt and hose and surveyed the chalk scar. Then, he had always begun the climb simply by taking a run at it. He was tempted now to ignore his years and wounds and take a run at it again — but that, he was forced to acknowledge, would almost certainly result in an early, ignominious downward slide. Better to be thrifty with his breath and scramble all the way, using embedded flintstones to give him a grip or a toe-hold where the chalk was steepest.

At first the climb went well, for his hands and feet instinctively sought their old lodging places. Even so, he soon became aware that it was more taxing than he remembered, and he was obliged to pause for breath halfway. The dry weather had loosened the surface, and as he progressed he had been sending down trickles of chalk and small flints. When he resumed the climb, he became aware that chalk and flints were beginning to slide down from another source — this time upon him, from above.

Very soon the slide became a shower. He had to stop and fling up an arm to protect his eyes. The small flints were becoming larger and sharper-edged, and when one of them caught him a dizzying crack on the side of the head he knew that this was no accident. The debris was not merely falling, but being kicked down on him. Once again, his brother was intending to do battle.

Almost caught off-balance, with his full weight on his weaker leg, Will clung with one hand to a flintstone while his other foot scrabbled in vain to find a toe-hold. Glancing down, he saw that there was a long steep way to fall. Glancing up, he saw that he was near the top of the mound where the massive figure of Gilbert waited, a stone gripped in either hand.

Were he still a boy Will would have acted without thought, swinging up lightly to the top of the mound and using his greater speed to dodge past Gib. But that was no longer feasible. For a man of impaired agility, who had come to pacify his brother rather than to challenge him, prudence was the only course.

Shielding himself as best he could from the debris that still came down, Will spat out a mouthful of chalk dust and sued for peace.

'Pax, Gib!' he shouted, hoping that his brother would remember that much at least of their schoolday Latin. 'Have done, I say . . .'

The kicking stopped. He looked up again. Gilbert had moved forward to the edge of the mound and stood towering above him, his great hands still gripping the missiles, his hair and beard wild. 'Pax?' he said venomously.

'I'll pledge no peace to a brother who spies on me!'

Will cursed himself for a fool. Had he a groat's worth of the prudence he had just prided himself on, he would not have made this climb. His perch was precarious, his leg ached abominably, and their brother was as violent as Meg had warned. He could neither retreat nor stay where he was. The only way to advance was by talking, and that as reassuringly as he knew how.

'I am not here to *spy* on you, Gib. Nor yet to do battle with you, for I have no cause. I've come merely to see the old keep, and to recall the merry times we had here.'

'Pah!' growled Gilbert. There was dark suspicion in his voice, but he turned away and flung his missiles elsewhere.

Will seized the opportunity to hoist himself up to solid ground. The old defensive walls that had risen straight from the top of the mound had been quarried away completely at this point, making a gaping entrance to what remained of the keep. Gilbert had disappeared, growling, among the ruins, and Will limped about for a few moments until the cramp in his leg had eased. His head was sore, and his left eye was nearly blinded by the blood that was trickling into it. Silently cursing Gib, he wiped away the blood with his sleeve and remembered, with a fleeting satisfaction, that the shirt was not his own but one of his brother's.

Gilbert had removed himself to the far side of the upper ward, and was now hurling stones at the jackdaws that made their habitation in the ruins. Will thought it politic to reassure him that it was indeed the old keep he had come to see, and so he made a point of wandering through what little was left of the hall and passageways. Many of the walls were no more than shoulder-high, and since his last visit, years ago, plants had sprouted thickly from crevices between the mossy stones. Pushing past them he sought and found another gap in the wall, opening on to a pathway that led down to the foot of the mound. He was glad to know of it, for he had no intention of returning by way of the precipitous chalk face — nor yet of climbing it again, with or without Gib's menacing presence.

His brother was still trying to stone the jackdaws. They circled high, just out of his reach, calling their noisy *kyow kyow*, and Gilbert shouted curses at them as he missed.

Before approaching him, Will went to the western side of the keep and looked out over the huddled, smoke-wreathed roofs and gables of the town. Firelight and the sounds of voice and horn and drum rose from the market place, which heaved with evening merry-makers, and the air was larded with the smell from a hundred feast-day cooking pots.

In the valley beyond the town stood the great grey bulk of the priory, secure in its precinct within its own high walls. It was only from up here, on the old upper ward of the castle, that the massiveness of the priory church and the extent and grandeur of the buildings that surrounded it could be seen as a whole.

From here, the contrast between priory and castle, the one so powerful in size and wealth, the other reduced to the farmstead that lay below this ruined keep, was only too clear. If Gilbert often came up here, as Meg had said, and brooded over the change in the Ackland family fortunes, small wonder he felt bitter.

But how far, Will wondered, had that bitterness led his brother? Certainly to a sullen, vicious temper. Worse, to madness? Worst of all, to the Devil's work of murder?

Shading his eyes against the crimson set of the sun, Will looked further west to where the road to Lynn went past the prior's tithe barn. He could glimpse the great roof of the distant barn, but the bailiff's house was hidden by trees. Was Walter Bostock indeed at Bromholm, as his wife Sibbel had supposed? Or was he the murdered man whose mortal remains, now corrupting within his shroud, awaited burial in the parish churchyard?

Will turned his gaze south to the rim of the shallow valley. He could see the line of the Peddars' Way, Roman-straight between tall hedgerows, rising over the downland sheep pasture of Bartholomew's Hills. The hills were too far distant for him to see the gibbet that stood at the crossroads, but he knew well enough that it was there. And so did Gilbert, for all that he rarely travelled to Swaffham and never beyond it.

The gibbet, and its purpose, was engraved deep in Will's memory. As soon as he was old enough to ride so far, their father had taken him and Gib to see a hanging.

Most of the townsfolk had had the same intention, and the press of onlookers was so great that by the time they arrived the miscreant was already hanging by his own weight. His arms were bound, but his legs still kicked feebly as his body revolved in the air, his tongue bursting from his mouth and his eyes bulging in his purple face. That, their father had told them sternly, was what happened to wrong-doers; and when the last breath left their bodies, their souls went straight to an even more dreadful punishment — the eternal torments of hell that awaited every unshriven sinner.

It was a fearful lesson, and one that Will himself had never forgotten. Young as they were then, he and Gib were well aware of hell. Not only did the priest speak of it constantly but they saw it for themselves, every saint's day and Sunday, in a painting above the chancel arch on the wall of the parish church. What was depicted there was the day of Doom, when good men would be separated from the wicked, and the mouth of hell with its fearsome teeth and furnace-red throat would gape open to receive unshriven sinners.

But had Gib, in a few moments of murderous madness, quite forgotten those lessons? Was it his own fate he came up here to brood on? For if he had indeed killed the bailiff, it was not only the possibility of discovery and being hanged that he would fear, but the certainty of being pitchforked by waiting devils into the everlasting flames.

Feeling a rare compassion for his brother, Will went in search of him. He found him still in the same place, throwing flints with aimless savagery at a tall fang of masonry, for the birds had made themselves scarce.

'How now, Gib?' he asked pleasantly. 'Is it

125

to be jackdaw pie for supper tonight?'

Gilbert scowled at him, determined to take offence at whatever his brother said. 'I'd marvel to see *you* hit more of them than I did.'

Will laughed. 'And I'd marvel with you, for your aim with a stone was always better than mine. What of archery, though? I'm sadly out of practice. Shall we go together to the butts tomorrow, as we used to do?'

Gib flung another flint, this time taking aim and sending it whistling accurately through an arrow-slit in the wall. 'Archery is a pastime for idle gentlemen who have nothing to do but travel and read books,' he said sourly. 'As for me, I am head of this family and its sole support, and I must work. Do not mock me with your pastimes, for I have leisure for none!'

Will shook his head. 'I come not to mock, but in friendship,' he insisted. 'And also to bring a message from Master Justice Throssell. He wants to know if any man of middle years is missing from the town, and asks me to ask you if all your servants are accounted for.'

Gilbert gave him a piercing look from under his shaggy brows. 'Why so?'

'A man was found dead in the river yesterday. Didn't you hear the news? It seems he was murdered.'

His brother bent to pick up some loose flintstones. 'Aye, so I heard,' he said indifferently. 'A stranger — a vagabond, by all accounts.'

'That may be so,' said Will. 'He's nameless, true, for his face was beaten beyond recognition. But the justice will not have him buried unknown, without ensuring that he's not from Castleacre. He has sent the constable to enquire throughout the parish for missing men.'

Gib made no comment. He had resumed his throwing and was preoccupied by it, taking aim at the arrow-slit with another flint. He missed, and cursed with greater vexation than such a failure warranted.

'Are all your serving men accounted for?' persisted Will. 'Those in your household, and on the fields?'

'How should I know?' snapped Gilbert, aggrieved. 'The men take every saint's day as a holiday, and will do no work.'

'They do so everywhere. But today's the holiday. Was any man absent yesterday, when the body was found?'

Gib shrugged for answer, and threw at a passing crow.

It was time, thought Will, to come to the point. 'The justice has had reports of missing men,' he said, 'but most have proved false. One man who's certainly absent from his home, though, is the prior's bailiff.'

About to throw again — massive weight on his back foot, right hand holding the missile poised behind his head, left arm forward for balance — Gilbert paused.

'How do you know that?' he growled, without changing his stance.

'I made some enquiries to aid Justice Throssell. I went along Priorygate, and so to the bailiff's house, but did not find him.'

Gilbert straightened, taking his time. 'You wouldn't expect to find the bailiff at this season, were you a tenant of the priory and tormented by him as I am!' he glowered. 'He's over at Bromholm for the reckoning.'

'So I heard,' said Will. 'His wife told me that he's accounted for.'

He spoke lightly, and his brother's response took him by surprise. Gilbert's face — so much of it as was visible between hair and beard — darkened. He became bull-like, hunching his great shoulders and lowering his head in anger.

'*You went to the bailiff's house and spoke with his wife?* God's death, is there no end to your prying! I know full well where Walter Bostock is — he's about his proper business. And you can go about yours, brother, for

128

you've outstayed your welcome here. Take your servant and your horses, and go!'

Will stood his ground. Blood from his cut head was trickling into his eye again, but he would not acknowledge the hurt by wiping his face.

'As you wish, Gib,' he said, humouring him. 'I came only for a week, but I won't stay where I'm not welcome. I'll leave tomorrow, and my child shall leave too. But first, I must ask Meg what's to be done with Betsy. No doubt our sister will have an opinion on this matter.'

Gib shifted at once. 'Aye, well ... ' he conceded gruffly. 'A week, did you say? Well, stay so long if you must — but I allow it only for Meg's sake. Listen to me, brother — '

He drew a great breath. His anger refuelled, his eyes glittering, he stabbed a thick finger in Will's face. 'Spy on me no more! And pry no more into Castleacre affairs, for you're as unwelcome in the town as you are in this castle.'

'That's not what I was told when I walked the streets this morning.'

'It's what I tell you now.' Gib gave Will's cheek a sudden, stinging, upwards slap, then brought away his hand and showed his brother the blood on it.

'You bleed already, Master William!' he jeered. He thrust his face closer, and Will felt the tainted heat of his breath. 'Spy or pry again, and by the Mass you will bleed more!'

Will clenched his jaw and his fists, but forced himself to turn silently away. He would not show his own anger, for his brother's eyes were those of a man who had caught a glimpse of hell.

* * *

Late that night, unable to sleep, Will rose from his bed, dressed, and slipped quietly out of the house. A full moon rode high over the castle walls. He walked by its light through the orchard, kicking at fallen apples and releasing their heady, fermenting smell. As he walked, thinking uneasily about Gilbert, he willed Ned Pye to make all possible speed to Bromholm and back with news of the prior's bailiff.

He had concealed his cut head from the rest of the family that evening by attending to it himself and changing his blood-smeared shirt. Meg had thrown him several anxious, questioning looks, but poor Alice had been with her in the parlour both before and after supper, and he had had no opportunity to speak to her.

130

As for supper itself, Gilbert had made it a thoroughly disagreeable occasion. The meal was a cold one, for most of the servants were either merry-making in the town or sleeping off a day's drinking. Gib, who hated to eat his meat cold, had attacked it savagely, railing throughout the meal at the solitary, clumsy old serving woman. Will had done his best to entertain Meg and Alice by telling them of outlandish foreign customs and manners, but his heartiness had been as forced as their amusement. It was a relief, now, to be out of the house and alone in the dew-drenched night.

All was quiet, apart from the distant bark of a dog fox and the hooting of an owl. After the long day of celebration, the whole populace of Castleacre — townsfolk, pilgrims and wayfarers alike — had fallen into an exhausted sleep. Ordinarily, Will would not have been able to leave the house at night without tripping over and waking some of the servants, for they slept on straw pallets that they put down wherever they chose. But tonight, though some of the men were sprawled, snoring, across the screens passage, they were so far gone in drink that Will could step over and even on them without making them stir.

The dogs seemed to be asleep too, both in

the house and in the yard — and that was strange. The door of the house was always left unbarred, because the dogs could be relied on to bark at any unusual movement.

When Will had first begun to grow tall and fidgety, the too-easily wakened dogs and servants had been a great inconvenience to him. Often enough he had wanted to sneak from the castle at night, against his father's orders. But there were some things that he had been glad enough to learn from his elder brother: one was that the servants could be forewarned with a wink, the other was that the dogs could be quietened with marrow-bones.

He turned and looked about him, listening. Then he saw a glimmer of light coming from the open door of one of the stables, over against the castle walls, and heard the muffled clop of ironshod hooves on straw-covered stone. One of the horses was being led out, by a large man who carried a horn lantern.

Will had no doubt that the man was Gib, even before he emerged into the moonlight and blew out the lantern. But what was he doing? Fleeing because he had committed murder?

From that distance, there was nothing Will could say or do to stop his brother. He watched Gib lead the horse hurriedly to the mounting block, heard the creak of the stirrup leathers as he settled himself in the saddle, saw him ride through the gatehouse, and heard him gallop away into the night.

10

Will rose in the grey mist before dawn, when cocks were crowing from every dung-hill in the castle yard and throughout the town. He had hoped to find that Gilbert had returned during the night, but his brother's horse was not in the stables.

'How now, Jacob?' he called, as the yardman stumbled from the gatehouse yawning and scratching. 'My brother's cob is not here.'

The old man seemed unperturbed. 'Aye, well — ' he mumbled through his toothless gums. 'Master Ackland sometimes rides out early to the fields.'

'But not at midnight, I think. Didn't you hear the hooves — or were you too full of ale?'

'That I was not!' protested Jacob, who would never admit to any negligence for fear of being turned off his work and out of his house on account of age. He splashed a handful of water from the horse trough on to his whiskery face, and wiped it with his sleeve. 'I heard nothing,' he said stubbornly.

Will gave a significant sigh, and shook his

head. 'My father, God rest his soul, always said that no man could ride through the gatehouse without your knowledge. But time passes, old friend . . . '

'Nay, Master Will!' Jacob caught him by the arm. ''Tis not that I *did* not hear,' he pleaded, his faded eyes fearful. ''Tis that your brother is my master and I dare not displease him. My best way is to hear naught, see naught and say naught.'

'So it is, then,' agreed Will, giving the old man a reassuring clap on the shoulder. He went into the stable to attend to his own horse, which had heard his voice and whinnied an enquiry. Within a few minutes, the sound of hooves came galloping up Castlegate street, and then Gilbert's voice shouted for the yardman.

Will stayed where he was, conscious that he was indeed spying but unrepentant so long as Gib's innocence was in any doubt. He waited until his brother had left the yard to go to the house, and then until old Jacob brought Gib's heavyweight cob back to the stable.

'You won't tell your brother that I spoke of him, Master Will?' Jacob begged as he unsaddled the horse.

'Never fear,' said Will. 'It shall be a secret between us.'

He lingered to pat the cob. It was sweating

after being ridden hard, but by no means exhausted. Wherever Gilbert had been that night, it was not far from Castleacre.

* * *

The mist was beginning to rise and the castle-dwellers were astir, though the servants went about their work sluggishly, thick of head and bleary of eye. Gilbert, in contrast, seemed at first in a better humour as he sat down to breakfast in the hall. He ignored his wife as usual, but spoke respectfully to his sister and almost with civility to his brother.

But this morning's harmony did not last long. The cook had spoiled the bread by dropping it in the ashes, and the egg pancakes were tough as saddle-leather. Gilbert shouted for hot meat, but when the gangling boy came running with a hurriedly roasted coney it was blackened on one side and raw on the other.

Gilbert's anger exploded like gunpowder. He cursed, threw aside the dishes, kicked the boy to the floor, and stamped out to the kitchen shouting abuse at the cook. Poor Alice flinched, her pale eyes wide with fear. Meg immediately led her sister-in-law from the hall, denouncing Gib's behaviour and saying that the two of them would breakfast peacefully in her parlour on wafers and a honeycomb. But as she left she glanced at Will, signalling that she wanted to speak to him.

'What did Gib say last night?' she asked, when she returned quickly to the hall.

'Nothing of any significance,' said Will. He had been tussling with a pancake, but now he gave up the unequal contest. 'It seems that he mistrusts me — he accused me of spying on him.'

'With reason?'

'Not without,' he admitted. 'But he's on the edge of violence, as you warned me, so I'll take your advice and leave him be. And now,' he added lightly, to give her no cause for alarm, 'for my own satisfaction, I intend to call on Gosnold the constable to hear whether the man I found in the river has been named. Justice Throssell means to have the corpse buried by nightfall, named or not — and that will put an end to the matter.'

As Will mounted his horse and rode out, he found himself regretting the absence of his servant. It was not Ned Pye's slapdash services he missed, for Meg had ensured that he was adequately cared for at the castle. But — though he did not mean to tell him so — he missed Ned's company, his irreverent loyalty, and their exchanges of opinion. Remembering the constable's insistence that the corpse was a stranger's and his haste to have it buried unknown, Will would have liked to hear Ned's opinion of Thomas Gosnold.

The early sun was no more than a haze behind the mist as Will rode along Castlegate. Weavers' looms were already clacking busily, and the women who sat spinning within their open doors called out greetings as he passed. But the refuse-strewn market place and Southgate street were silent and deserted, save for scavenging dogs and those revellers who lay snoring beside the ashes of last night's bonfires. None of the alehouses and shops had opened their doors as yet, though judging by the oven smells the bakers were astir.

Hoping to find the constable at his Southacre farm, Will cantered down beside the priory wall to the river, and splashed across the ford. Southacre stood well back from the Peddars' Way, and to the east of it, screened by trees and approached along a track. The farmhouse, timber-framed between high gable-ends of flint and brick, had been built by the priory nearly a hundred years before to house its long-established tenants, the Gosnold family. With all its barns and outhouses and orchards, the farmstead was of greater extent than the Acklands' castle, even including the ruins. But Will acknowledged this to be fitting, for the Gosnolds were wealthy enough to own the great flocks of sheep that grazed the wide downland of Bartholomew's Hills, where the roads crossed and the gibbet stood.

As Will approached the gateway to the farmstead, Thomas Gosnold came pounding out on his horse, shouting over his shoulder a fierce injunction to his men to work harder. From the half-hearted thump of flails that came from his threshing barn, it seemed that his servants were in no better condition for work after the feast day than Gilbert's.

Will raised a hand and called a greeting. 'Give you good day, master constable!'

Surprised to see him, Thomas Gosnold hauled his heavy horse to a standstill. He was equally courteous, as they sat their mounts side by side and head to tail, but his sharp blue eyes were unmistakably wary in his florid face.

'Good day to you, Master Will Ackland. What brings you to Southacre?'

'Mere curiosity,' said Will lightly. 'I come to ask if you've put a name to the murdered man?'

The constable sat square upon the dignity of his office. 'That is a matter for the law — as you should know, sir, from your studies in London. I shall make my report to Master Justice Throssell in due course. No doubt he'll tell you of it when he sees fit.'

It was a just reproof, and Will gave a nod of acknowledgement. 'But if you recall, master constable,' he pointed out, 'it was I who sent you word of the body in the river. Knowing my interest, Justice Throssell told me yesterday that two men of the parish had been reported missing. Since then, I've heard that a third man is absent.'

Thomas Gosnold's eyes, small above his heavy jowls, narrowed further. His reddish hair bristled below his cap.

'A third man?'

'So I'm told.' Will turned his horse and brought it back to stand beside the constable's. 'The first, as you know, is one-armed old Tom Pardew, whose corpse it cannot be. The second was drunken Jack Broach, who has been found. The third, who is certainly absent from Castleacre, is the prior's bailiff.'

'Walter Bostock is not missing! Whoever says so, lies!' said the constable fiercely. 'Every tenant of the priory knows he's gone to Bromholm — '

'For the Michaelmas reckoning — so my

brother tells me. And every tenant thanks God for his absence, according to Gilbert, for Walter Bostock watches too closely and exacts too much in tithes and rent.'

'Pah!' The constable kicked his horse into motion. 'Master Ackland's anger against the prior's bailiff is well known, and does him no credit. For my part, I have naught to complain of. Walter Bostock does his duty to the priory, as I do mine to the law.'

He urged his horse to a canter, but Will caught up with him. 'And the murdered man, master constable? Is anyone from the parish unaccounted for?'

'None!' asserted the constable. 'As I said from the first, the corpse is a stranger's. We'll bury him unknown, and that will be an end on't. Good day to you, sir!'

Will checked the pace of his own mount and watched Thomas Gosnold thunder away towards Bartholomew's Hills, his horse's hooves leaving a green track in grass that was white with heavy dew.

Despite the constable's hopes, Will's interest in the murdered man could not end with the burial. He would not be easy in his mind until he was sure that the corpse was not Walter Bostock's. But while he was waiting for news from Bromholm, he could at least take a closer look into the circumstances of the man's death. And he would begin with an examination of the rags the corpse had been found in, before they were buried with him.

★ ★ ★

Hob the sexton and Hob his son had, it seemed, been celebrating the feast of St Matthew late into the night. Will found them snoring prodigiously in a sheltered corner of the churchyard, earthy and hairy as two moles, their heads pillowed on the mound of a grave.

Glad of their absence, for he could do without their inquisitive help, Will entered the mortuary. It was dimly lit by a fallow candle, placed in front of the tall wooden cross, and the gloom was tainted with the first sweet-foul smells of mortal corruption.

Will crossed himself in the presence of the corpse, lying humped under its shroud, and then retrieved the man's rags from the corner where they had been thrown. Carrying them out into the daylight, and away from an overshadowing yew tree, he spread them on a grave and went down on his haunches to examine them.

The blue woollen hose had been made for a man more full-bellied than the corpse. They

142

were of medium quality, such as a yeoman or an impoverished gentleman would wear — but they were not Gilbert's, for the darns on either knee were clumsily done, and both Meg and poor Alice prided themselves on their handiwork. Below the knee, both legs were in tatters. This had given the garment the appearance of being ragged, but Will could now see that it had been slashed with a knife.

The shirt — made for someone considerably taller than the dead man — was of a different origin. Stained as it was from close contact with the corpse, its quality was unmistakable, for it was made of the finest linen delicately pleated and stitched. Though it was well worn, in that the linen was thin in places with a slight fraying at the neck, there was neither patch nor darn. Both sleeves were ragged, as was the lower half; but once again the garment appeared to have been deliberately slashed.

Will sat back on his heels and considered what he saw. The shirt was of finer quality than he himself had ever possessed, and certainly better than any of Gilbert's. Better too, he judged, than his godfather would wear, for though Lawrence Throssell was the wealthiest man in the parish he was always modest in his attire. A shirt of this quality would have been owned by a knight, or more probably a nobleman, and there were none such this side of Swaffham. If, as Will supposed, the garments had been put on the corpse after death, how had such a shirt come to be here in Castleacre?

The answer lay, without doubt, in the widespread fame of the priory. Many pilgrims who came here were of high rank, not only knights and nobles but even, some years ago, Queen Katherine herself with all her retinue. She had stayed in the prior's guest house on three occasions, on her way to the holy shrine of Our Lady at Walsingham.

But it was not only pilgrims who enjoyed the hospitality of the priory. Travellers of every rank stayed here too, and there was undoubtedly a coming-and-going of men who wore fine linen shirts. Such guests would, it was hoped, make generous gifts to the priory. And what would be more natural than for a departing nobleman to discard a worn shirt, in the knowledge that the monks would put it to charitable use? It was the duty of all Christians to feed the hungry and clothe the naked, and there were always beggars at the priory gates.

So far, Will thought, his argument was sound. A would-be murderer planning to disguise the body of his victim — or needing to disguise it after the deed had been done — would know that anonymous garments were to be had from the almonry. They would be serviceable, but he could slash them to give the corpse the appearance of a vagabond's.

But there was more to it than that. The victim would have been clothed when he was set upon. What had been done by the murderer with the man's own clothing, including his boots?

The church bells had begun to ring, and Will looked up. The priest would be preparing to say Mass, as he did every day, though there was no obligation for parishioners to be present save on Sundays and holy days. But it was an obligation upon the old beadsmen from the almshouses to pray every day for the souls of their Throssell benefactor and his family, and now — cloaked, capped and badged, and clutching their rosaries — they were entering the churchyard in tottering procession.

Will quickly added his own prayer for Anne to theirs, then gathered up the ragged clothes to return them to the mortuary. But it occurred to him that the shirt, foul as it was, might yet provide some further information. Rather than allow the whole garment to be thrown into the grave, he drew his knife from

145

his belt and cut off a piece of the pleating at the neck. Before leaving the churchyard he concealed the scrap of linen in a convenient chink of the stone wall.

★ ★ ★

Castleacre was creaking into life as Will rode down again towards the river. On their feet at last after the excesses of the feast day, entertainers and pedlars were setting out for the next town. Pilgrims, uplifted by their candlelit glimpse of new blood on St Matthew's bones, and assured of a remission of their sins, were going buoyantly on the next stage of their pilgrimage. All of them made their way down Southgate street, where the keepers of food shops and taverns and alehouses stood outside to cry their trade, doing their best to delay the departing customers with pots of ale or to sell them pasties to sustain them on their journey.

Will rode with the wayfarers as far as the ford, where he caught a final sight of the dancing bear as it shambled away in its chains to its next performance. Splashing across the river, he turned immediately west along the wooded bank. A short path had recently been hacked and trodden along here, for this was where the constable's men, sent from

Southacre, would have retrieved the dead body from the water. Will dismounted, and hitched his horse to a low branch of an ash tree, out of the way of those who were crossing the ford.

He had become increasingly uneasy that Gilbert might be charged by default with murder. If — God forbid — Walter Bostock could not be found at Bromholm, it would be assumed throughout Castleacre that the corpse was his, even though he might have met with some accident elsewhere. But if clothing or other possessions were to be found in or near the river, they could be shown to Sibbel Bostock. If she could not identify them as her husband's, then Gilbert could not be accused of murdering him.

Will had seen the good condition of the victim's feet. The man was a rider, and his possessions would have included a horse with harness, saddle and saddle-bags. The murderer might well have taken the horse and sold it in another town, but the saddle-bags and their contents would be too easily identified. It seemed to Will that the murderer would have wanted to rid himself of them, and of his victim's clothing, as soon as possible.

He looked about him, swatting as he did so at the insects that buzzed round his head.

Most of the trees stood well back from the river, apart from the pollarded willows that liked to dip their roots in the water. Both banks, on either side, were overgrown with seeding thistles and willow-herb, and with bushes bearing an abundance of hips, haws, sloes and blackberries. There were any number of places where clothes and boots and saddle-bags could have been concealed. And apart from the banks there was the river itself, deep-edged with reeds and thickly grown with water-weed.

The prospect of searching single-handed was daunting. Again, Will missed Ned Pye — and felt aggrieved when he thought of him, even now riding across Norfolk like a gentleman. But this task was too important for the honour of the Ackland family to be shirked.

His horse, surrounded by a dance of insects, was stoically swishing its tail and stamping to drive them away. Will hung his doublet on the pommel of his saddle, cut himself an ash plant, and began to beat along the tangled river bank, searching as he went.

The going was uneven, squelchy in some places and impenetrable in others. Down here in the valley the day was airless, with a richly thick smell of damp earth, river weed, mushrooms and ripe berries. Insects clustered round Will's sweating face, and burrs and floating seeds clung to his clothes. Brambles, reaching out to catch hold of him, declined to let go. But he was wearing his least-good shirt and hose and cared nothing for the damage they sustained as he continued his search, making his way along both banks of the river above and below the ford.

His task was enlivened by wayfarers who called out greetings to him as they crossed the river, and also by the birds that gathered to feed on seeds and berries, and rose in great flocks when he disturbed them. But he found nothing of interest, and as the morning lengthened so did his thirst.

When the noonday bell rang, Will returned to his horse and led it to the ford to drink. Noticing that one of its shoes was loose, he led it up Southgate street and left it with the farrier until later in the day.

He had intended to refresh himself at the sign of the Angel, until he saw two old friends dozing over their sticks on a bench outside the Green Man. They were both rheumy of eye and did not at first recognise him, although they had spent their lives in the service of his family.

'Well met, Luke!' he exclaimed. 'Well met, George! You know me — Will Ackland, home at last. Shall we drink a pot of ale together?'

149

The old men, their fading embers stirred into life by his greeting, touched their caps respectfully and champed their sunken mouths with pleasure. Luke, who had been a shepherd, was long in the face and lean in the shank. A man of few words, as shepherds are, and those words always the same, he contrived to croak them with a meaning suitable for every occasion. George, the livelier of the two, had been cook at the castle. Still rounded from a lifetime of tasting and supping, he was grievously short of breath.

Will called to the landlord for hot mutton pasties and ale, and they all drank deep. As the old men savoured their food, they recalled their days at the castle.

'You were a young rogue, Master Will!' wheezed George. 'I mind the time you were six years old, and I beat your backside with a ladle for stealing raisins.'

'So you did,' agreed Will. 'And I hollered, for the ladle was hot, having just come out of the broth. And my mother came and beat me again, thinking I had fouled my hose!'

'Ah, Jesu, how the whole kitchen laughed . . . ' George wiped his eyes, and Luke gave a creaky chuckle: 'Ho-ho — 'tis as I say!'

Then the cook sobered. 'My duty to your

sister, Dame Margaret,' he said hoarsely. 'But as for Master Ackland your brother — in truth I know not what your father, God rest his soul, would have thought of his conduct.'

The shepherd agreed, with a solemn shake of his head. 'Aye — 'tis as I say . . . '

'He has much on his mind,' said Will, by way of apology.

'He's too free with his anger. And 'a has too loose a tongue. Forgive me for blunt speech, Master Will — an old servant's privilege. But your brother Gib is like to be hanged afore he's much older.'

Will gave him a guarded look over his pot of ale. 'How so?'

'Why, 'a has threatened in this very alehouse to kill the prior's bailiff. And' — the cook struggled for breath — 'and now there's a man found murdered in the river, the bailiff is gone, and Gilbert Ackland is said to be the miscreant!'

'Aye, aye, 'tis as I say . . . ' intoned Luke sorrowfully.

'This is naught but rumour,' Will protested. 'No man has reason to believe the prior's bailiff is dead. And I'll wager my brother is not the only tenant who has spoken against him.'

The shepherd raised his old head, suddenly

151

hopeful. "Tis so! As I say . . . ' he informed his friend.

George gave a grudging nod. 'Aye, there's not a tenant who hasn't spoken ill of the bailiff — no, not even the constable himself. But Gilbert Ackland was the only one to threaten him.'

He paused to gather his breath. 'Mark our words, Master Will,' he wheezed, and the shepherd, doleful again, nodded his agreement. "Tis Walter Bostock who lies murdered. And when your brother's tried for the evil deed, there's none in Castleacre will speak for him.'

11

Will loped down to the river again with a new sense of urgency. Some evidence of the murder must lie there, and he intended to find it. Whether or not it would point to his brother was no longer his chief concern. If Gib had indeed committed murder, then he must suffer for it. But Will could not allow him to be considered guilty without any evidence at all.

Now that St Matthew's feast was over, the number of travellers on the Peddars' Way had shrunk to an everyday level. With none to observe him, Will stood on one of the stepping stones and surveyed the ford, the dusty road on either side, and the nearby trees. It would not have been difficult for the murderer, guessing when his victim would ride that way, to have lain in wait, detained him on some pretext, and stabbed him without being seen.

Disposing of the body would have been more difficult. The fact that it had been left in the river convinced Will that only one man was involved in the murder. Had there been two, they could have carried their victim well away from the road and either buried or concealed him. But a solitary murderer might well have decided to take advantage of the river by pushing the body in, and letting the fast-flowing water carry it away downstream.

If so, the barrier of the fallen bough had spoiled his plan. Perhaps it was only then, with the body held fast within sight of the ford, that the murderer had hit on the plan of destroying his victim's face and changing his clothes. And that made it more likely that he would have hidden the dead man's own clothing somewhere nearby.

Will had already searched both banks. Now it was time to search the river itself. He splashed downsteam, across the shallow ford, and then waded on, thigh-deep in the invigoratingly cold water, to the place where the bear had found the body.

The fallen bough, stretching more than halfway across the river, had gathered an accumulation of dead branches and reeds, together with oddments dropped by wayfarers as they crossed the ford. Will heaved aside the branches and sorted through the debris, but the only items he could recognise were a shoe with more hole than sole, a tattered blanket, and a leather hat whose brim and crown had parted company.

He waded on downstream, in and out of the shade of the pollarded willow trees. Their roots spread wide in the water and provided any number of hiding places, and where the banks were treeless there were concealing growths of reed and tangled watermint. Will zig-zagged from one side of the river to the other, prodding every likely place with his ash-plant, while coloured dragonflies hovered and hummed over the water and kingfishers dived in brilliant flashes of blue, emerging from their living larder with dinners by the beakful.

Not noticing where he trod, he took an occasional plunge up to his armpits when the river bed deepened unexpectedly. It was during one such sudden dip, by the southern bank, that he found what he had been looking for. Grabbing at a tree root to keep his balance, he saw that a saturated bundle of cloth was crammed into an underwater hollow between that root and another.

With some relief, not least because the coldness of the water had begun to make his weaker leg ache, Will tossed the bundle up on to the bank and hoisted himself after it. Shaking out his find, he spread the garments on a bush and examined them.

The clothes were too sodden for their colours to be discerned, but everything was of

155

good yeoman quality: a cap, a sleeveless leather jerkin, a doublet, a shirt, a pair of hose; no boots, but a pair of boot-hose. It was certain that they belonged to the murdered man, for a knife thrust had penetrated jerkin, doublet and shirt. And there was little doubt that these clothes had been hurriedly exchanged for others, for some of the garments had been roughly slit from top to bottom for ease of removal.

Whether they had belonged to the prior's bailiff, though, was another matter. Sibbel Bostock would be able to give an instant yea or nay when she saw them — but Will could not approach her with so alarming a question unless he had reason to doubt that her husband was alive.

Until Ned brought news from Bromholm, there was nothing to be done with the garments. Will rolled them up again and stowed them in a cleft in a nearby ash tree, slashing the bark with his knife so that he could find it later.

★ ★ ★

His search was only half-completed. The murdered man's heavier possessions — in particular his saddle-bags — were still undiscovered. Walter Bostock would have

156

been carrying in his bags the rent rolls for the priory's lands at Bromholm, and if these were found there could be no doubt that he was the victim.

The simplest way for the murderer to have rid himself of the saddle-bags would have been to throw them in the river. In such a swift current they could well have been carried some distance before finally sinking. Will slid into the water again, and resumed his downstream course.

This time he concentrated on the river bed. Though the water was brilliantly clear, it contained deep layers of weed that wavered in the current, offering concealment. As he went, Will slashed at every clump of weed with his staff, disturbing shoals of tiny fish and sending spotted trout gliding away with an easy flick of their tails.

He was so intent on peering into the water that he was not at first aware that the river had emerged from trees and scrub, and was now running between green banks. When he looked up, he saw that on his left was grazing land tenanted by Thomas Gosnold. Some of the constable's cattle were clustered at a drinking place, and they raised dribbling heads and blinked in mild surprise as Will came wading through their water.

The right bank — where a heron stood in

the shallows like a tall grey sentinel, poised to strike at fish or frog with its pick-axe beak — formed the southern boundary of the priory's precinct. Beyond the meadow where the monks' dairy herd grazed, there rose the splendour of the priory itself.

It was years since Will had seen the priory from this river viewpoint. He stood still for a few moments, under the sound of the bell that marked the ending of the monks' afternoon Choir Office, and leaned waist-deep against the current while he admired what he saw.

The monastic buildings, added to over the centuries and now clustered together in all their diversity of age, shape and material — stone, flint and red tile; buttress, arch, corbel, roof, gable and traceried window — gave the appearance of some noble foreign town, overtopped by the tower of the great church.

The nobility of its appearance was apt, for the Cluniac order had always attracted men of aristocratic birth to the religious life. Nicholas de la Pole, who had been prior of Castleacre for as long as Will could remember, had Plantagenet blood in his veins, and the long face and narrow nose that went with it.

Cluniac monks did no manual work. As all

Castleacre knew, their work was to praise God in solemn splendour, and to pray for the welfare of the living and the dead, especially for their own benefactors. They lived within a framework of attendance at the seven daily Choir Offices, from Matins at two in the morning to Compline at dusk, and the rest of their time was required to be spent in private prayer and study.

There had of course been some backsliding over the centuries, and all Castleacre knew that too. Some monks had found it impossible to keep their triple vow of poverty, chastity and obedience, and the townspeople enjoyed repeating and embroidering the old scandals. But those who had the benefit of being employed at the priory were inclined to be tolerant of the monks: 'After all,' they reminded each other, 'they are but men, as we are.'

The Castleacre monks were few in number now, no more than a dozen where there had once been thirty or more. The roughest of the manual work was done by lay-brethren, who lived in obedience in return for a lifetime of food and shelter. But demands upon the priory's hospitality, from guests, travellers, pilgrims and the poor, were so great that many craftsmen and additional servants had to be employed.

From where he stood, Will could see some of them as they went about their business among the various domestic buildings on the river side of the priory. Laymen were not permitted there unless they were employed, and he had not realised how extensive these buildings were — workshops, stables, store-houses, dairy, laundry, granary, malthouse, brewhouse, and the great kitchens with their smoking chimneys. The air was heady with a mingled brew of malted barley and hops, for Castleacre priory was famed for its beer.

Thirsty again, Will closed his eyes for a moment, the better to breathe in a good draught. A small explosion of sound made him open them abruptly. The solitary heron had sprung into the air with a clap of its huge wings and was now circling, its neck drawn in and its long legs trailing behind, before flying further downstream.

Its sudden flight had surprised someone else. It seemed that while Will had been standing in the river, another man had been lying absolutely still, face down, on the low bank at the water's edge. He was now half raised, one sleeve rolled high above a bare arm, his face turned away from Will and up towards the sailing bird.

He was wearing a dark garment, but he was not a monk for he had no tonsure; probably a

160

lay-brother. And Will had no doubt about what he was doing there. He himself had once lain equally still on that very bank in the company of some idling monks, every one thrusting a bare arm deep into the achingly cold water as they competed to be first to tickle a trout.

His memory was sharpened by a numbing ache in his leg. He had been in the river long enough. And besides, he wanted to speak to the trout-tickler, who might well have caught sight of the murder victim's saddle-bags as he gazed into the water.

'Ho there, brother!' he called pleasantly, raising an arm in greeting as he waded towards the bank.

Startled, the man turned his head, stared for a moment, and then scrambled to his feet. Will recognised him at once, for all that he had not seen him since they were both boys. There could be no mistaking that great head, the face pale under a shock of dark hair, and the squat body allied to those long spidery limbs. Jankin Kett's widowed mother Miriam had been nurse to the Ackland children, and he had been brought up with them at the castle.

'Jankin!' cried Will with pleasure as he reached a shallow and limped out on to dry land, with water showering from his shirt and hose. 'Well met! You know me — your old playfellow, Will Ackland.'

But Jankin was staring at him with something like dismay. He had been a simple boy, and Will could not tell whether he knew him or not, but he was clearly not disposed to linger. Turning away he began to run clumsily across the meadow towards the priory, dodging among the dairy cows, his feet hobbling in ill-fitting boots, his long arms flailing, his thin legs pumping awkwardly up and down under his coarse knee-length tunic.

Hampered by his own numbed leg and his sodden boots, Will could at first do no more than stumble after him. For the moment he had forgotten his purpose, and was intent on nothing more than renewing his acquaintance with Jankin. Miriam Kett had died when her son was twelve years old, and Will's father had placed the boy in the care of the priory for the rest of his life.

'Jankin!' he cried again, his pace quickening with use as he followed him, to the disturbance of the cows. But Jankin would not stay. He ran across one of the causeways spanning the narrow channel that carried a flow of water past the domestic buildings, and disappeared among the racks of drying linen on the laundry green.

There was so much linen, from church,

guests and monks, that the racks were crowded with surplices, rochets, sheets, tablecloths, napkins, shirts, drawers and towels. Jankin was flailing about among them, evidently in a state of great agitation. Having caught up with him Will bided his time, with an eye on the laundry yard beyond. There, two lay-brethren were scrubbing out the great stone washing troughs, closely supervised by a brawny, red-armed laundress from the town.

Knowing that the office of priory laundress had been fiercely guarded by generations of women of her family, Will was not surprised by her roar of anger when she caught sight of Jankin among her clean linen.

'Out, hog!' she bellowed at him, her face ruddier than her arms. 'You have no business here. Out of my yard this instant — out, out, you whey-faced loon, or the sub-prior shall be told!'

And then she saw Will, and her humour changed instantly.

'Ho-ho — who have we here?' she said with a throaty chuckle, allowing Jankin to edge past her with nothing more than an absent back handed swipe and a cry of *hog!* to encourage him on his way. She looked Will up and down, so entertained by the condition of his clothes that she failed to recognise him.

'How now — are you soaked to the skin?' she enquired with a lecherous twinkle in her eye. 'Come into the laundry house, my fine young man, and I'll soon strip off those wet garments . . . '

Will laughed. 'I fear the task would prove too much for you, Mistress Harbutt,' he said, and with a quick side-step he passed her and followed Jankin, leaving the laundress to stare after him with dawning, discomfited recognition.

Behind the laundry house was a maze of cobbled alleyways that connected the various domestic buildings. Will paused. Of Jankin there was no sign, until he erupted fearfully from a doorway amid a volley of cabbages and onions, oinking noises and shouts of *Out, hog, out!*

He glanced back the way he had come, saw Will, and stumbled on down an alley at the back of one of the great buildings of the priory. The alley led out to the open, giving a glimpse of scythed grass and an oak tree beyond. No sooner had he set foot outside than he stopped abruptly, turned round in a flurry of elbows and knees, and ran back blindly into Will's restraining arms.

'Friend Jankin — I mean you no harm,' said Will, trying to calm him. But the man's eyes held a dumb animal's fear. He resisted

164

strongly at first, for his shoulders had far more power than his skinny limbs suggested. But then, as Will continued to reassure him, he stopped struggling and glanced back towards the end of the alley.

'Leave me be!' he begged, in a deep, hooting voice. His flat white face and tousled hair were damp with sweat, and his snub nose drooled like a child's.

'Come, you know me,' said Will persuasively, though he still gripped his thin arms. 'We were boys together. We used to tickle trout in the pool above the stepping stones — remember?'

Jankin took another anxious look over his shoulder. 'Leave me be! Let me go, Master Will — '

'I have one question for you,' Will persisted, 'and then you shall go. When you first saw me, I was searching the river for a pair of saddle-bags. Have you seen them — in or out of the water?'

'No, Master Will, no! God's blood, I've seen nothing.'

'Think, Jankin! I need to know, for a foul murder has been done and my brother Gilbert may be falsely accused.'

But Jankin was beyond listening. Pleading, he began to struggle again.

Will would not let him go. 'You remember

Gib — and my father,' he coaxed. 'And Meg, who was always kind to you. We had some merry times when we were young together, and your mother, God rest her soul, was our nurse. We are your family . . . '

Jankin's eyes were screwed tight, and tears began to roll down his moon-flat face. But he would only shake his head.

'The priory is my mother,' he hooted mournfully. 'The sub-prior is my father.' And with a sudden wrench he freed himself from Will's grasp and fled blindly through the doorway from which he had been ejected. What impelled him was the rapid approach of a monk, tall and thinly forbidding in his all-black habit, who hissed with authority *Back to your work, both of you!* as he came gliding near.

12

The monk's cowl was over his head and Will could not see his face, but he wore at his breast a plain wooden cross suspended from a thong of leather. There were two members of the Castleacre chapter, men of learning, who had been ordained priest before taking their vows. One was Prior Nicholas, who was now growing old, and the other was sub-prior Arnold.

The sub-prior was responsible for discipline within the priory. Sternly obedient to the Cluniac rule himself, an ascetic where the prior was not, Arnold was held in awe by the servants from the town — and in fear, so it seemed, by the lay-brethren.

Glancing down at his own shirt and hose, not only sodden but stained and torn as well, Will could take no offence at being mistaken for the meanest servant. After all, he had made the same mistake with Sibbel Bostock. But he did not intend to let it pass.

'I am Will Ackland, Father Arnold,' he said courteously, 'younger brother to your tenant at the castle.'

'Indeed?'

The sub-prior spoke in a dry, austere voice. He pushed back his hood sufficiently to give Will a direct glance. His dark eyes burned deep in his gaunt, high-cheekboned face, betokening long hours of prayer, little sleep, and much fasting. 'Then your father was one of our many benefactors. We remember him daily in our prayers. But I must tell you, Master Will Ackland, that the rule against laymen entering the priory precincts holds good for gentlemen as well as others. What brings you here? And why were you detaining one of the lay-brethren?'

Anxious to avoid trouble for Jankin, Will repeated that he had been searching the river for a pair of saddle-bags washed downstream from the ford. He had trespassed on the priory precinct, he said, thinking that one of the servants might have caught sight of the bags in the water. 'And then, seeing Jankin Kett, whose mother was my old nurse, I followed him and put the question. He tried to avoid me, and that was why I detained him — he was not at fault for speaking to me.'

The sub-prior, standing erect and still with his hands folded within the sleeves of his habit, gave him an uncomfortably piercing look. It would go hard, Will reflected, for any monk, lay-brother or servant who tried to conceal anything from him.

168

'Do you suggest that these saddle-bags had been stolen?'

'No, I do not,' said Will, firm on Jankin's behalf. 'There was no question of theft. I believe the bags were thrown into the river, upstream from here, to hide the evidence of a crime. Had they been found within the priory precinct, it would be by chance. Nothing more.'

The sub-prior made a fractional inclination of his head, by way of acknowledgement. 'Then this crime has naught to do with the priory?'

'Not to my knowledge,' said Will. Certainly the priory would be involved if its bailiff should prove to be the victim. But without that proof it was better to say as little as possible.

The sub-prior gave him another piercing look. 'And Jankin Kett — had he seen the saddle-bags you seek?'

'No, he had not.'

'Then be assured that they are not within the priory precinct, Master Will Ackland, and trespass here no more. Follow me, and I will show you the way to the outer gate.'

The sub-prior drew his cowl over his face, turned and swept away down the alley. Will followed, still dripping river water but holding his head high. When they emerged from between the walls, he found that they were out in front of the fine range of buildings that formed the best of the priory's guest houses, and the prior's own imposing lodging.

The whole of this area, fronted by the expanse of shorn grass and the single oak tree, was walled to give the prior and his guests privacy. A stone gateway led to the wide space in front of the priory church, which towered over all the other buildings.

Outside the prior's lodging, departing guests of high rank — a nobleman and his lady, by the richness of their garments and accoutrements, and the number of their attendants — had just mounted their horses and were taking their final leave. The sub-prior motioned to Will to wait, and they stood back with deference while the prior, uncowled and white-haired, raised his hand in a farewell blessing.

Will remembered Prior Nicholas as a large man with a commanding presence, proud but not haughty. Much of his time in earlier years had been spent in travel on affairs of the Order, and occasionally — because of his family connections — in the service of the Crown. But advancing age had confined him to Castleacre, where he delighted in entertaining guests. These were chiefly the high-born and wealthy, who could be expected to increase the priory's endowments, but he also sought the company of anyone who could bring him news of church and state.

'Ah, Father Arnold,' he said, pausing as he made his way back to his lodgings on the arm of one of his household attendants. His black habit, in contrast with the sub-prior's, was made of the finest cloth expertly tailored, and his priest's cross was heavy with gold.

The prior's greeting had been civil, but no more; the deep bow over folded hands that the sub-prior made in return was a formal acknowledgement of obedience. There was, it seemed, no amity between the two monks.

Since Will last saw the prior his long Plantagenet face had drooped into heavy jowls that were reddened with good living. His nose was still narrow as an eagle's, but his eyesight was evidently poor. Glancing at Will, he failed either to recognise him or to notice his dishevelled appearance.

'Is this a guest of your own, Father Arnold?' he continued, the remembered boom of the lordly voice now somewhat muted. 'A rare event, indeed.'

The sub-prior lifted his head to answer, tightening his thin lips. 'This is Master Will Ackland, Father Prior,' he said reluctantly.

'Richard Ackland's son?' Interested at once,

Prior Nicholas extended his ringed hand, and Will approached and made a reverence.

'Good, very good! You are welcome here, Will Ackland,' the prior announced, displeasing the sub-prior still further. 'Your godfather told me, when last I saw him, that you were on your way home from your travels.'

As boys, Will's father and godfather had learned their Latin at the priory in the company, among others, of Nicholas de la Pole. He had later been sent away to Eton College. But when eventually he returned to Castleacre as prior, he had renewed acquaintance with his early schoolfellows.

'You were lately in Rome, so Lawrence Throssell told me!' The prior sounded both envious and eager. 'He shall bring you to dinner with me before you return to London, for I must hear all.'

Will thanked him, and he turned at once to the sub-prior. 'And as you are acquainted with Master Will, Father Arnold,' he said graciously, 'you must join us.'

The sub-prior said nothing, but his bow conveyed stiff displeasure.

'Oh, fear not, fear not,' said Prior Nicholas, with what sounded like an outburst of pent-up irritation. 'I shall not require you to eat. Mortify your own flesh if you will — but do not spoil my pleasure

172

in offering my guests good food and wine, in return for congenial company.'

★ ★ ★

By the time Will had squelched through the town to the farrier's, collected his horse and ridden it back to the castle, his clothes were beginning to dry on him. His doublet was still on his saddle, where he had left it while he searched the river. With his thoughts on nothing but the likelihood of his brother's involvement with the murder, he rode through the gatehouse in stained and crumpled shirt and hose, and still-sodden boots.

He was taken by surprise to find that all was bustle and importance within the castle yard. As at the prior's lodging, departing guests were being bidden farewell. Meg, with Alice beside her, stood outside the door as they mounted their horses to wish them Godspeed.

The castle guests, a man and a young woman, had none of the trappings of nobility. Even so, they were evidently persons of some consequence. They were dressed in riding clothes that befitted a rank higher than that of gentleman, they had fine horses, and they were accompanied by two grooms and a servant.

'Master Will — Master Will!' hissed old Jacob excitedly from where he stood within the gatehouse, treading from foot to foot in his anxiety to be of service, but with nothing to do. One of the grooms was bending to offer his linked hands to his master as a step up to the saddle, while the other held a horse at the mounting block so that his young mistress could settle herself side-saddle and arrange her gown.

'Tis Sir Ralph Corbyn!' continued Jacob, taking Will's reins in shaking hands as he dismounted. 'He's been here a good hour — thinking to see you, or so I hear. Master Ackland's been away all day, no one knows where, and Mistress Meg is displeased by your absence . . .'

Will himself was displeased that he had missed an hour of his visitor's company. Sir Ralph, a knight whose family had long held lands at Oxmead, to the south of Swaffham, was a member of Parliament for the county of Norfolk. He was an old friend of Lawrence Throssell, who had taken his godson with him to Oxmead on several occasions in the past.

Will strode to greet the knight as he eased himself into his saddle. 'Your pardon for my absence, Sir Ralph,' he said, inclining his

174

head as a mark of respect. 'Had I known you were here . . . '

'Ha, Will! Well met,' said Sir Ralph, dismissing the apology. 'I am glad to see you back in England,' he added, bending down to offer his hand. He was some ten years younger than Justice Throssell: a wiry man of medium build with a close-clipped greying beard, fierce springy eyebrows and a sharp pair of eyes.

'I called on Lawrence Throssell on my way home from Lynn, and he told me you were here. You must give me the latest news from Westminster, Will, for Parliament has not sat these nine months. Come to dinner at Oxmead — tomorrow!'

'Gladly, sir,' said Will. But then a woman's voice intervened, young but pleasantly low.

'Not tomorrow, father, for we are bidden to dinner at Cressingham. The day after . . . ?'

'Ha, I had forgot Cressingham. What good fortune, to have a daughter to remind me!' Sir Ralph turned in his saddle and beckoned her to ride forward. 'You remember Julian, my youngest child? No doubt you'll find her grown since last you saw her.'

Will recalled her as a plump, high-spirited girl — agreeable in appearance, at twelve years old, but no more — whom he had teased and chased in the Oxmead garden.

175

But the slender young woman now nearing twenty, who sat her horse with an easy grace as she approached, had grown in beauty. He made to doff his cap, and discovered to his chagrin that he had lost it somewhere by or in the river. Bowing instead, he glanced down at himself and saw with dismay that his appearance was little better than a vagabond's.

Julian Corbyn was dressed as became her creamy-pale skin, in a green velvet riding cloak. She wore a hooped head-dress, set well back from her forehead in the French fashion that Anne Boleyn had introduced to the Court, so that her hair was revealed at the front instead of being hidden in the English way under a close cap and a gabled hood. Her features were delicately formed, and her hair and eyes were the bright brown of sweet chestnuts newly emerged from their green husks.

Silenced by admiration, and vexed by his own poor showing, Will could only bow again and say, 'Mistress Julian.'

'Master Will,' she returned with grave acknowledgement, though her lips twitched with a smile too near amusement for his comfort.

'On Sunday, then, Will,' said Sir Ralph, clearly anxious to be on his way. 'Ride over to

Oxmead directly after Mass. We have matters of great importance to discuss — though no doubt,' he added indulgently, 'my daughter will vex you with questions about the dress and manners of France and Italy.'

'I shall indeed,' said Julian. 'What other subject could be of interest to me?'

She spoke demurely, as a good daughter should, but there was a wilful light in her eye. 'I must ask Master Will about the appearance of gentlemen, especially,' she added, 'for I hear that in France and Italy they dress very fine . . . '

She gave Will a smile at his own expense, and rode out through the gatehouse. He stood staring after her, so dazed that he hardly heard his sister's exasperated cry: '*William Ackland!* Where have you *been?*'

13

Meg questioned him all the way back to the house, though Will would only say that he had been tickling trout at the river.

'*In* the river, more like!' They had entered the hall, and she ceased her scolding long enough to order the servants to pull off his sodden boots and bring him hot water and towels.

'No — bring me a flagon of ale first!' Will instructed them. He was in an excellent humour, and gave an affectionate greeting to Alice who had re-entered the hall before them. She was now sitting at the table, where she was sorting a strew of herbs. The air of the great room was sharp with chervil, onion, tarragon and fennel, mingled with the smoke of burning logs.

Alice looked up at Will, her features plain and pale in comparison with Meg's, and gave him a small, rare smile. Ever since their attendance at Mass on St Matthew's day, when he had lent her his arm, she had been less shy with him. And no doubt Gilbert's absence for the whole day had made her feel more at ease.

A servant brought ale, and Will took it and stood with his back to the great fireplace, knee-deep in slumbering dogs. His spirits unaccountably high, his aching leg forgotten, his clothes steaming in the warmth, he raised the flagon and drank deep.

But Meg had still not finished her complaints. Though she sat down with Alice and resumed the sorting of the herbs, for her hands could never rest, she delivered herself of her opinion.

'Your conduct is not fitting for a grown man, Will Ackland — let alone one who's a gentleman, and very near a barrister. I spent two hours or more, as we sat in my parlour with the Corbyns awaiting your return, praising you for your knowledge and the statecraft you'd learned on your travels. I hoped Sir Ralph would look on you favourably, and give you some advantage at Westminster when you're called to the Bar. But then you come home as tattered and soaked as a vagabond after a rainstorm! What must he have thought of you?'

'You need have no fear of that,' Will assured her. 'Sir Ralph is too wise to judge a man by a trivial disarray in his appearance.' Then he grinned at her. 'But I thank you for what you said of me, Meg, for he's invited me to dinner on Sunday.'

She stopped in her task, a great bunch of thyme, ready for drying, in her hands and a look of relief on her face. 'Aah . . . ' she said, on a long breath. 'Then I'm very glad for you.'

'And I,' said Alice. 'Mistress Julian Corbyn,' she added artlessly, with all the authority of someone who had once travelled as far as Swaffham, 'is more beautiful than anyone I have ever seen . . . '

He affected indifference. The women glanced at each other, endeavouring not to laugh.

'Even if her father failed to notice your appearance,' said Meg, 'Mistress Julian did not. From what we saw, you pleased her not at all.'

'Ha!' said Will with confidence. 'No matter, for I'll dress finer than any man in Norfolk on Sunday!' He stepped over the tangle of dogs and cats and began to strut about the hall, flagon in hand, reviewing in his mind's eye the peacock clothes he had bought on his travels.

'I shall wear my blue-embroidered shirt, and my French doublet of murrey-red with the sleeves slashed to show the pink lining. And the dark — no, the paler of the blue hose. And the boots of Florentine leather, and my feathered cap of black Italian velvet.'

'Shall you, indeed?' said Meg dryly. 'And where, pray, do you keep all this finery?'

'Why, in my travelling chest — '

Will stopped abruptly, his confidence foundering. He slapped his head with the heel of his hand. 'Mass,' he groaned, 'I had forgot! I left the chest at Gray's Inn. All I have here is what I stand in . . . '

'Not so. You have what you brought for saints' days and Sundays.'

'That's not good enough for Oxmead!'

'But surely' — Meg pretended to be puzzled, but her eyes mocked him — 'Sir Ralph will not judge you by your appearance? Did you not say just now that he's too wise for that?'

Will scowled, temporarily silenced. His sister turned to Alice. 'I do believe,' she said, 'that William plans to go a-wooing . . . '

'That I do not!' he protested, but they only teased him the more. He slammed down his flagon, stalked out to the screens passage, and shouted for a servant. He missed Ned Pye, who always seemed able to conjure up whatever was needed, however unpromising the circumstances. Ned would have ensured that he went to Oxmead well dressed — and would have given him a companion's support into the bargain.

There was so much raucous laughter from

181

the direction of the kitchens that Will had to shout a second time before the gangling boy, Lambert, came at a run. Needing help to remove his boots, Will sat on the heavy bench against the wall of the passage and anchored himself to it while the boy tugged.

'Is the cook drunk again?' Will asked with resignation.

'He is but merry, sir,' panted Lambert, taking a fresh grip. He had long outgrown his clothes, and his shirt-sleeves and hose came nowhere near his raw-boned wrists and ankles.

'And what's the cause of such merriment?'

Lambert kept his head down as he wrestled with the first soaked boot, staggering back as it came off, boot-hose and all. Recovering his balance he seized immediately on the second. The noise from the kitchens increased, and Will repeated his question.

'Why, nothing . . . A — a bawdy jest, sir,' Lambert mumbled as he heaved away. His long narrow chin was downy with an unshaven first beard, and splotched with pimples. His eyes were reddened, as were those of all the servants who worked in the smoky kitchens. But there was a great unease in them, and Will knew that there was something he was trying to hide.

Freeing himself from the boot with a final

182

kick, Will stood up, barefoot, and seized Lambert by the shoulders. 'The truth, boy!' he demanded. 'I've heard bawdy jests in plenty, but none to cause so much laughter before supper time. Tell me the truth.'

'Sir — ' said Lambert wretchedly. He hesitated, then burst out: 'Master Ackland is the cause. He's been gone since breakfast, when he beat the cook sorely. And now we hear he's fled the town — and the cook is glad of it!'

Will stared at the boy. 'Fled?'

'Aye, sir.' Lambert would not meet his eyes. 'On account of having murdered the prior's bailiff . . .'

'God's blood!' exploded Will, angered by the spreading rumour and more so by the fear that it might be true. He flung the boy aside, but seized him again before he could fall.

'Listen to me, Lambert Catchpole. There's no one in this town — not the justice of the peace, nor the constable, nor any other — who can say who the dead man is. As for your master, I have no doubt he'll return before nightfall demanding his supper. And woe betide the cook, and all of you, if it's not ready — and done exactly to his liking!'

★ ★ ★

By the time Will had changed his damp clothes and returned to the hall, he found it empty. It was a room that always darkened early, and the distant sound of women's voices told him that they had moved to Meg's parlour, where daylight lingered longest.

He was glad to be alone with his anxiety. Restless for Ned's return from Bromholm, he strode about, kicked the log on the hearth into flame, and conferred with the dogs. But presently Meg came looking for him. 'Betsy is with us,' she said, and so he was eager to follow her.

His womenfolk had, it seemed, taken it upon themselves to provide him with garments fine enough to wear at Oxmead. From the clothing and stuffs piled on the table in the window, it appeared that they had ransacked every chest in the house. 'Not just for your benefit, neither,' his sister pointed out. 'We have the honour of the family to consider.'

Before he would look at any of it, he went to his daughter. Under the eye of her nurse Agnes, she was exploring the tumbled contents of the great oak chest in the parlour, her plump arms buried deep in old velvets and satins.

'What have we here, Betsy?' he asked, kneeling beside her. The smell of dried lavender floated up from the chest as he discovered a gown of deep blue that had belonged to his mother, and one of emerald green that Meg had worn when she was young. 'Do you know the names of the colours?'

Shy again at first, she gave him a half-smile and a nod.

'Well then: what's this?'

'Green,' she said instantly.

'Good. And this?'

'Blue.'

He smiled. 'I see you know them all. One more, then.'

Betsy hesitated. Her budding lips tried to frame the 'y' of 'yellow', but found it difficult. Undaunted, she looked him mischievously in the eye.

'Red!' she asserted. And then she chuckled, knowing that he knew she was teasing him, and he stroked her hair fondly and went to join her elders.

Meg and Alice had decided that they had time enough to make him a new shirt, out of some fine linen that Meg had put by, inset at the neck with a band of many-coloured embroidery they had found. As for doublet and hose, Alice offered what her husband had been married in, and had never worn since.

'Gilbert will never know,' she said, though there was some apprehensiveness in her voice.

'He cannot wear them again, for he's grown too fat,' said Meg. 'They'll be large for you, even so — but we can have them altered to fit.'

'I'll not wear Gib's hose!' Will declared ungraciously.

'Then you must make do with your Sunday pair,' snapped Meg, out of patience with him. 'But you need not turn up your nose at his doublet. It's as fine as any Norfolk gentleman could wear, for I ordered it from the best tailor in Lynn.'

It was indeed a fine garment, made of light blue velvet with bands of darker blue braid in the front and on the wide-puffed upper sleeves. Will tried it on, admiring it but finding it far too large at the waist. The women fussed round him, pinching and pinning it.

'I thank you both,' he said. 'But who is to alter it? There's no time to take it back to Lynn.'

'Young Dickson, here in Priorygate, will do it,' said Meg, removing a pin from her mouth. 'He's a much better tailor than his father was — why, I hear that the prior himself has some of his clothing made by

186

him. If young Dickson's tailoring is good enough for my lord prior, it should be good enough for Master Will Ackland. There . . . '

She stood back to judge the alterations, conferring with Alice over the placement of a last pin. 'You look very handsome, Will,' murmured his sister-in-law.

His sister snorted. 'At least he'll do the family no discredit,' she conceded. 'Now, Agnes shall take the doublet straight to the tailor, so as to lose no time in the unpicking. And you must call there tomorrow morning, Will, for a fitting.'

As they divested him carefully of the pinned garment, and wrapped it in a cloth, Will caught sight of Agnes's wholesome face. She was a good-hearted young woman, and always ready to be of service, but her expression now was one of dismay.

She said nothing beyond a small 'Aye, madam,' as she took the bundle Meg gave her, but her eyes were cast down and her mouth was tight. Will followed her out of the parlour and caught her up in the hall.

Some of the candles had been lit, and the tablecloth was in place, but the three serving women who were supposedly setting the supper had gathered in a muttering huddle, pewter plates and drinking cups and loaves of bread clutched to their aproned bosoms. As soon as Will entered the room they fell silent and scurried about their work, giving him covert glances.

He ignored them. 'What's amiss, Agnes?' he asked quietly.

She looked away from him, her eyes wretched. 'Oh, sir — I dare not go out, for fear of what folk will say! Here's Master Ackland fled, and the whole town calling him a murderer — '

The sound of hooves galloping into the castle yard made everyone in the hall look up, and stand as if frozen. Collectively — including even the dogs, or so it seemed — they held their breath.

Then the front door burst open and a great bellowing for attention reverberated through the house. His brother had not fled after all, and Will had never been so glad to hear his voice.

But it seemed that something untoward had happened during the day, for Gilbert bore the unmistakable marks of a brawl. He walked with a cautious stiffness, as though his back pained him. There was a bruising on one of his cheeks, and on the other, extending across his forehead, was a livid weal.

Gilbert refused, that evening, to speak of it — or indeed to speak at all, except savagely to the servants. But Will took note that his brother did not leave the castle again that night, nor yet early the following morning.

14

After breakfast, when the priory bell was ringing for the monks' Chapter Mass, Will went out under an overcast sky to call on the tailor in Priorygate.

He chose to walk rather than ride. Unwilling to believe that all Castleacre considered his brother a murderer, he wanted to meet the eyes of everyone he came upon. But where yesterday there had been smiles and greetings, today there were none.

Townspeople pointed him out covertly, turning away at his approach or busying themselves so as to avoid speaking to him. True, Dickson the tailor rose from where he sat cross-legged in the window of his shop and attended to him eagerly, but he was a young man intent on building up his business.

While he was in the shop, with its coloured clutter of half-finished garments and reels of thread, Will negotiated for the making of a new cap for his visit to Oxmead, in place of the Sunday cap he was now wearing. He had persuaded Meg to let him have a good piece of the emerald green velvet from her discarded gown, and she had laughed and found him a peacock's feather to go with it.

The tailor promised that all would be ready by the next morning, Sunday, before Mass. Will left the shop with rising spirits. As he stepped out again into the street, a woman's voice, deep and warm, hailed him.

'Why — Master William Ackland!'

He would not have recognised Sibbel Bostock except by her voice. The woman who was approaching him from the direction of the priory gatehouse was properly attired as the wife of a yeoman. Her gown was of a seemly length, and her hair was entirely hidden by her linen undercap and her gable hood. She carried an empty basket on her way to the market place.

Will's spirits sank again. He returned her greeting with the briefest courtesy, for he was reluctant to speak to her. With reason, he felt uneasy in her presence. It seemed that, living out of the town as she did, the bailiff's wife had not yet heard the rumours. Would the townspeople be quick to inform her, he wondered, that it was her husband who had been murdered, and his brother who was the murderer?

But he could not part from her at once, for she might later think of his haste as an admission of Gib's guilt. Better, he decided, to deny that part of the rumour by making conversation with her.

'Young Dickson is a good tailor, I hear,' he said, conscious of a stiff formality in his voice. For all that her lustrous black hair was now completely hidden, Sibbel Bostock was a remarkably handsome woman. The black eyes, in the strong brown-skinned face, seemed larger and more bright than he remembered.

'An excellent tailor,' she agreed. 'And perhaps I can be of assistance to you, Master Will? Should you need any fine cloth or velvet for Dickson to make up, my husband's aunt has the best you can buy this side of Lynn, at her shop by the church in Swaffham. She will be sure to give you a fair price if you mention my name.'

Will muttered his thanks. The image of the mutilated corpse hovered unbidden before his mind's eye. Was it her husband who had been buried unknown before dusk yesterday, with only the constable, the sexton and his son to attend him during the last rites?

His unease doubled as Sibbel Bostock continued, smiling and lowering her voice confidentially though there were none to hear.

'I have placed an order with Dickson, secretly, for a new cap for my husband. The prior's bailiff is like most men — except young gentlemen such as yourself, of course — and always favours his sad old cap ... Now there'll be a new one for him, will-he-nil-he, when he returns from Bromholm!'

Will smiled as best he could, feeling compassion for a good wife who might well, unknowing, have been a widow for some days. 'And when will that be?' he asked, for something to say.

'Tuesday at best, or Wednesday more like. Unless of course he's delayed on business for the priory. He may be required to go to Thetford, or even further afield.'

They had conversed enough, he hoped, for her to doubt any rumour she might hear about Gilbert. Possibly she would hear nothing, for the townspeople might shun her as they so often shun the newly bereft, not knowing what to say beyond *God ha' mercy*. But to make it plain that Gib had not fled, Will said that his brother was waiting for him to return and discuss a matter of business. He bade her farewell and walked quickly back through the town, his head held high and looking neither to right nor to left.

In the castle yard, he found Jacob hissing through his toothless gums as he rubbed down a strange horse. It was near exhaustion, and white with sweat where Jacob had not yet reached.

'Is Ned Pye returned?' Will asked, half eagerness, half dread.

'Aye, sir — he's now indoors, eating and drinking his fill.' The old yardman snuffled with amusement. 'But I wager he'll be standing up to do it, for he's been a long time in the saddle.'

Will ran to the house and in through the front door to the screens passage. 'Ho there, Ned!' he shouted.

His servant appeared, making his way slowly and exaggeratedly bow-legged through the archway from the kitchens. He was chewing a mouthful of food and carrying a flagon. His chin was unshaven, his eyes were bleary from lack of sleep and his yellow hair clung to his forehead, darkly matted with sweat.

Will beckoned Ned into the hall, occupied only by the old dogs stretched on the hearth in front of a smouldering bough. 'You've done well,' he said, clapping him on the shoulder. 'Sit down and tell me your news.'

'I'd sooner stand,' said Ned ruefully. Grimacing, he rubbed his behind. 'Mass, I'm as raw as a sliced onion!'

He paused to swallow ale, and Will guessed that the pause foretold bad news. 'You did not see Walter Bostock?'

'No, Master Will. As you feared, he's not at Bromholm.'

The hall, with its heavily beamed ceiling and hazy window glass, was always dull when the sun did not shine. Under today's overcast sky it seemed to gather gloom, foretelling a long dark winter.

Ned drained his flagon before taking up his story.

'I heard the news first from two disorderly monks, drinking at the sign of the Sun in North Walsham. They'd been sent — or so they said — from their priory at Bromholm to find whether the bailiff was on his way, for he was late. I rode on as far as the priory to make sure, but Walter Bostock had not arrived. On the way back I enquired wherever I stopped to change horses, but none of the innkeepers had seen him since last Michaelmas.'

The news was no worse than Will had expected, but to hear it told was a grievous blow. He shook his head in dismay. 'Now, good St Christopher . . . ' he muttered, invoking the aid of his favourite saint as he always did in time of trouble.

'I doubt there's much the saints can do to help,' said Ned bluntly. His low opinion of the church had been reinforced by the

Lutheran beliefs he had heard during their travels in Europe, though Will had observed that Ned was instantly devout whenever they'd had cause to fear for their lives. 'This will go ill for your brother — unless you discovered anything to his advantage while I was away?'

'All I found,' said Will despondently, 'were the murdered man's own clothes, hidden on the river bank. The bailiff's wife has yet to be shown them, for proof, but I've little doubt they were her husband's.'

Then he gained new hope. 'But proof that the bailiff was murdered will not be proof that Gib was his murderer,' he declared. 'If my brother is falsely accused, I must clear his name. You stay here and sleep, Ned, for you've earned it. I'll collect the dead man's clothes, and take them to Sibbel Bostock.'

'That's the constable's work, surely?' said Ned.

'True, in different circumstances. But if Gib is not guilty, the murderer must be one of the bailiff's other enemies. From what I've heard, he was wished ill by all the tenants of the priory — and the constable is among them.'

★ ★ ★

196

Ned Pye volunteered to postpone his much-needed sleep. Privately, having been cuffed about the ears by Gilbert Ackland without reason at their first encounter, he had no objection to seeing him condemned for murder, guilty or no. But just as it was his master's duty to defend his brother, so it was Ned's duty to support his master. And besides, preoccupied and seemingly unaware of her as Will Ackland was, Ned thought it unwise to leave him alone in the presence of Mistress Sibbel Bostock.

As for Will, he concealed his pleasure at the prospect of his servant's company by refusing to take him unless he first shaved himself. Leaving Ned grumbling, Will rode down to the river, beat his way along the southern bank, found the ash tree he had marked, and retrieved the dead man's bundled clothes. By the time he returned to the market place he discovered Ned standing outside the Woolpack inn, where he had made the final exchange of horses. Clean-shaven, give or take a few bloody nicks, Ned was holding the reins of his own nag in one hand and using the other to raise a new-filled pot of ale.

Will did not hurry him. Anxious though he was to hear Sibbel Bostock's verdict on the clothes, he wanted to give her time to finish her buying and return home. But Ned had a prodigiously wide throat and was soon ready to mount, though he groaned loudly with discomfort as he lowered himself on to the saddle.

Ignoring his complaints, Will led the way across the market place and along Priorygate. He looked about him as he rode, to ensure that they did not pass Mistress Bostock, and as he did so he realised that the townsfolk were no longer shunning him as they had done earlier.

But on that occasion he was walking. Now that he was mounted, and could no longer meet their eyes, the townsfolk did not hesitate to stare at him, and nudge and whisper and point him out to each other. If he could not soon clear Gilbert's name, he reflected grimly, he would feel no more welcome in Castleacre than his brother.

Once clear of the town they cantered along Priorygate, meeting and passing carts that took produce to the prior's tithe barn, or corn to be ground at the mill, or goods to and from the river wharf. The gates in the wall that gave access to the great barn stood wide today, and the two men were able to ride straight through and along the track that led to the bailiff's farmstead, and the thatched house backed by the clump of oak trees.

Fowls were scratching round the open door, and dogs gave warning of their arrival. Sibbel Bostock came out at once. She was still wearing her seemly gown, but she had removed her hood and loosened her under-cap so that her long dark hair tumbled about her throat.

'Master Will Ackland!' she cried with pleasure. 'I had not thought to see you again so soon.' She gave Ned one glance, and dismissed him. 'Will you not come in this time, sir, and refresh yourself?'

'I fear that I'm the bringer of bad news,' he said gravely. He dismounted, and unstrapped the bundle from his saddle. 'I think it best that we stay outside, Mistress Bostock, so you can see clearly what I have to show you.'

He undid the bundle, and Ned helped him to spread the garments out on the furze bushes by the farmstead gate. The clothes were stiff and dark from their long immersion, and still damp from having been rolled together. 'Do you know these garments?'

'That I do not!' she said with distaste, but Will urged her to look more closely. She turned them over, held them up to the light, saw the cuts in them and looked at him with puzzlement in her great black-polished eyes. 'No,' she repeated. 'How should I know such rags?'

Will's errand was made more difficult by the conversation he had had with Sibbel Bostock only that morning. 'These are not rags,' he explained, to save her pride. 'These were good garments, cut from a body found in the river three days ago. Did you not hear it spoken of in the town?'

She drew away from them immediately. 'I heard of the murder yesterday, from the miller's wife. If the garments belonged to the dead man, what has that to do with me?'

'The bad news I bring, Mistress Bostock, is that your husband did not reach Bromholm. He is missing. I am here to ask if these garments are his?'

The glow of health drained from Sibbel Bostock's face. 'No!' she protested, crossing herself fervently and invoking a litany of saints. 'My husband cannot be dead! If he's not at Bromholm he must be about the priory's business elsewhere.'

'I fear not,' said Will.

'But these garments are not his!' Her voice, husky at all times, broke upon her tears. 'Indeed, Master Will, I do not know them . . .'

For his part, he did not know how to deal with her distress. 'I must tell you,' he went on, wishing he could have left this errand to the constable, 'that I saw the body, and it bears a blemish that will serve for proof. Did your husband have a birthmark, Mistress Bostock? A patch of crimson skin on his behind?'

Anguished, she had begun to take short, agitated steps this way and that, squeezing and plucking at her hands. Now she stopped abruptly, lowering her eyes in confusion.

'Why — I — I cannot say,' she protested. Her long full throat flushed as darkly red as the dead man's blemish. 'My husband the bailiff has always been a hard-working man. We go to bed when it is dark, and rise before dawn.'

'But in summer . . . ?' Will persisted, intent on obtaining the proof he needed. 'Surely in summer, when the nights are so short that a hard-working man cannot get enough sleep between dusk and dawn . . . ?'

Sibbel Bostock would not look up. 'Sir,' she said with modest dignity, lifting one hand to her throat, 'I do not know the ways of gentlemen. My husband the bailiff is not of yeoman birth, but the son of a poor husbandman. How else should he go to bed, at whatever time of year, but in his shirt?'

Will heard Ned Pye give a snort of suppressed laughter, and glanced at him with a scowl.

'I shall not add to your distress, Mistress Bostock,' he told her. 'I must have an answer,

201

but I will seek it from the bailiff's own family. He has an aunt in Swaffham, you said . . . ?'

She looked up instantly, her eyes wide with unease, her fingers entwining the lustrous strands of hair that hung at her throat. 'You have no need to trouble yourself, sir! I — I was made wretched by your news and tried to disbelieve it. In truth, my husband had just such a mark from birth. And now — may God have mercy on his soul — I must accept that he is dead.'

15

Leaving the bailiff's widow lamenting, Will and his servant escaped at a gallop. They did not stop until they had passed the tithe barn and regained the road.

Ned burst into laughter as soon as he had breath for it. 'Ha — a modest, virtuous wife indeed! Why, a man going to bed with Mistress Bostock would need no shirt to warm him, however icy the weather . . . If her husband didn't know she's a whore, he was a fool.'

Will agreed. But it was a matter that gave him cause for concern rather than amusement.

'I have been blind, Ned! I was sure it was anger against the bailiff's exactions that led to the murder. But now I can see there was jealousy in it.'

'You were slow to recognise her for what she is,' said his servant critically. 'I knew what kind of refreshment Mistress Bostock offered as soon as we first clapped eyes on her.'

'You should have told me, then, for you knew I had matters of more importance on my mind.' Will raised an eyebrow at him. 'Or did you hope to take up her offer yourself?'

'I intended to!' said Ned, denying the memory of the ringing box on the ear she had given him. 'All that prevented me was your sending me straight off to Bromholm.'

But Will was still vexed by his own failure to see that Sibbel Bostock herself could well have been the reason for the murder. 'Only this morning,' he recalled, 'when she told me she had ordered a new cap for her husband, I believed it a sign of fondness . . .'

'A salve for her conscience, more like!'

'True. And now she knows he's dead, she needs to appear modest and grieving or rumour may spread through the parish.'

They turned their horses towards the town, riding at walking pace.

'What was it that opened your eyes?' Ned asked with a grin. 'Mistress Bostock's repeated offer of refreshment?'

'No — it was her sudden modesty. It did not suit so bold a woman. When she gave me a glance from under her lowered lids, I knew she was merely playing the virtuous wife.'

A cart laden with grain was approaching, on its way to the tithe barn, and they moved from the crown of the road to let it pass. The carter was well known to Will, who raised a hand in greeting. But the man drove past with a covert stare as his only acknowledgement.

Will frowned, but not against the carter. 'What troubles me is that this only goes to prove the case against my brother. When we first called on Sibbel Bostock, she'd already heard of me — and from whom, if not Gib? There was also something he said when I first came home. We were speaking at supper of the King and Anne Boleyn — '

'King Henry's black-eyed whore,' said Ned with a chuckle. 'She and Mistress Bostock are alike in more ways than one . . . '

'Yes, for they can both bewitch men. My brother took the King's side: *If a man can have no satisfaction from his wife*, he said, *he's entitled to seek it from another.* And where has Gilbert been, when he's absented himself these past nights and days, if not in the arms of Walter Bostock's wife? He has a motive far stronger than mere resentment of tithe for wanting the bailiff dead.'

'So he has. But just as he's not the only tenant with cause to hate the bailiff,' Ned pointed out, 'I'll wager he's not the only one to fall under the spell of Mistress Bostock.'

They rode on past the priory gatehouse and were immediately slowed by an oncoming crowd of beggars, the wretched poor, the lame and the blind, all scuttling early to the priory for the midday dole. The sight of so many battered faces stirred Will's memory.

'My brother,' he remembered, 'came home yesterday evening bearing all the marks of having been in a brawl . . . Merely a drunken one, perhaps — but I noticed that he did not go out again at night.'

'Aha — a quarrel with a rival for Mistress Bostock's attention?'

'I shouldn't wonder,' said Will, his hope renewed. 'If we look for another man — probably a tenant — with recent injuries, we may yet find something to brother Gib's advantage.'

* * *

At the market place, they parted. Will told his servant to wait for him outside the Woolpack inn, and to keep his eyes and ears open. He himself turned left into Northgate street, for the time had come to inform Justice Throssell of his findings.

As soon as Will was shown into the hall of his godfather's house, Lawrence Throssell came hurrying in long-gowned dignity to greet him. The old gentleman tumbled out anxious questions, interspersed with pressing invitations to dinner and — when Will declined — instructions to his servant to bring malmsey wine and ginger cake to the parlour.

'But what of the prior's bailiff, godson?' he asked for the third time, pausing on this occasion to listen to the answer.

Will gave him all the information he and Ned had gathered, but made no mention of their opinion of Sibbel Bostock. They had already agreed that they would speak of this to no one. Adultery and fornication were offences against church law, and if the churchwardens were to suspect her they could summon her before the archdeacon's court. Will had no wish to call down any punishment upon her. After all, with church law extending far into the unswept corners of everyday life, which man or woman was not at some time guilty of one offence or another?

As Justice Throssell listened, he had been nibbling absently at the ginger cake that he loved for its hotness in the mouth. Now, his authority in no way diminished by the crumbs of brown dough sprinkled on his sparse white beard, he made his pronouncement.

'It grieves me to say this, Will, for the love I bear you and the Ackland family. But my duty is clear. The constable tells me that your brother was already suspected throughout the town of having murdered Walter Bostock. Now you have brought me proof of the corpse, I must issue a warrant for the suspected offender's arrest. The constable must bring Gilbert Ackland before me to answer the charge.'

'Sir,' said Will. 'I understand your duty. But will you allow me, for the sake of my family's pride, to bring Gilbert before you myself without need of a warrant?'

Justice Throssell was wary. 'Do you think he will come?'

'I'll make sure he does, sir.' Will was less confident than he sounded but he continued boldly, for Meg's sake rather than for Gib's. 'And if you should remand him for trial at the next Quarter Sessions, will you allow me to stand surety for him, instead of committing him to the town gaol?'

The justice slowly shook his head. 'In truth, Will, if you were a man of substance I would gladly do so. But murder is a grave charge. What surety can you possibly offer to weigh against it?'

'Neither property nor land, sir, as you know. But when I travelled in the service of a nobleman, I saved my salary to pay for my final year of study at Gray's Inn. It's not a great deal — but it's all I have, and it means as much to me as a fortune to a wealthy man.'

'Well, then — you may stand surety for your brother if you wish. But I hope for your sake,' Justice Throssell added in warning, 'that your trust in him is not misplaced. I can show you no favours. If Gilbert should flee, your money will be forfeit.'

Will swallowed his unease. 'Sir,' he agreed, rising to his feet. 'I'll go and find him now.'

Justice Throssell trotted beside him to the door. 'Bring your brother before me as soon as you can. But mark me, Will — if you have not persuaded him to come within two hours, I'll have him fetched by the constable's men. And if he's already fled, I'll authorise a hue-and-cry and have him hunted down, Ackland or no.'

★ ★ ★

Prising Ned Pye away from the Woolpack, where he was teasing the hostess with flattery in the hope of being quietened with a free refill of ale, Will returned with him to the castle.

'Is my brother at home?' he called to the yardman, as they clattered through the gatehouse amid the usual commotion of dogs and fowls.

'Aye, sir' croaked Jacob, taking their horses as they dismounted. 'Master Ackland's been about the yard in an evil humour all morning. He stamped off not so long ago in the direction of the old keep.'

'I must go up there and speak to him. I hope to bring him down with me, and the three of us will then ride into the town together. Have his horse saddled and ready, Jacob.'

Ned had been listening with some scepticism. 'I doubt your brother will be brought down so easily,' he said as they went through the herb garden and round the side of the house towards the upper ward.

'I must try to make him see reason. If I can't — if he prefers to flee — then he must take the consequences. But at least I shall have told him what the consequences are.'

Aware that Gilbert might be looking out from the old keep, they kept their voices low and made soldierly use of natural cover as they approached the great earthwork. Ned Pye stared up at the precipitous scar, the chalk a brilliant white against the darkly overcast sky. '*That* is the way you climbed when you confronted your brother the other day? With your leg weakened from wounds? I wonder you didn't fall and break your neck.'

'I climbed it often enough when I was a boy.'

'That proves you're no wiser now than you were then,' said his servant severely. 'Surely you're not going to climb it again?'

'No, I've learned my lesson. Last time, my

brother saw me climbing and became enraged, thinking I was spying on him. This time, with two of us, our tactics will be different. I shall take the path that winds up through the scrub and emerges on the far side of the keep. I'll draw Gib's attention by calling to him as I go. Meanwhile, you will climb up on this side, unseen, to give me support.'

'*I* am to climb the cliff?' Ned was indignant. 'Ha — I might have known it! Servants must always expect the dangerous tasks ... Well, if I reach the top without breaking my own neck, what am I to do then?'

'Stay out of sight, and come to my help only if I call. I may need you if Gib becomes violent.'

'And if he sees me while I'm making the climb?'

'He'll kick flints down on your head, I shouldn't wonder. If he does,' Will advised, 'your best plan is to duck.'

16

A westerly wind had risen, loosening the first drops of rain from the heavy clouds. Will left the cover of the orchard trees and made an open approach to the upper ward.

'Ho there, Gib!' he called loudly, before taking to the path that snaked up the scrub-covered side of the earthwork. 'Where are you, brother?' he went on, pausing occasionally in his brisk pace. 'Gib, I say — are you up there?'

There was no answer. Reaching the top he began to search the ruins, and found Gilbert leaning his arms on a chest-high stretch of broken wall, gazing out over the roofs of the town in a brooding silence. Approaching rain had already obscured the great grey bulk of the priory, but the bell for the noonday Choir Office made its powerful presence, visible or not, known throughout the valley.

Will joined his brother, standing beside him and leaning his own folded arms on the wall. 'Shall we go to dinner?' he suggested.

'I'll eat my dinner when I please,' Gilbert growled, without turning his head.

'Why not, since you're the master here?'

said Will, humouring him. He fell silent for a few moments. The rain, sweeping across from the west, dashed against their faces, but neither brother moved.

'No doubt you've heard what's being said about you in the town?'

'Ha!' said Gilbert with contempt. 'The fools say I killed the prior's bailiff — but the murdered man cannot even be recognised!'

'That was true until this morning. But Justice Throssell has now heard that recognition's been made. The corpse is undoubtedly Thomas Bostock's.'

Gilbert's head jerked round towards his brother, his cap and his beard streaming with rain. What little could be seen of his weather-worn face had paled, making the bruising on one cheek and the livid weal on the other more clearly visible.

'*Undoubtedly?* How can that be?' he blustered. 'I heard it said that the face of the corpse was battered beyond all knowledge.'

'So it was. But Justice Throssell has now been told that Walter Bostock had a distinctive birthmark on his body — and so had the corpse. There's no longer any doubt, Gib. The prior's bailiff has been murdered.'

Gilbert flung himself away and began to stride up and down between the broken walls, but with some caution, as though his back

213

pained him. 'Then may his soul burn in hell,' he muttered, 'for he deserved to die — '

He stopped abruptly in mid-pace. 'But I did not kill him!' He strode back to Will and thrust his thick finger to within an inch of his brother's face. 'Mark me: I am not his murderer!'

'Do you swear it?'

'Aye — by the Holy Cross of Bromholm!'

Will was heartened by his brother's use of one of the most solemn and binding of all oaths. Even coming from a man who practised his religion only when it suited him, it carried conviction.

'Then who is the murderer, Gib? Do you have evidence against anyone?'

Gilbert turned away impatiently. 'If I had, I'd have told you before now. The murder could have been done by any one of the priory's tenants. They all hated the bailiff, though most were too cunning to say so — the constable especially. Aye, you'd do well to suspect the constable!'

'Then I'll do what I can to find some evidence. But meanwhile, the charge has been laid against you. Master Justice Throssell requires you to attend him at once to answer to it.'

'*To attend him? To answer a false charge?* God's blood, am I to be treated like a common suspect!' Gilbert's face was so purpled with rage that his injuries hardly showed. 'Never! The Acklands were lords of this valley for two hundred years, and I'll not be summoned to attend a mere magistrate.' He stabbed his finger at Will again. 'Go back to Justice Throssell, brother, and inform him that I am not guilty.'

Will shook his head. 'Gib,' he said patiently, 'I cannot do that. The law requires you to answer in person to the justice of the peace. All I can do for you is to keep you company. Otherwise — '

Gilbert thrust his wet face menacingly close to Will's. 'Otherwise what? *Make* me go, will you, little brother?'

'Why should I trouble?' said Will, folding his arms. 'The choice is yours. If you're not willing to come with me to the magistrate, he'll send the constable and his servants to arrest you and take you there by force.'

'*The constable — by force?*' Gilbert let out an infuriated roar. 'God's death, I'd sooner leave Castleacre than submit to that! Out of my way!'

Will stood his ground. 'If you flee, you'll only harm your cause. Listen to me, Gib — '

But Gilbert was beyond reason. His instant response was to strike out at his brother. Will saw the ham-like fist coming and jerked his

215

head aside, but the glancing blow was fierce enough to rock him back on his heels. Gib turned and broke into a pounding run, making his way in the driving rain round the outer passage of the keep towards the top of the path.

But Will was by far the more agile of the two, despite his old wounds. He cut off a corner of the keep by vaulting over one broken wall, and then scrambled up another, cursing when his boots slipped on the wet flints and he cracked his knee. As he stood up on an empty window embrasure just above head level, he caught a glimpse of Ned Pye leaning comfortably in a sheltered corner, keeping an eye on what was happening.

The empty window was one of the many vantage points Will had used in his youthful single combats with his brother. As Gib ran by below, Will leaped on to his heavy shoulders and wrapped his arms round his brother's neck, bearing him to the ground.

'Now will you stay and listen to me,' he panted, kneeling astride and pinning him face down on the grass-grown passageway.

Gilbert slammed his hands impotently on the wet turf. 'My back is hurt — get off me!' he protested through gritted teeth.

'Pains you, does it?' said Will callously, exploring the tender, swelling flesh on his

216

own cheek with cautious fingers. 'How did you come by the damage — and to your face as well? Brawling, were you?'

'What's it to you? My horse put a hoof in a rabbit hole and threw me into a bush. Get off me, do you hear!'

Gilbert gave a sudden heave of his great shoulders and rolled over, breaking Will's hold and elbowing him in the ribs for good measure. Lumbering to his feet he set off again towards the path. Will followed him at a run, flinging himself forward to seize Gib round the knees, at the same time thrusting the weight of his shoulder behind his brother's thighs. Hobbled, but carried forward by his own momentum, Gib thudded to the ground and lay there winded.

This time, Will intended to make sure that his brother heard him out. Gilbert's cap had fallen off in their struggles. Sitting astride his shoulders, Will seized his attention by grabbing a handful of the rain-matted hair at the nape of his neck and pulling back his head, making him roar a protest.

'Quiet, Gib, and listen. Flee if you will, for I'll not try to stop you again. But remember this: if you flee, it will convince the justice of the peace that you must be guilty of the murder.'

He paused, wiping the rain out of his eyes

with his sodden sleeve while he waited for his words to sink in.

'Do you understand? If you did not commit the crime, you must go before Justice Throssell and plead not guilty. And then, on the strength of your solemn oath' — he eased his grip on his brother's hair — 'I'll set about finding the real murderer.'

'Ha!' snorted Gilbert. 'What chance have you of that, when it's most likely the constable himself? And meanwhile, you expect me to lie in that stinking town gaol, awaiting trial? Never!'

'Then you must do as you please,' snapped Will, out of patience at last. He released Gilbert's hair and stood up, rubbing his cramped thigh. 'I've told Master Justice Throssell that if you'll agree to be bound over to appear at the next Quarter Sessions, I'll keep you out of gaol by standing surety for you. But if you'd sooner flee, and be hunted down by hue-and-cry — then go, and the devil take you.'

The rain had begun to ease. Will strode towards the path, trying not to limp, and Gilbert hurried after him.

'Not so hasty, brother. In truth, I did not know you had any surety to offer.'

'I have a few savings. But mark me, Gib: I can't return to my studies at Gray's Inn without them. If you flee, you'll deprive me of both my money and my profession.'

With some effort, Gilbert formed his features into an unaccustomed expression of gratitude. 'On my oath, I shall not flee. And you're welcome to stay here as long as you please — aye, and at my expense!'

It was strange to think that the enraged brother who had ordered him from the castle two days ago had now become a suppliant, following anxiously on his heels as they descended the narrow winding path through the scrub. Will muttered his thanks for the invitation to stay, but avoided any more discussion.

With a full year's study still to complete, he needed to return to London for the start of the Michaelmas law term. He hoped to set off from Castleacre in four days' time, on Wednesday; at the latest on Friday.

It was not lack of money that would prevent him from going. Meg would undoubtedly be willing to release him from his bond by standing surety for Gib herself. But duty to his family required him to stay until he had discovered the true murderer.

As everyone knew, the solemn process of the law was no guarantee that justice would be done. If Gilbert remained the suspected offender, his plea of not guilty at the

Quarter Sessions would be of no avail. There was good evidence that he had threatened to kill the bailiff, and the jurymen — chosen for their local knowledge and likely acquaintance with the facts of the case — would almost certainly find him guilty.

Until their grandfather's day, convicted felons who could read had been able to escape hanging by pleading benefit of clergy. But murderers were no longer given that benefit. The only thing that could save Gib from being hanged would be the discovery that another man had committed the crime. Small wonder, then, that he was suddenly anxious for Will's help.

They had reached the foot of the mound. Will turned to reassure his brother, and saw that Ned Pye was following them down the path at a discreet distance, wisely preferring not to descend by way of the chalk cliff.

'Be of good cheer, Gib!' he said, concealing his own unease by slapping him over-heartily on the back. 'I'll find the murderer as soon as I can, with my servant's help. Ned is a good man to have at your shoulder in perilous times, and he'll be as loyal to you as he is to me.'

Despondent, muddied, yesterday's bruises evident on his pale cheeks, Gilbert nodded his thanks. Will glanced down at his own dishevelment and let out a great chuckle.

'By the Mass, Gib, we'll be in trouble when Meg sees us! Let's meet her wrath together, for I dare not face her alone!'

17

'*Stand forward, Gilbert Ackland!*'

For a moment Will feared that his brother would refuse to comply. The two of them, as presentable as a vexed and anxious Meg had been able to make them in a hurry, stood at one end of the great oak table in Justice Throssell's hall, where they had been ushered by the sturdiest of his servants. The justice himself, stern under his skull cap, had just entered from the parlour to take his seat at the far end of the table. It was his steward, acting as his clerk, who gave the command, and Gib drew a fierce breath and clenched his fists in impotent fury at being summoned by a servant.

Thankful at least that the constable was not there to witness Gib's humiliation, and perhaps to gloat over his own escape from justice, Will gave his brother a nudge. With great reluctance, Gib took a step forward.

The justice of the peace looked up severely, giving no sign that he knew either of them. 'Gilbert Ackland,' he said, his piping voice surprisingly strong, 'you are charged with a grievous felony, in that you did murder Walter

222

Bostock, bailiff to the prior of Castleacre. How say you to the charge? Are you guilty or not guilty?'

Gilbert squared his great shoulders. 'I am not guilty, sir!'

A log shifted on the hearth, sending up a crackle of sparks. Everyone present watched in a tense silence as the justice's clerk wrote down the plea in his careful, cramped hand, his quill scratching on the parchment.

'Then I commit you for trial,' continued the justice, 'at the next Quarter Sessions in Bishop's Lynn. Is there any man here who will stand surety for you until that time?'

'I will, sir. William Ackland,' he added, to make it clear that he was not presuming upon his relationship with Justice Throssell, nor yet his long acquaintance with his godfather's steward. He stated the sum he could pay, the justice agreed, and he went forward — not without misgiving — to sign away his life's savings on the strength of his uncertain-tempered brother's oath.

Then the justice solemnly ordered Gilbert to remain within the parish at all times, and within his castle walls from dusk to dawn. He would be allowed to leave the castle in order to attend Mass on saints' days and Sundays, and to walk or ride once a day round his own fields. But he was forbidden to go on any other man's land, or to enter any inn, alehouse, shop or private dwelling, on pain of immediate imprisonment.

'Do you understand these conditions?'

Gilbert's tension was near-mutinous, but he forced himself to mutter, 'Aye, sir.'

'Very well. The court is risen.'

The steward held open the door that led to the parlour, and Master Justice Throssell trotted out with immeasurable dignity. Avoiding each other's eyes, the brothers turned to leave. The justice's other servants shuffled awkwardly out of the way, uncertain of their role now that the court proceedings were over. But the steward, a neat, precisely clean-shaven man, dropped his clerk's formality and came hurrying back down the hall to escort his master's godson to the front door.

'Master Will . . . ' he said, with evident sympathy for his predicament.

'Robert . . . ' acknowledged Will. He lingered, while Gib went out to the street where Ned was waiting with their horses. 'I expected to see the constable here, ready and willing to clap my brother into gaol.'

'Justice Throssell sent to inform him of the hearing, sir. But the constable — knowing that you'd agreed to stand surety and his presence would not be needed — begged to be excused. It seems he's injured, after being thrown by his horse.'

Will was immediately interested. 'Thrown, was he? Is he badly hurt?'

'That I don't know, sir,' said the steward, who had been schooled in diplomacy by his master. But he allowed his eyebrows to rise eloquently. 'From all accounts he's expected to survive.'

Hopeful that the constable's so-called accident had happened at the same time as Gilbert's, Will hurried outside to join his brother. There he found that a noisy crowd — Castleacre's usual spectators, the very young and the old, the idle, the simple, and the women who always carried their spindles with them so that they might earn as they stood gossiping — had gathered by the well on the opposite side of Northgate. From their disappointed mutterings, it seemed that they had hoped to enjoy the sight of Gilbert Ackland being dragged off to the town gaol.

Ned had kept Gilbert as far from them as possible by bringing the horses close to Justice Throssell's door, and placing his own mount nearest to the crowd. Gilbert himself, still unmounted, was incoherent with rage and humiliation.

'Go home,' Will advised him. 'I'll stay and speak to them, for we cannot be whispered about and pointed at every time we pass through the town.'

His brother was unsure of himself after enduring the indignities of the magistrate's court. 'Do I go alone?' he mumbled.

'Why not?' said Will. 'I'm not your gaoler. You've given me your oath, and keeping it is a matter for your own conscience. Mount up and go, or your dinner will be ruined.'

Gilbert hastened away, and Ned manoeuvred his horse so as to dissuade the crowd from running after him. Will mounted his own horse and approached them with an easy smile, knowing that they had not assembled out of any particular hostility towards Gilbert. They had been drawn, as always, by the excitement of a happening; any happening. There was no malice in their hope that it might lead eventually to a hanging.

'Friends!' Will addressed the gaping, upturned faces. There was some hooting in response, but no real disrespect for none had reason to dislike him. 'You deserve to be told the truth of what has happened. Walter Bostock has indeed been murdered.' He was forced to pause by a swelling murmur of satisfaction that the rumour had been right, and a cheer or two from the disaffected. 'And whoever did the foul deed must be found.

'My brother Gilbert has just appeared

before the justice of the peace *of his own free will*. True, he has in the past been heard to utter threats against the prior's bailiff' — jeers, laughter, and cries of *hang him!* Will raised his voice — 'but can there be any man among us who has never made an alehouse threat? Gilbert Ackland has pleaded not guilty to the charge of murder.'

Will paused to allow them time to vent their ribald disbelief. It occurred to him that one or other of them might be aware of something that would lead him to the murderer, and he wondered for a moment whether to offer a few groats for the information. But Castleacre folk could be endlessly inventive if they thought it would be to their advantage, and it would be wiser not to tempt them.

His horse, confronted by the noisy crowd, was stirring restlessly. He reined it in and raised his voice again. 'Hear me out! For my brother has sworn a sacred and binding oath by the Holy Cross of Bromholm that he is innocent of this charge.'

The noise abated instantly, as he had known it would, for there was no one who did not respect that oath. Indeed, there was a muted murmur of *Aye, aye.*

'I am standing surety for my brother,' Will continued, 'and I do it gladly. Though I have urgent business in London, I shall remain here until the Quarter Sessions, if need be. My intention is to discover the real murderer before then. In the meantime, friends' — he looked down at them with a wry affection — 'since you have known me all my life, I hope you will still greet me when we meet, for I do not expect to stay in Castleacre long!'

★   ★   ★

Will and his servant sat in the parlour of the Woolpack inn, where the other customers were travellers rather than townsfolk.

'I thought you'd forgotten our dinner,' complained Ned, drawing his knife from his belt and attacking a lukewarm mutton pie. 'I was near to eating my horse — except that the poor old nag would be too tough . . . What do we do next, Master Will?'

'We give our attention to Thomas Gosnold the constable. As a tenant of the priory, he has as much reason as my brother to hate the bailiff. And then, there are other pointers to his possible guilt.

'First, he told me he had no complaint against the bailiff. But we've both heard from townsfolk that he has spoken ill of him. Secondly' — Will paused to chip some cinders out of the piecrust before attempting a bite — 'when I went with Justice Throssell to view the corpse, the constable was over-anxious to declare the man a vagabond and to have him buried unknown. True, he might merely have wished to save himself trouble. But the injuries he's said to have will strengthen the case against him, if — as we think — the murderer was Sibbel Bostock's lover.'

'One of 'em,' said Ned, lowering his pot of ale.

'Aye, one of 'em. It's beyond belief that both Gilbert and the constable should have been thrown from their horses on the same day. If it seems likely that they fought each other, I'll confront Gib and find out more.'

'Ah — so we ride to Southacre after dinner, to discover what the constable's injuries are?'

'Not 'we'. You must go without me, for I'm known there.'

'Good — I'll do better on my own!' grinned Ned, relishing the prospect. 'I'll present myself at the kitchen door with a tray of ribbons, and tease the information out of the women servants . . .'

'Do as you will, as long as you arouse no suspicion.' Will pushed aside his half-empty trencher and wiped his knife clean with bread. 'And while you're at Southacre, I'll find out more about the shirt the bailiff's corpse was wearing.'

★ ★ ★

Will rode to the northern side of the churchyard and collected the scrap of shirt that he had concealed in a chink of the wall. Stained as it was, there was no mistaking the fine quality of the linen, and the delicacy of the sewing. And the reason he had saved that particular scrap from the neck of the shirt was that a letter N was elaborately embroidered on it.

It seemed that the message he had given the crowd outside the justice's house had already spread, for he was greeted in the usual friendly way as he rode across the market place. The priory bell was ringing to signal the ending of the monks' early afternoon service of Nones as he cantered along Priorygate, but it ceased as he turned in through the gatehouse. Giving the porter a nod, he dismounted and tied his horse's reins to a tree behind the building. Then, instead of taking the wide path that led down to the great west front of the priory church and the prior's lodging, he struck off instead to the east, along the way used by day-servants and beggars.

This way led first to the almonry, from where the daily dole was distributed, and then to the pilgrims' lodgings. It continued past the lay folk's cemetery, round the east end of the church and the monks' cemetery, and on past the infirmary to the domestic buildings of the priory.

The morning's rainclouds had blown over, and the lay-brethren who worked at the laundry were busy on the drying green, spreading the last of the day's wet linen on racks to take advantage of the wind. The laundress herself, alone in her yard now that the great washing troughs had been emptied, rested on a bench in a sheltered corner, her large red hands in her lap, her legs stretched out wide under her old gown.

Doll Harbutt looked weary. Her linen cap was awry, her plait of greying hair had tumbled down on one shoulder, her skirts were soaked with washing water. But it was not only weariness that had overtaken her. She seemed subdued, very different from the vigorous woman with the lecherous laugh who had offered to strip him on his previous visit.

Will gave her good day. Startled, openmouthed, she raised one brawny red arm and clutched her bosom in surprise.

'Master Will Ackland — I had not thought

to see you here again!' A wave of colour mounted her throat, only to be lost in the everyday crimson of her face. She half-rose to her feet. 'Had I recognised you yesterday, sir,' she apologised, 'I would not ha' spoken so . . . But there,' she added with a touch of her former spirit, ''tis not every day a young gentleman walks into my yard, soaked to the skin and bold as you please!'

Will laughed. 'I took no offence, as you see, for I've come again to ask your advice.' He sat down on the bench beside her and handed her the scrap of linen. 'This was part of an old garment — do you know who it belonged to, Mistress Harbutt?'

'Old indeed.' She grimaced, holding it at arm's length, either to keep it from her nose or to see it more clearly with weakening eyes. Then, 'Aye,' she announced, 'that I do! I cannot read, but that letter stands for Nicholas. 'Tis from a shirt that once belonged to my lord prior. His linen is always of the finest, and always marked so.'

'What happens to the prior's linen, after it's no longer fit for his own wearing? Does it go to the almonry for distribution to the poor?'

'I' faith it does not!' The laundress was indignant. 'My lord prior's garments are too good for them!' She hesitated, then gave Will a defensive sideways glance. 'What with all the important guests, and the household linen and church linen — not to mention all the monks changing their shirts and drawers in honour of St Matthew's Day, even though they'd been worn little more than a month — my work is never-ending. Can you wonder if garments sometimes get lost in the wash?'

'I shouldn't wonder at all,' Will assured her, straight-faced. 'You work hard for the priory, Mistress Harbutt, and are entitled to some perquisites — as is your husband.'

She was shocked. 'My George is but a poor herdsman — I would never let him wear what my lord prior has worn! No, sir: I allow the best garments to go to none below the rank of yeoman. I have an arrangement with all the tenants' wives — excepting Master Ackland's, of course,' she added hastily.

Will thanked her for the information, and rose to go. Doll Harbutt planted her hands on her knees and heaved herself to her feet, her expression subdued again.

'We've had a sad event here at the priory today, Master Will. Young Jankin Kett, one of the lay-brethren — you and your family know him of old — '

'Jankin?' Will felt a lurch of alarm somewhere deep within him. 'What has happened?'

'He's dead, sir.'

233

She gave a long, heartfelt sigh. Shaken, Will crossed himself and murmured a *God ha' mercy*...'How did he die?'

'Drownded, poor simpleton. One of the monks took a walk by the river after Chapter Mass, and saw him afloat. 'A must have fallen in and could not swim.'

'True, he could not,' said Will slowly, through lips that felt numbed. 'I tried to teach him when we were young, but his limbs were all awry.' He shook his head. 'Poor Jankin — he loved the river. We used to tickle trout together. That was what he was doing when I first saw him yesterday. I tried to speak to him, and followed him through your yard, but he would not stay.'

Doll Harbutt snuffled, wiped her nose with the back of her hand and sat down again, suddenly overcome. 'That was when I last saw him. 'A was harmless, sir, harmless . . . and yet I shouted at him and beat him round the ears. We all did it, servants and some of the other lay-brethren as well . . . When they brought him up from the river this morning, I was so grieved for the poor mooncalf that I laid his body out myself.'

'Had he been dead long?' asked Will. 'Had he begun to stiffen?'

'No, sir.' She paused, then added in a

broken voice: 'The bruises we gave him were plain enough, all round the back of his neck . . . '

'I must go and see him,' said Will. 'Where is he lying?'

'In the nave, sir. He's to be buried after Vespers.'

Her helpers were returning from the green with baskets piled with dried linen. The laundress still had the remainder of the day's work to do, but evidently she had a greater burden. She caught Will by the sleeve and looked up at him with haunted eyes.

'Do you think, sir,' she whispered hoarsely, 'that Jankin took his own life because we made him wretched? If so, he's gone straight to hell, and his sin will be on our heads too.'

Will sought to reassure her. 'No, Mistress Harbutt,' he said firmly. 'I do not believe that Jankin would have taken his own life.'

18

The priory church was never empty. At this time of the afternoon, when the monks were engaged elsewhere in meditation, reading or study, there might be no one there at all. But a benevolence of saints was always present, their carved and painted images looking down from every altar, niche and corner; and silence was never complete, for the walls seemed to encompass the echo of centuries of plainchant and prayer.

The great candles that were used to light the church during High Mass, revealing the vivid colours of the wall paintings and the brilliance of the gold and silver and jewels with which the statues were adorned, were now extinguished. The carved and painted bosses, distantly high in the roof of the nave, were lost in the gloom. But Will could see two candles burning in the north aisle, beyond the pillars that separated it from the nave, and there he found the body of his boyhood friend.

Jankin was at peace, there was no doubt about that. Lying on a bier in his white shroud, with only his face visible under his shock of dark hair, he looked little older than when he had first been put into the care of the priory. All the fear and anxiety had been smoothed from his moon-flat features by the hand of death.

But even though Will had some idea of Jankin's wretchedness, he refused to believe that he had drowned himself. Self-destruction was a sin so great that the thought of it could not be borne. Whatever private misgivings they might share with the laundress, everyone at the priory, monks and lay-folk alike, would prefer to attribute Jankin's death to an accident.

What concerned Will, however, was not misgivings but guilty knowledge. The bruising on the back of the neck that the laundress had observed suggested a different cause of death. And if that were so, the truth would be kept hidden somewhere within the priory.

He was just finishing a heartfelt prayer for the repose of his friend's soul when he heard the swift approach of sandalled footsteps, and saw from the corner of his eye the swirl of a black habit. He knew at once, without looking up, that its wearer was the sub-prior. But the nave of the church was the one part of the priory that was always open to laymen, and there was no need for apology.

'An untimely death, Father Arnold,' he said

as he rose to his feet. 'And a grief for my family — Jankin's mother was our nurse, as I think I told you.'

The sub-prior inclined his head fractionally by way of acknowledgement. His cowl was pushed back, revealing his gaunt face, but his deep-set eyes were lowered. 'Jankin idled by the river when he should have been at work,' he said in his austere voice. 'No doubt he fell in and was unable to swim.'

'Perhaps so,' said Will. 'But he was mistreated by the other servants, I saw that for myself when I was here yesterday. I understand there is bruising on the back of his neck. Could he have been held under water in some incident — some horseplay — do you think?'

The sub-prior raised his eyes and gave Will a single, burning glance. 'How should I know that?' he said with disdain. And turning abruptly, he swept away towards the Quire.

★   ★   ★

Will rode back to the castle and found Ned Pye waiting for him, sitting astride the parapet of the bridge over the ditch with his back against the outer wall of the gatehouse. He was juggling with pebbles to pass the time, and looking pleased with himself.

238

'Here's news to hearten you!' he cried, jumping down and taking the horse's bridle. The castle dogs, accustomed to Will by now, came rushing out without much barking and fawned round his legs as he dismounted.

'The constable's servants,' Ned went on, 'tell me that he came home yesterday with a fine black eye! Mistress Gosnold was so angry with him that she hasn't spoken to him. And he hasn't left his yard since then, for he's too ashamed to be seen.'

'Excellent news! What else do they say about the constable?'

Ned grinned. 'They say he has a whore somewhere, for he sometimes rides out o'nights. And no one knows where he might be during the day . . . '

It could be nothing more than servants' gossip. What with his flocks and herds and his duties as constable, Thomas Gosnold had reason enough to absent himself from Southacre. But the black eye certainly suggested a brawl, and perhaps a rivalry with Gilbert Ackland.

'My brother's at home, I hope?'

'Aye, and comforting himself with ale. He shambles about the yard like a caged bear, and snarls at everyone he comes across. That's why I'm here, out of his way. Old Jacob has gone into hiding.'

'He's a wise man. And we'd best stay here too, if we're to talk without interruption.'

Ned hitched the horse's reins to a rusted hinge that had once supported one of the castle's great outer doors. 'The servants aren't best pleased with you, Master Will,' he said, evidently agreeing with them. 'They think you should ha' let your brother be clapped into gaol, guilty or no, to give them a few weeks' peace.'

Will let that pass.

'Keep your fleas to yourself, sirrah,' he commanded an over-friendly hound, pushing the animal aside with his boot and slapping his bitten calf. He joined Ned on the parapet, drew up his heels out of the dogs' way, and rested his arms on his knees in thought.

'I must persuade Gib to tell me the truth about the brawl. But even if we know that they've both enjoyed Sibbel Bostock's favours, we need more than that to connect the constable with her husband's death.'

'I could start by finding out what happened to the bailiff's horse,' suggested Ned. 'It can't ha' disappeared — I'll wager it's been sold. I'll visit the farrier before supper and ask him to describe it.'

'Do that,' Will agreed. 'And what of the other possessions the bailiff had with him when he set out? All I've found so far are his

240

clothes — except for his riding boots. There's his saddle and harness to find, and his saddle-bags, and the rent rolls for the priory's lands at Bromholm. If we can trace any of them to Southacre, we'll have a good case against the constable.'

'*We?*' objected Ned in an injured voice. 'Who is this *we?* It seems that I'm expected to do it all myself, since you are riding out on pleasure tomorrow . . .'

Will had almost forgotten that he was invited to dinner at Oxmead. Almost, but not quite, for the image of Julian Corbyn had come to mind, delightfully unbidden, on several occasions during the day.

'I do not go on pleasure,' he informed his servant austerely. 'Sir Ralph Corbyn is one of the Members of Parliament for Norfolk. He could be of assistance to me when I become a barrister.'

'Ha!' crowed Ned. 'You needn't try to deceive me. I've heard how you pestered the womenfolk to deck you out in finery for the occasion! You're going a-wooing — and without my approval . . .'

Will repaid him for his impertinence by tipping him off the parapet, though he took care to dump him on the bridge rather than down into the ditch.

'Enough of your grumbling,' he said. 'And

241

you need not grin like an ape, neither. As for the tasks — you told me not two hours ago that you'd rather do them alone than in my company. Besides, it's in your interests as much as mine to discover the murderer. The sooner my brother's name is cleared, the sooner we can return to London.'

Ned stood up and brushed the dust of Castleacre off the seat of his hose. 'Amen to that,' he said fervently.

★ ★ ★

An uneasy quiet hung over the yard. Even the geese and the dunghill roosters seemed subdued as Gilbert Ackland, morose as a captive bear, prowled within the confines of his castle walls.

Will approached his brother in the orchard, careful not to give the impression that he was cornering him. For his part, Gib knew better than to receive his benefactor with a snarl; but his bitterness towards the rest of the world was undisguised. Only the news of the constable's black eye seemed to give him any satisfaction.

Will guessed that his brother had kept his liaison with Sibbel Bostock a secret for fear of the long reach of church law. Had word of it got to the churchwardens' ears, he would

242

have been summoned before the archdeacon's court and either heavily fined or sentenced to imprisonment for adultery. But that was now of small significance. Finding himself in danger of being hanged for murder, Gib was at last prepared to answer his brother's questions, though he did so with resentment.

Yes, he had fought with Thomas Gosnold yesterday — and Sibbel Bostock had been the cause.

It was at Michaelmas the previous year that he had first accepted her invitation to taste her elderberry wine. Since then, he had visited her whenever her husband was away on priory business.

'That must have given you a double satisfaction,' suggested Will. 'Not only did you enjoy Mistress Bostock, but you cuckolded your enemy the bailiff into the bargain.'

'Aye — it pleased me well at first. Then I began to suspect that I had a rival. Sibbel denied it . . . but I've been in torment these past few months. Then, yesterday — '

Gilbert snatched a ripe apple from a tree and hurled it viciously against the castle wall, where it splattered on impact.

'I found Thomas Gosnold with her! By God — if I'd already murdered the bailiff I would ha' killed the constable too.'

Will tried to give his brother some consolation. 'I doubt that you and the constable were the only men to enjoy her favours, Gib. Mistress Bostock offers a taste of her elderberry wine to any man who's to her liking. And if we're to discover the murderer, we must know every one of them. Do you have reason to suspect anyone else?'

Gilbert swelled with rage. The priory bell had begun to ring for the early evening service of Vespers, but he had no difficulty in making himself heard above its sound.

'God's blood — haven't I already pointed you to the murderer? Thomas Gosnold had reason enough to want to rid himself of the bailiff. Aye, and he had opportunity, too. And the authority to escape justice by claiming the body was unknown. Have the constable arrested, and let me go free!'

Will gave him a few moments to calm himself. 'So that you can return to Sibbel Bostock's arms?' he suggested, not unkindly.

Gilbert's outburst had abated. He turned his great head towards his brother, his eyes wretched amid the tangle of his hair and beard.

'I' God's name,' he said in a broken voice, 'I *love* the wench . . . She bewitches me. I cannot leave her be . . .'

Recalling the lustrous black-eyed charms of

Sibbel Bostock, Will had no difficulty in understanding. It seemed to him that his brother was as much in thrall to her as King Henry was to Anne Boleyn, a woman made in a similar mould. And how it would end, for man, monarch or mistresses, he could not begin to guess.

19

At supper, Will told the family of the death of Jankin Kett, though not of his ill-treatment nor of the likelihood that others had played a part in his drowning. Meg was sad for a time, less perhaps for Jankin himself than for their vanished childhood of which he had been a part. Even Gib muttered a *God ha' mercy*. And by the time Will had finished explaining to them that Jankin's death had been an accident, he had almost come to believe it himself.

He slept lightly and was up and about by Sunday cock-crow, eager for the meeting with Julian Corbyn that the day would bring. Ned Pye was eager too, heartened by the prospect of returning to London as soon as he could find the bailiff's murderer. He went whistling about his duties, cleaning his master's boots until they shone, sharpening Will's knife to a fine edge for shaving, and fetching a second basin of hot water without too much grumbling.

The whole valley was blanketed by September mist as the Ackland household set out to join the rest of the parish at

Mass. Too weary to make the journey, Alice remained at home with her rosary; but Gilbert went with them, wanting to escape the confines of the castle and no doubt hopeful of catching sight of Sibbel Bostock. As for Ned Pye, he rode off on his own, intent on taking advantage of the mist and the Mass by exploring Southacre while the constable and his household were in church.

Afterwards, Will changed from his Sunday clothes into his finery. As he came down from the stair-turret to re-enter the hall he found that every female in the castle had gathered to take a look at him, the older women servants murmuring approval, the younger ones blushing and giggling in answer to his raillery.

Agnes had brought Betsy to see her father, but his fine appearance made her shy again. She peeped out at him from a doorway, and hesitated when he called to her. 'Come, sweet Betsy,' he coaxed, bending down with his hands outstretched, but she would only laugh and run away.

His sister and Alice were waiting for him in the hall: not in order to admire him, Meg pointed out firmly, nor yet to receive his thanks, but simply to ensure that he was fit to be seen at Oxmead.

'I despair of you, William Ackland . . . ' She sighed as she looked him over. 'You'd be almost presentable, if it weren't for that great bruise on your cheek. It passes belief that a man of your learning should choose to brawl with your brother! A Cambridge Master of Arts, indeed . . . I cannot imagine what Sir Ralph will think of you.'

'He'll think me a lucky fellow, to have a sister so careful of my welfare,' he teased her. 'And have no fear about the bruise — I'll wear my new cap over one eye, so the feather will hide it.'

'Have done,' said Meg crossly. 'And listen to me, for I have more care for your welfare than you realise.'

She put one hand on Will's arm and walked with him to the door of the hall.

'Mistress Julian,' she said as they went, 'is as beautiful a maiden as you'll find — and a match for you in spirit. But do not lose your heart to her, Will. She is not for you.'

He began to protest that he had no thought of it, but his sister cut him short. 'When Sir Ralph was here, he told me of the good marriages he had secured for all three of his older daughters. He has no son-in-law without wealth, nor below the rank of knight. As for Julian, he dotes on her. He would never allow his beloved youngest child to marry a penniless gentleman. And besides — '

'What else?' said Will ungraciously, thinking that Master Justice Throssell had not been so censorious when he'd asked for the hand of his daughter. But then, the justice was his godfather, and no doubt regarded him with indulgence.

'Sir Ralph,' Meg warned, 'already has a marriage in mind for Julian — to the second son of his near neighbour, Lord Stradsett.' She gave her brother's arm a consolatory squeeze. 'I'm sure he made a point of telling me this because he thinks well of you. He does not want you to go to Oxmead under any misapprehension.'

Numbed by disappointment, he made no reply. They had reached the open front door, and his horse stood groomed and ready in the yard. Old Jacob led it forward, and Meg gave her brother an encouraging smile as he prepared to mount.

'I know you'll make a good impression on Sir Ralph. And, Will — '

'What now?' he glowered.

'As you go through Swaffham, be so good as to buy me a lemon if you can find one — there've been none to be had in Castleacre all summer.'

Will left the castle in a towering ill-humour, urging his mount across the bridge and through the town at a pace that sent people and livestock scattering.

It irked him that everyone in the household assumed that he was going to Oxmead in the hope of wooing Julian Corbyn; and it irked him even more that they were right. But what he had just heard from Meg had thrown him into confusion. Though his head understood only too well, his pride rejected his understanding.

He thundered across the ford and south on the Peddars' Way. It was good to be riding out again, after spending so long at Castleacre, and the activity soon began to restore his spirits. So did the sun: it had sucked up the early mist, and the September light was now as golden-warm as honey ... or as the remembered glow in Julian's eyes. Dismissing Meg's warning, he rode on with fresh hope.

He eased his horse's pace as the road climbed Bartholomew's Hills, and made amends for his haste through the town by acknowledging other travellers along the Way. At the crossroads, the long-dead corpse dangling from the gibbet gave him a moment's apprehensiveness on Gilbert's behalf. But, crossing himself as he passed it, he felt confident of establishing his brother's innocence. There was good reason to believe that the constable had murdered the bailiff, and it was reassuring to know that Ned Pye was even now searching for proof of Thomas Gosnold's guilt.

Before long he reached Swaffham, a market town bigger than Castleacre, with an arguably finer parish church but with neither castle nor priory to give it importance, let alone a shrine to bring pilgrims and prosperity. He found the lemon Meg wanted, though in truth it was a poor wizened thing and not worth the price. Then he sought out the draper's shop that Sibbel Bostock had told him of, and revealed to the bailiff's aunt that her nephew was dead.

The aunt, a busy old widow with a sharp tongue, was neither grieved by Walter Bostock's death nor unduly surprised to hear that he had been murdered. He'd always been a man who made enemies, she said. And he was miserly with his money — why, he'd never spent so much as a groat in her shop . . .

Will took the hint and, at the cost of sufficient sky-blue cloth to make Betsy a cloak, he learned something more about the bailiff and his wife. Then he rode on, as far to

251

the south of Swaffham as Castleacre was to the north, and so came to Oxmead.

The village, in flatter land than Castleacre, well wooded and near a slower river, consisted of little more than the church and rectory, a few farmsteads and a huddle of cottages. All the land hereabouts, and more elsewhere, had belonged to the Corbyns for generations. Sir Ralph's father had chosen the site fifty years ago for the building of a great square red brick house, and as Will rode towards it he could see the battlemented turrets of its gatetower rising high above the intervening trees.

Though the gatetower was fortified, and approached by a bridge over the moat that surrounded the whole building, these apparent defences were nothing more than symbols of prosperity and pride. The waters were shallow, casting delicate reflections on the walls that rose directly from them; the mullioned windows were large so as to let in the light. For all its warlike pretence, Oxmead Hall was a mansion built in and for times of peace.

Eager to set eyes on Julian again, Will dismounted under the gatetower, left his horse with a groom and walked through to the great open court that stood square in the centre of the house. His host, Sir Ralph, emerged from the main doorway on the opposite side of the court and came forward to meet him, spare, trimly bearded and formidably sharp-eyed.

'A word with you, Will, before we go in,' he said when they had exchanged greetings. 'It concerns my daughter.'

'Sir?' said Will stiffly, thinking that Sir Ralph meant to warn him off in person. But it seemed that it was not Julian's future marriage that her father had in mind.

'She has known you since she was a child,' said Sir Ralph as they paced the court together, 'and I believe she has hopes of you as an ally. She speaks demurely of wanting to discuss foreign modes of dress with you, but she does not deceive me.

'Whenever I am absent from Oxmead — and in winter, when the dampness cannot be borne — Julian accompanies her mother, my lady wife, to Norwich. They stay with her brother, Alderman Mancroft, and his wife. But there are dangerous ideas abroad in Norwich, heresies imported from the Low Countries, and I fear my daughter may have caught the infection. These notions must be uprooted from her mind, Will, and I rely on you to help me. I have already informed her of her folly. Before you leave here, I want you to take her aside and persuade her of it.'

'I am at your service, sir,' said Will solemnly, concealing his pleasure at being given her father's permission to speak to Julian in private. The approach of a party of horsemen prevented any further conversation. At their head as they clattered across the bridge rode an elderly man with a flowing grey beard, a nobleman by his dress, followed by attendants and grooms.

'Ah, my good friend and neighbour Lord Stradsett!' said Sir Ralph with satisfaction. 'He's hampered by deafness but he likes to have company about him — and to remind me of his interest in Julian on his son's behalf. No need for you to attempt to speak to him. You'll find that nods and smiles will serve you well.'

* * *

Sir Ralph and Lady Corbyn were known throughout the county as good hosts, and there were always guests at their table. On this occasion, besides Lord Stradsett and Will, there were also Alderman Augustine Mancroft, a portly, dignified man, and his taller, thinner wife, on a reciprocal visit from Norwich. The youthful household chaplain, Father Woodiss, was present too, but he was largely disregarded.

254

Will was instantly aware of Julian as he entered the great galleried hall in the wake of Lord Stradsett; and she, he believed, of him. But as was proper he paid his first courtesies to Lady Corbyn, a comfortably rounded woman, so secure in her rank that she was still content to wear the outmoded gable hood.

Mistress Mancroft, her long-faced sister-in-law, was spikily conscious that she and her husband had no standing in the county of Norfolk. But she compensated for this by wearing more fashionable clothing than her husband's sister, including the new French hood that Julian also wore. As Will soon discovered, Mistress Mancroft never tired of pointing out that in Norwich, the largest city in the kingdom after London, her husband was one of the leading citizens by virtue of his wealth as a merchant, his importance as an alderman, and the fact that he had twice been mayor.

Will released himself from their company as soon as he could, and sought out Julian. She greeted him with a lively grace, the bright brown hair that was spread over the shoulders of her blue gown delighting his eye; but her attentions were principally confined to Lord Stradsett, leaving Will downcast. His spirits did not lift until after the horns had sounded

255

for dinner, when Julian chose to walk beside him as they went through to the smaller hall.

'Your appearance is much finer than when I saw you last,' she told him with a smile. 'The purple of that bruise on your cheek goes well with your doublet . . . Tell me, is fist-fighting one of your usual pastimes?'

'Only when I argue with my brother,' he said lightly. 'You should see *his* bruises.'

'Worse?'

'Much worse.'

They laughed, acknowledging pleasure in each other's company, and then were separated. Sir Ralph took the centre of the long table, with Lord Stradsett and Lady Corbyn on one side of him and Will and the chaplain on the other. Julian sat opposite her father, with her uncle and aunt on either side. Men servants bustled about the hall, offering each diner a silver basin of water and a towel. The household dogs prowled round in hopeful uncertainty, with the exception of one small hound that sat alert on Lady Corbyn's lap, confident of being fed with the choicest morsels from the many dishes that crowded the table.

Before the dinner was served, Sir Ralph called on his chaplain to say grace. Father Woodiss, who had effaced himself until now, made the most of this opportunity to be heard and gave a blessing in such lengthy Latin that Sir Ralph cut short the flow with a firm *Amen*.

Julian immediately addressed Lady Corbyn, with apparent innocence. 'Do you not regret — as I do, mother — that the chaplain's eloquence is wasted on those of us who have no Latin? After all, you named me for Dame Julian the anchoress of Norwich, who wrote all her prayers in English. And that was more than a hundred years ago.'

'Have done,' said Lady Corbyn uncomfortably, but Julian's parade of innocence continued.

'Across the North Sea, as I've heard, there are some who not only use prayer books but even read the Bible in their own tongue! Can that possibly be true, Master Will?' she said, turning to him.

Her lively brown eyes had mischief in them. But he knew from what her father had said that her intent was serious, and so he made a diplomatic answer. 'They do things differently in foreign countries, Mistress Julian.'

Sir Ralph slammed his palm on the table. 'Those you speak of deny the authority of the church. They are heretics, in any language!' he said fiercely. 'I forbid you to make mention of them. Especially in front of my Lord Stradsett,' he added, disregarding the fact that his lordship was about to embark on a partridge, succulently roasted with garlic, onions and pears, and had no notion of what had been said.

'You know full well, daughter,' Sir Ralph continued formidably, wagging his finger at her, 'that the word of God has been handed down in Latin, and is interpreted for us by the church. It always has been so, and always will be, and there's an end on't. Now be silent.' He raised his voice at the servants: 'Wine for my lord, I say! Bring us more wine!'

Soundly rebuked, Julian sat with her head lowered, eating little. Will, gazing at the glowing colour of her hair, hoped to offer her the support of a smile, but she would not lift her eyes. She appeared outwardly obedient, taking no further part in the conversation, but a rebellious patch of red burned on either cheek.

Lady Corbyn diverted attention from her daughter by pressing her guests to taste other dishes. As the partridges and capons on the table were replaced by venison and roast ribs of beef, conversation turned from harvest, rents and taxes to the never-ending problem of beggars and vagabonds. But soon, as at every other table in the country, they began to discuss King Henry's proposed divorce.

Their sympathies lay, as did those of most people throughout the land, with the wronged Queen. Their anger toward Mistress Anne Boleyn was all the stronger because she was Norfolk-born, and they spoke censoriously of her as Nan Bullen. Mistress Mancroft described her as 'a brazen hussy'; the alderman as 'the King's whore'. They appealed to Will, who had been in London most recently, for the latest news of her, and he told them on good authority that she now had her own apartments near the King's at Hampton Court, and was always referred to as 'the Lady Anne'.

' 'Lady' indeed!' protested Lady Corbyn, her feathers ruffled.

'But at least,' said Sir Ralph, 'she helped to bring down Cardinal Wolsey. We should be grateful to her for that.'

There was immediate agreement, for no one present had a good word to say for Thomas Wolsey. He had risen from humble origins ('His father was nothing more than a butcher of Ipswich!' sniffed Mistress Mancroft) to become the most powerful of the King's subjects, not only Lord Chancellor but also a Cardinal of the church, and the Pope's representative in England.

The grumbles against him were many. The

Cardinal was an unchaste priest, with a concubine and at least one child. The Cardinal had strengthened the power of the church in this country, to the disadvantage of men of honest endeavour. The Cardinal was corrupt, taking bribes in return for favours, and making use of the revenues of the church to become the richest man in the land. The Cardinal had lived in great splendour, and had more courtiers about him than the King.

'But for all that,' pointed out Sir Ralph, 'it was the King's favour — and latterly Anne Boleyn's — that kept him so high. He gave King Henry the great new palace he'd built at Hampton Court in the hope of retaining that favour; but to no avail. When it was withdrawn, he was bound to fall.'

Lord Stradsett, who had himself been at Court in his younger days, had been straining to follow the conversation with a hand cupped to his ear.

'A man cannot serve two masters,' he pronounced, in a booming voice that made his beard-hair flutter. 'When Wolsey sat in judgement last year on the matter of the King's divorce, he was acting for both Pope and King. He could not please both. He failed to obtain the divorce, and so the King stripped him of office.'

'And of all his other palaces, lands and

goods,' said Alderman Mancroft with satisfaction. 'With all that wealth to replace what he lost by the last French war, the King should have no need to raise our taxes!'

'It should keep him in funds — and his mistress in jewellery — for a year or two at least,' agreed Sir Ralph dryly. 'I heard that she and the King were taken by boat, in disguise, to Wolsey's fine new house by the Thames near Westminster, so that they might gloat over the treasures it contained.'

Lady Corbyn clucked with disapproval. 'But what has happened to the Cardinal since his fall?' she asked.

'He was imprisoned, for exercising the power of the Pope in the King's realm.'

'But where imprisoned? In the Tower of London?' asked Mistress Mancroft with unbecoming eagerness, for she knew that few emerged from that dread place.

'No, no — ' said Sir Ralph. 'At least, not yet.'

'But he will be executed?' his sister-in-law persisted.

He shrugged. 'If the King wills it. Though I hear Wolsey's ill, and may not live to reach the Tower.'

'Ah me,' sighed Lady Corbyn, not with sympathy for Thomas Wolsey but in fearful wonder at the workings of Church and State.

'That anyone so great — and standing so high in the King's favour — should fall so far . . . '

Lord Stradsett tugged his beard. 'I would not be a courtier in these uneasy times, for all the riches in Christendom. In King Harry's younger days, we always guarded our tongues on pain of dismissal. But now, I hear, they have a new watchword: 'The anger of the Prince means death.'

20

'Your father's hospitality is too generous,' said Will as he and Julian escaped from the house into the sunlight. 'I thought dinner would never be done . . .'

'And such gloom in their conversation! But at least he has granted me leave to talk to you before you go. Oh, Will — I am happy to have you here at Oxmead again.'

Freed from her father's observation she laughed, plucked up the front of her skirts and ran lightly across the brick bridge that spanned the moat. Will stood for a moment under the shadow of the gatetower, watching her; barely conscious of the green smell of the water as it lapped against the walls, but piercingly aware of the swirl of Julian's russet hair against her throat as she turned, smiling, to look back at him.

He hurried after her, quickening his pace to a run as she crossed the mown grass beyond the bridge and entered the gardens, where he had used to chase her years ago. This time, though, she was not hiding but waiting for him. Her lightheartedness had been replaced by a solemn air.

'I have something to tell you that no one else must hear. Promise me that whatever we speak of shall be our secret?'

'Does it concern your betrothal?' he asked warily.

Julian was indignant. 'No — I am not betrothed! If you thought me attentive to his lordship before dinner, that was only to deceive my father. Francis Stradsett is a nincompoop. I'd sooner enter a nunnery than have him as a husband.'

Will's hopes burgeoned as they walked together through gardens smelling warmly of box and sweet-briar and sun-ripe apples. But, dazzled as he was by her nearness, he had wit enough to conceal his pleasure.

'Then I hope your father does not take you at your word,' he teased her, 'for I think you'd like the life of a nun even less.'

She shook her head impatiently. 'No matter. What I want to ask, Will, is whether you ever saw Mistress Anne Boleyn when you were in London?'

'Only at a distance.' He began to speak of the appearance of the King's mistress, but Julian cut him short.

'Everyone here condemns her out of hand. But in Norwich, there are some who speak in her favour. She is a learned lady, I believe?'

Forewarned by her father, Will was

guarded. 'Anne Boleyn is clever, certainly. She was trained at the French court, and speaks and reads their language.'

'I've heard that she often reads the Bible in French. She has a French translation, imported to this country for her own use.'

'Has she? I have no knowledge of that.'

Julian turned on him with a passionate impatience. 'But surely you know *why* it is in French? It has to be in a foreign language, because English translations of the Bible are banned in this country.'

'So I've always understood,' he said patiently.

'Well, then — when Anne Boleyn becomes Queen, she will persuade the King to allow us to read the Bible in English!'

Will thought it desirable, but unlikely. 'Perhaps . . . ' he said.

Her bright brown eyes sparked with irritation. 'Oh, you've grown so cautious! Surely you cannot agree with such a ban?'

He would not make a direct answer, for fear of giving her encouragement. 'When did you become interested in such matters?'

'Last winter, when I stayed with my uncle in Norwich.' Julian hesitated. 'There is a young man — ' she began, and then turned abruptly away to hide the blush that was staining her cheeks.

Will felt a sudden stab of discomfort, entering sharp as a knife between his ribs. He suspected what it might be; but he refused to admit to jealousy, even to himself.

'What of him?' he asked with a show of indifference.

Julian explained, all in a rush, that the young man had been destined for the church. But finding himself at odds with the church's authority, and needing to make his way in the world, he had lived for a time at Alderman Mancroft's house while he learned the spice trade. They had, she admitted, sometimes talked together.

She said it with great seriousness, and Will was instantly alarmed. He knew that Alderman Mancroft, a merchant grocer, imported Eastern spices from the great depot at the port of Antwerp. And it was through Antwerp that many of the forbidden books — including Tyndale's New Testament in English, printed of necessity in Germany — were smuggled into England.

'Does this young man travel to and from Antwerp?' he demanded. 'Has he brought back any English Bibles — or any books written in English against the church?'

Hot-cheeked again, though for a different reason, Julian raised her head and stared at him defiantly. 'I shall not say.'

Will was angry now. Not with Julian, in her ardent innocence, but with this pernicious young man — Edmund she called him — who had burdened her with his beliefs.

As Will knew, there were men in London and at Cambridge — as well, no doubt, as others scattered throughout the country — who sought these books. But the church would come down with great severity upon any who bought, sold, read, possessed or copied them. Those who did so were careful to keep their activities a secret from all except 'known men'.

This wretched Edmund was a fool, and a dangerous one, to have disclosed his mind to Julian. Where else besides her father's house had she given hints of her beliefs? Who else besides his guests had heard her? The church, like the King, had informers everywhere. If she did not hold her tongue she was at risk of being questioned by the archdeacon's officers, and they would not take *I shall not say* for an answer.

As for Edmund himself, a traveller to and from Antwerp, no doubt he was already being watched. When the time was ripe he would be seized, and charged with heresy. And surely Julian knew what would happen then? The books in his possession would be burned, and he himself might well be burned with them.

But Edmund's likely fate was a matter for him alone. Will's sole concern was for Julian. Fierce in his anxiety for her, he seized her by the shoulders.

'You must never again say anything against the authority of the church! You risk too much by doing so. As for that young man, he's already in great danger. He was wrong to take you into his confidence, and you must have nothing more to do with him. Do you understand?'

Julian pulled angrily away.

'Let me go! What right have you to tell me what to do?'

Then her expression changed, from anger to realisation and from realisation to contempt.

'Oh — but you've come as my father's lackey, haven't you? That was why he invited you here, to try to talk me out of my beliefs! But you cannot — and I will never abandon Edmund. So go your ways, Will Ackland, and do not return to Oxmead, for I have no wish to see you ever again.'

21

Half-blinded by the smart of humiliation and anger, Will thundered away from Oxmead and did not pause until he reached Swaffham market place. Then he slowed his horse to a walking pace and began to gather his wits.

He had no need, he told himself, to fear for Julian's safety. She was young and foolishly wilful, but she had her father to protect her. As for her evident attachment to that wretch Edmund — but no, he would not dwell on it. He would put her out of his mind, and dismiss his desire for her as an episode of Michaelmas madness.

(If only she were not so well endowed with grace and beauty . . . If only she had not stood so fragrantly close when she confided in him . . . If only he had not grasped her slim shoulders, and felt their warmth under his hands . . .)

Will urged his horse on, and forced his thoughts towards Castleacre.

There was still his brother's innocence to be established. Had Ned, he wondered, been able to find the proof they needed of the constable's involvement in the bailiff's murder? If so, the constable would be charged, all suspicion would be lifted from Gilbert, and Will would no longer be required to stand surety for him.

The prospect was invigorating. It would remove the burden of anxiety from the whole family, and Will himself would be free to resume his own life. He looked forward to setting off with Ned for London, where there were interests and friendships to be renewed at Gray's Inn. And he recalled that when he and his fellow law students tired of their books, a short ride across the fields would take them to the village of Islington, where there were always red-cheeked country wenches eager for dalliance.

(But what of that, when Julian was so wondrously fair?)

He crested Bartholomew's Hills and saw the familiar shallow valley of the Nar lying before him, dominated by the great tower of the priory. As he skirted the gibbet he saw that Ned was waiting for him further ahead, opposite the Walsingham turn. It was his servant's mare (in truth an ageing creature) that Will recognised first, grazing placidly beside the hedgerow. Ned himself was seated on the grass, his back against a tree, exchanging greetings and jests with travellers on the Peddars' Way.

'Ha, Master Will!' Ned jumped up, smirking from ear to ear. 'What news from Oxmead?'

'None that I'll share with you, Jackanapes,' retorted Will as he dismounted. 'What of Southacre, though? Did you find the bailiff's horse in the constable's stables?'

Ned pulled a glum face. 'No, I did not. Nor did I find the Bromholm rent rolls. I looked through all the saddle-bags in the harness room, but they were empty. In truth, there's nothing at Southacre to connect the constable with the bailiff's murder.'

Will's hopes of an early solution to the mystery slid down into his boots. He had been sure of the constable's guilt — as sure, no doubt, as the constable had been of Gilbert's. If both were innocent, then who had done the deed?

Ned embarked on a tale of how he had spent the day, wearing himself out — not to mention his poor old mare — by visiting every stable in and near Castleacre in search of the bailiff's horse. But Will observed a grin hovering on either side of his mouth, and cut him short.

'Then you have discovered it? Where?'

'Why, in the bailiff's own stable, snug as you please! Sibbel Bostock said it had been found and brought back by one of the lay-brothers.'

'Brought back when?'

'Yesterday, she said, soon after you'd been to tell her of her husband's murder. But she was lying. The bailiff's horse is the only one in the stable, and there's more than a day's worth of recent dung on the straw.'

'Good!' said Will with satisfaction. 'Then Mistress Bostock has lied to us throughout, for I learned this morning that she and her husband had little regard for each other. The bailiff's aunt told me that Sibbel had never thought Walter Bostock good enough for her. She wanted to have servants, like a proper yeoman's wife, and it vexed her that he would not allow it. For his part, Walter was angry with her because she had borne him no children, and was undutiful towards him. Knowing this, we have reason enough to go and talk to her again.'

Will was about to re-mount when it occurred to him that Ned might have compromised the coming encounter.

'When you visited her this morning, did you by any chance sample her elderberry wine?'

Ned hesitated. Reluctant as he was to lose his amorous reputation, this was not an occasion for boasting. 'In truth,' he admitted,

272

'she made me no offer.'

'That's just as well,' said his master, 'for we have some stern questions to put to the bailiff's widow.'

★ ★ ★

Sibbel Bostock showed no surprise when Will and Ned Pye rode up to her door. It was almost as though she expected them. She seemed subdued, in both manner and appearance. Her hair was hidden by her linen cap, her feet were shod, her skirts concealed her ankles. She held her eyes modestly low and said little, beyond ordering the dogs to be quiet; but she made no pretence to a widow's grief.

Will did not pay her the courtesy of dismounting.

'Mistress Bostock,' he said. 'My brother Gilbert Ackland is accused of the murder of your husband. He has sworn by the Holy Cross of Bromholm that he is innocent. I am here to clear his name by discovering the real murderer.'

Sibbel Bostock glanced up at him warily, her wide eyes a brilliant black against the sunburned hue of her skin. She raised one hand towards her magnificent throat. She was, Will observed, almost as handsome as he remembered; but with Julian's delicate fresh beauty still in his eyes, Sibbel's now seemed coarse.

'Then indeed, sir,' she protested, 'you have wasted your journey, for I cannot help you.'

'I think you can. By living out here, with no neighbours to pry, you have been able to fornicate without fear of being reported to the archdeacon. No, you need not deny it. My brother has admitted to being one of your lovers, and I think Thomas Gosnold is another. No doubt you have others — and I believe it was one of them who murdered your husband. Who was it, Mistress Bostock? Someone from within the priory precinct?'

Sibbel Bostock's cheeks burned crimson. 'I have no lover within the precinct!' she protested.

'A would-be lover, then. An ardent admirer. Tell me, which of the lay-brothers was it who returned the bailiff's horse?'

'I do not know. They all wear the same garments — I cannot tell one from t'other.'

'What else was returned to you? What of the Bromholm rent rolls that the bailiff would have been carrying when he set out?'

'I know nothing of them. The saddle-bags were brought back empty, save for the few needments my husband took with him. The horse was his own, and was rightfully returned to me because it is now mine. I have naught to do with the priory.'

'No?' Will raised his eyebrows. 'But you look to it for protection, I have no doubt?'

Sibbel Bostock lowered her eyes. She would say nothing more, but the flush of blood that suffused the column of her throat was eloquence enough.

★ ★ ★

The bailiff and all other day-workers were answerable to the cellarer of the priory. He was a monk second only in importance (or so he believed) to the prior himself, for he had charge of all temporal matters: lands, properties, leases, rents, wages, mills, work-shops, granaries and provisioning.

Brother Walstan had been cellarer for some ten years, and had become increasingly tetchy under the burden of his responsibilities. The room where he worked was near the almonry, and accessible to the priory's tenants, but there were few who would willingly interrupt him.

Will was saved from his anger by the fact that Brother Walstan, a man with a long nose and a quick, harsh voice, had known and respected his father. Even so, walled in as he was by three centuries of cobwebbed account books, and with his tonsured head bent over page after page of figures, the monk was reluctant to waste time. He nodded an acknowledgement when Will commiserated over the priory's loss of the bailiff, and frowned when he heard that Gilbert Ackland had been charged with the murder. But when Will explained that he was endeavouring to clear his brother's name, the cellarer began to drum his fingers on the table.

'The charge is a grievous matter for your family,' he agreed. 'But what has it to do with me?'

'By your leave,' said Will, 'I need to know if the bailiff took the rent rolls with him when he set out for Bromholm?'

'Certainly.' But then the cellarer stilled his fingers. 'In truth I was angry, believing he was wasting his journey, for the rent rolls were returned to me later that same day. I thought the bailiff had carelessly dropped the saddle bag containing them, and had ridden on without it. But as we now know, he was dead before he left Castleacre.'

'What of his horse? Was that found at the same time?'

The cellarer shook his head impatiently. 'Walter Bostock's horse is no concern of mine. It is one of the very few items within this precinct for which I am not responsible.'

He took up his quill with a dismissive flourish, but Will persisted.

'Who was it who found the rent rolls and returned them to you?'

Brother Walstan sighed, his irritation ill-concealed.

'It was Jankin Kett, the simpleton who was put in the priory's care by your father. He burst in here just before Vespers on St Matthew's Eve, carrying a saddle-bag and mumbling that he'd found it near the river. He pulled out the Bromholm rent rolls, dropped them on this table, and ran away with the bag.'

'He said nothing more?'

'Nothing. He has since drowned, as no doubt you know. And the dead, I am glad to say, are not my responsibility either.'

The cellarer dipped his pen in the ink with an air of satisfaction. Almost as an afterthought, he crossed himself and added a hasty *God have mercy on his soul*, before bending again over his account books.

* * *

Will joined Ned Pye, who was waiting with the horses, and they had a swift discussion before parting. Ned fastened the reins to a post and strolled off to the stables in search of idle conversation. Will took the servants' path round the east end of the priory church, and fetched up once again in the laundress's yard.

Today, after the busyness that had followed St Matthew's feast, there was no sign of linen, wet or dry. Doll Harbutt was alone, and in good spirits. Queen of her kingdom, she sat at ease in the late afternoon sun refreshing herself from a foaming pot.

She greeted her visitor with eager surprise, awed by the quality of the clothes he was wearing. 'Why, 'tis Master Will again! Shall you join me in a drink of beer, sir — the priory's finest brew?'

'Gladly, Mistress Harbutt. Though I must not come here so often, or we shall be the talk of the precinct.'

Doll gave a great guffaw, but the crimson of her face deepened with pleasure and her broad hips swayed from side to side as she went into the laundry-house to fetch another pot. Will drank to her health, enjoying the flavour of hops as a change from hopless ale. Then he made to seat himself companionably on the edge of an empty washing-trough, but she hastily dusted a place for him on a bench out of consideration for his finery.

The week had been an eventful one at the priory, he commented, what with the feast, and Jankin Kett's death, and the news that it was the bailiff who had been murdered.

The laundress shrugged. 'In truth I never liked the man. There's none I know who'll mourn him, Mistress Bostock included. But I'll not believe,' she added fiercely — less, Will thought, from conviction than from a desire to assure him of her support — 'that your brother, Master Ackland, would ha' murdered him.'

'What makes you think Mistress Bostock does not mourn her husband?' Will asked.

'Why, because Walter Bostock beat her sorely. Knowing they had no servant, and seeking work for my youngest daughter, I sent her to their house early this summer to offer her services. But she heard the bailiff chastising his wife, and took to her heels for fear o'being beaten too.'

Doll Harbutt grimaced. 'Well, there,' she added. 'The common law allows a husband to chastise his wife. Some men are quicker to take advantage of it than others, and some are heavier-handed. But there's various ways a wife can have her revenge . . . '

'I don't doubt it,' Will agreed, with a lugubrious air that hid his eagerness for more information. 'Tell me, are you well acquainted with Mistress Bostock?'

'Not I! She takes pride in being the bailiff's wife, and holds herself aloof. I did hope at first that she might become a good customer o'mine. She sought me out, on the recommendation of the miller's wife, and I let her have one of the prior's shirts at a very reasonable price. But I think she had too high an opinion of herself, for she never came again.'

'Mistress Bostock is a handsome woman,' said Will. 'To those who have a liking for a dark complexion,' he added dismissively, for the laundress had sniffed her distaste. 'No doubt she has many admirers?'

'Ha!' said Doll Harbutt. 'Men will always make fools of themselves, hankering for what they can't have. I've seen many a burning glance being cast in her direction when she appears in the precinct — and not only by the lay-brethren.'

Will gave her a swift look, and she chuckled indulgently. 'Well, well — a monk is but a man, when all's said and done. Keeping the vow of chastity must often be a struggle. Who shall blame them if their thoughts are no purer than any other man's, eh, Master Will? But I'd best say no more on that subject!'

Knowing her to be a loyal servant of the priory, Will would not press her. 'How does Mistress Bostock conduct herself within the precinct?' he asked.

'Very seemly, to my knowledge. I've never heard of her giving an encouraging word or smile to any man. Excepting Jankin Kett, may God ha' mercy on his poor troubled soul.'

'Jankin?'

'Aye. It seems that Mistress Bostock had some business at the almonry, a month or so ago, and as she left she met Jankin face-to-face. He stood gawping at her, and she gave him a smile — out o' charity, what else? But Jankin, poor fool, found himself in love.'

Doll Harbutt paused to pour beer thirstily down her throat, and then wiped her mouth with her brawny forearm.

'After that, it seems, he began to go looking for her. The next I knew of it, the bailiff came rampaging after Jankin, saying he'd been spying on his wife. He chased him round these buildings — such a hue-and-cry you've never heard — caught him just over there, on the drying green, and gave him as good a whipping as I've ever seen. Aye, the poor mooncalf.'

Subdued, Doll wiped a single tear from her eye and comforted herself with another gulp of beer. Will was suddenly hopeful on his brother's behalf, but uneasy on his old friend's.

'Jankin was hobbling when I followed him through your yard t'other day,' he said. 'He was wearing a pair of riding boots that were too small for him. Do you know how he came by them, Mistress Harbutt?'

'They were too good to be his own, for sure. I'd never seen him in them before. They were well worn, but made of good leather — as I have cause to know, for I pulled them off him when I laid out his body. It was a tussle to get them off, but there: it caused him no pain.'

'Could you not have cut them off?' said Will, regretting that such indignity had been visited on his friend's corpse.

'*Cut* them off, sir?' Doll Harbutt was astonished by the suggestion. 'What, ruin a yeoman pair of boots, with years of wear still left in them? Indeed not! I shall take them home — they'll fit one or other of my sons, give or take a pinch.'

Will drained his pot and stood up. 'Would you lend me the boots for an hour, Mistress Harbutt? I'd like to know how Jankin came by them. The cobbler in the market place once told me that a wrinkled boot is like a face, he can always put a name to its owner.'

'Borrow them and welcome, sir.' Doll fetched them from her laundry-house, and

Will put a final question.

'When I was chasing Jankin, all the other servants were shouting *Hog* at him.' Doll had shouted it herself, as he remembered, but he would not remind her of it. 'Why was that, do you suppose?'

'Because 'a drank pig's blood,' she answered promptly. 'Not every day, you understand, nor yet every month. But once or twice a year, when he heard the squealing and knew the blood would be foaming hot, he'd steal into the slaughter-house with a jug.

'Not that Jankin was the only one to drink it,' she added fairly. 'I've known slaughter-men who made their breakfast of it. But Jankin always tried to hide what he was doing. He wouldn't stand there and drink it down like a man, but sneaked off to sup it in private. That was why folk shouted at him, to let him know we knew.'

'Can you recall when he drank it last?' asked Will.

'Why yes — a day or two afore he died. A lot of hogs were being slaughtered then, as well as other beasts, on account of the number of guests and pilgrims to be fed. It must ha' been the squealing that tempted him, poor simpleton.'

The bell had begun to ring for Vespers

from the great tower overhead, insistent in its calling. Will mouthed his thanks, dropped a silver groat into his empty beer pot and strode off, dead man's boots in hand, in search of Ned Pye.

22

By the time the bell stilled, the two men had walked their horses almost as far as the priory gatehouse.

Ned's news was that he had learned why Jankin Kett had been disliked by the day-servants and the other lay-brethren. It was not merely that he was set apart by being simple. Jankin had been the sub-prior's messenger, and he was suspected — rightly or wrongly — of spying on his fellows.

'I thought he must be under Father Arnold's protection, even though he feared him,' said Will. '*The priory is my mother*, he told me, *the sub-prior is my father*.'

'But from what I've heard,' said Ned, 'the others mistreated him more for enjoyment than out of suspicion. They didn't wish him dead. They think he drowned himself out o' wretchedness, and now they're feeling the guilt of it.'

'And so they should,' said Will sternly, 'for they gave him reason enough to be wretched.' He paused. 'But Jankin had reason to hate the bailiff, after the whipping he got. Loath as I am to believe it of him, I begin to think he could have been Walter Bostock's murderer.'

Ned's response was enthusiastic. He was eager to have done with all this mystery and set off back to London.

'Aye, you're right! I've heard how Jankin was strong in the arm, and how he'd lash out viciously when he was tormented too far. No doubt about it,' he concluded cheerfully. 'It was Jankin Kett who murdered the bailiff — and then drowned himself on account of it.'

Will made no reply. They mounted their horses at the gatehouse and turned towards the town, but he was absorbed in thought and would ride no faster than at walking pace.

'The bailiff set out on his journey before dawn on St Matthew's Eve,' he said, half to himself. 'We know that Jankin returned the Bromholm rent rolls to the cellarer later that same day. Most likely it was Jankin who returned the bailiff's horse to its stable, at the same time.

'True, this could have been mere chance. Perhaps Jankin really did find the horse, saddled and running loose. But if so, knowing it was the bailiff's, why did he not raise an alarm?'

Ned had no patience with lawyers' reasoning. 'By the Mass, we know why — because he was guilty!'

'But where's your proof, you knave? I cannot go to the justice of the peace and tell him that Ned Pye says so! No, our best hope lies with the boots Jankin was wearing. If the cobbler knows them to be the bailiff's, they must have been pulled off his corpse when his clothing was exchanged. The most likely man to have done so was his murderer. It's not proof positive, but it should be enough for Justice Throssell to make a posthumous declaration of Jankin's guilt.'

Ned Pye thrust out his paw impatiently. 'Then let me take the boots to the cobbler, and have done!' His voice took on a hopeful croak as he added, 'As I recall, his shop is next to the Woolpack inn.'

'Aye, I'll meet you there. Be off with you, for I still have some thinking to do.'

Ned set off along Castlegate at a gallop, the dust-clouds obscuring his horse's heels. Will followed slowly, his spirits tugged between relief at clearing his brother's name, and regret that it had to be at the expense of their boyhood companion. Besides, nothing was ever as simple as Ned imagined.

Will had no doubt that Jankin had the strength to pull the bailiff off his horse and knife him. And then, when his blood was up, he might have battered the bailiff's face in revenge for the whipping he'd been given.

But, knowing Jankin, Will could not believe that the whipping would have caused him to commit murder.

Jankin Kett was not violent by nature. Nor was he cunning. This murder had been planned: first to coincide with the bailiff's absence, and then to prevent identification of the corpse, should it be found. Jankin was capable of none of this. He might well have struck the blows and changed the garments, but the guilt was not his alone.

The greater part was surely Sibbel Bostock's. She was without doubt a clever woman, one who knew how to captivate men and bend them to her will. (Interesting, he thought in passing, that she should share that ability with the woman she so much resembled, the King's mistress Anne Boleyn.)

Sibbel Bostock had reasons of her own for wanting revenge on her husband. Knowing that Jankin doted on her, she might well have encouraged his hatred of the bailiff and persuaded him to commit the murder. Certainly she had lied with cunning, purporting to be a virtuous wife awaiting her husband's return when most probably she knew he was dead.

And now poor Jankin himself was dead — but not, Will was convinced, by his own hand. Had Sibbel brought about his death for fear that he might reveal her part in her husband's murder? Had she persuaded another lay-brother, one who admired her and despised Jankin, to dispose of him on her behalf?

By now Will had reached the market place, and there were greetings to be exchanged with shopkeepers looking for custom, and with drinkers outside the alehouses. He dismounted at the Woolpack, dismissing the hopeful loiterers who competed to hold his horse. In a few moments his servant emerged from the cobbler's shop, with the boots in his hand and a great grin on his face. Will beckoned the pot-boy.

'We were right!' Ned crowed. 'These are the bailiff's boots. The cobbler has often repaired them and will swear to it.' He seized one of the pots the boy was carrying, and took a great draught.

'That's your brother proved not guilty and your duty done, Master Will,' he announced as he lowered the pot to draw breath and wiped his mouth on his sleeve. 'When do we set off for London? Tomorrow at dawn?'

'Not so fast. I'm bidden to dinner by the prior tomorrow, in company with my godfather. We'll leave here the following day — but only if the bailiff's murder is finally resolved.'

Ned's round face lengthened with disappointment. 'What's still in doubt?'

'Sibbel Bostock's part in it is still in doubt. I'm convinced the plan was hers, but we have no proof as yet.'

'That we have!' protested Ned. 'I know for a fact that she lied over how long her horse had been back in the stable.'

'By the quantity of dung? That's only your word against hers. A Jackanapes from London against the wife of the bailiff of the prior of Castleacre?'

'By your leave!' said Ned indignantly. 'Besides, she's a whore. You have only to call on your brother's evidence to prove that.'

'He'd give no evidence against her. How could I ask him to? It would mean admitting his own adultery, and then being called before the archdeacon's court for punishment. No — with Jankin gone, taking the truth with him to the grave, we have nothing against Sibbel Bostock except suspicion. As long as she continues to deny everything . . .'

And then an almost-forgotten fact lifted his hopes. 'By the Rood, Ned, I think we may have her yet! Leave your ale, man, and mount up.'

Fired with eagerness, Will made to vault into the saddle as he used to do. But his weaker leg, having lost some of its spring, refused the jump, leaving him to curse and scramble. Once aboard, though, he went dashing across the market place and into Priorygate street. Ned poured the remains of the ale down his throat and followed, just in time to catch the reins his master threw at him as he dismounted outside the tailor's shop.

When Will emerged it was with a grim smile.

'Now I have proof of her deceit!' he said. 'A proven lie to confront her with. Take those boots back to the laundress at the priory, with my thanks, while I return to the bailiff's house and get the truth from Sibbel Bostock.'

★ ★ ★

'In God's name, sir!' The bailiff's wife had changed to her workaday attire and stood in her farmstead with her skirts hoist above her bare feet, her hair flowing free and a runt of a piglet tucked under one bare arm. She held her handsome head high, her black eyes sparkled with indignation and her sun-browned cheeks glowed with rising blood. 'Every word I've told you and your servant is the truth!'

Still mounted, Will looked down at her sternly. 'Not so, Madam. I recall that we met

291

by chance yesterday morning, outside Dickson the tailor's shop in Castlegate. I asked when you expected your husband the bailiff to return. On Tuesday or Wednesday, you told me. And you added that in his absence you had ordered a new cap for him. I believed you, thinking it the act of a fond wife.

'But you lied. I have that on the authority of young Dickson himself. He tells me that you gave him no order for a cap, nor indeed for anything else, for you have never set foot inside his shop. What say you to that, Madam?'

Sibbel Bostock's head drooped. Her rich dark hair swung forward, half-concealing her flushed cheeks. The piglet fell squealing from her slackened arm. 'Indeed, sir . . . ' she faltered.

'Indeed, Mistress Bostock. You lied to me then, just as you have lied to us at every encounter, to hide your knowledge that your husband had been murdered. But I have reason to believe that you not only knew of the deed, you were privy to it.'

'No sir!' Sibbel Bostock raised her head and shook it in denial, her hair swinging about her throat, her eyes flashing. 'I knew nothing of it until — until — '

Swift as bird to change course, she turned back from vehemence to meekness. Faltering, she twisted long strands of her hair in her fingers. Her bearing was anxious, her tone humble, but Will was aware that her eyes watched him with calculation from beneath modestly lowered lids.

'In truth, sir,' she confessed, low-voiced, 'I did lie when I told you I was unaware of my husband's death, and I am deeply sorry for it. But my only intent was to protect Jankin Kett. The poor fool doted on me. My husband whipped him savagely for it, and Jankin took his revenge.

'He came to me on St Matthew's Eve, bringing back the bailiff's horse and saddle-bags. At first he would not say what had happened, but when I pressed him he admitted he had knifed my husband and left his body in the river. My only thought then, sir, was to save the poor fool from hanging.'

Will interrupted her. 'Your *only* thought, Mistress Bostock? If your first concern was not for your dead husband, but for his murderer, then I think you intended his death.'

'It was not so!' Sibbel Bostock moved closer to Will. His horse shifted its hooves and tossed its head, but she caught at his stirrup leather and raised her great dark eyes to his.

'Oh, sir, I cannot grieve for my husband,' she said in a throaty murmur. 'He used me ill, sir, very ill — as you would know if you saw the marks on my body. Yet I never asked Jankin to kill him, I swear it. That was the poor fool's own doing. I told him only that the corpse must not be recognised, or he would be suspect throughout the precinct. I gave him some of my husband's clothes, which I first slashed into rags, and told him to dress the corpse in them and to destroy the features with a heavy stone. And that is all I know of the bailiff's death.'

'I think not,' said Will grimly. 'What of the Bromholm rent rolls that your husband carried with him? You told me not an hour ago that you knew nothing of them, yet Jankin returned them to the cellarer. Someone must have instructed him in that, for he would not have had the wit to do so of his own accord. Then later, when I began my enquiries, someone arranged for Jankin himself to be drowned. Who was that someone, Mistress Bostock? You, I do believe.'

His horse stamped with impatience, but Sibbel Bostock changed her grip from his stirrup to his boot and clung to it, gazing up at him with eyes that were darkly desirous. 'No, sir!' she murmured, her voice breaking. 'Oh, you would not think me guilty, if you only knew how ill-used I have been — Dismount, I beg you, and let me give you proof of my innocence.'

Her nearness and shamelessness disturbed him. He could not tell whether to believe her or not, but her lustrous eyes were captivating. He swallowed, understanding how it was that Gib and the constable and poor Jankin had all been in thrall to her, for he himself was near to being bewitched.

And then he remembered Julian Corbyn, and the thought of her fresh young beauty filled him with distaste for Sibbel Bostock's charms. But he did not draw away from the bailiff's widow, for he saw how he might turn her wiles against her in his search for the truth.

'Very well,' he said sternly, glad that Ned Pye was not there to see him dismount and follow Mistress Bostock towards her house. But he took good care not to cross the threshold.

23

It was still too soon for Will to reveal to his family the extent of what he knew, let alone what he guessed, but as soon as he returned to the castle he said enough to put them all in good heart. The rest of it — the truth of the whole matter — he intended to discover when he went next day to the priory.

Supper was a far more cheerful meal than usual, Gilbert even going so far as to give his brother an affable nod before embarking with enthusiasm on yet another hot mutton pie. But for Will himself, conversation was difficult.

Meg and Alice, knowing nothing of his abrupt departure from Oxmead, were agog to hear about his visit — and most particularly about Mistress Julian Corbyn. What had she worn, they wanted to know? What had she said to him? Had she approved of his finery, was she betrothed to Lord Stradsett's son or no, had she spoken to Will in private; what had she *said*?

He parried all their questions as lightly as possible, but with a downcast heart. Since his return from Oxmead, the urgency of clearing his brother's name had enabled him for the most part to put Julian from his mind. But now, the teasings of Meg and Alice had reopened the parting wound that Julian had given him.

He left their company as soon as he could do so without displeasing his sister. Pacing about the darkened castle yard — to the accompaniment of firelit boisterousness from the kitchen quarters, where Ned was no doubt entertaining the serving women — he forced his mind to dwell on nothing but tomorrow's visit to the priory: on what he needed to learn, and from whom.

Unavoidably, that meant thinking of Sibbel Bostock. And now he knew at first hand how she could enthrall men, it was hard to prise her image from his mind.

But it was Julian Corbyn he thought of last thing at night, and again first thing in the morning.

★ ★ ★

Gilbert spoke to Will very cordially at breakfast, inviting his brother to accompany him on the daily ride round his land. Will had little interest in farming. But the air was clear and fresh, and with time to spare before leaving for the priory he was glad enough of a reason to ride out.

He had rarely known his brother in so talkative a mood. Gilbert showed him every field and its boundaries, and described in some detail how he intended to manage it the following year: whether by ploughing and sowing, and with which crop, or by leaving it fallow with sheep to dung it. Will strove to be friendly, asking questions to show that he took an interest, and evidently this pleased his brother.

'We'll make a gentleman farmer of you yet!' said Gib, giving him a sideways glance from between his shaggy hair and his beard as they rode back through the castle gatehouse and dismounted. But Will merely laughed, and went in search of his daughter.

He soon saw her, running through the herb garden towards the barns followed by her nurse. But before Will could join them, Meg emerged from the house and waylaid him. She wore a look of contrition.

'I am sorry I teased you over Julian last night. I hoped I had prepared you for disappointment — but not so, it seems?'

He gave a wry shrug. 'You could not know, Meg. Julian told me she scorns Lord Stradsett's son, and I was hopeful. But it seems that she secretly admires another.' He paused, choosing his words carefully for the truth was too dangerous even to be hinted at. 'I angered her, I fear, by saying too much. Now she does not wish to see me again.'

'Ah, Will,' said his sister kindly, giving his arm a sympathetic squeeze. But she followed it instantly with a firm shake, and words that were firmer still.

'The sooner you secure Gib's release and go back to London, the better. We've been thankful for your presence here, none more so than Gib and poor Alice. We shall all miss you. But there's no occupation for you here in Norfolk, let alone in Castleacre. When do you leave?'

'Tomorrow, all being well.'

'I am glad to hear it, for your sake. Now I'll keep you from your daughter no longer. You'll find her with Agnes, collecting eggs. Ask her if she can count them. I've tried to teach her as far as ten, but I doubt you'll persuade her to venture beyond five.'

Meg gave him an affectionate smile and swept back to the house. 'Betsy!' Will called as he approached the barns, and he was delighted when she hurried out to greet him, cautiously cradling a speckled egg in her cupped hands.

He went down on his haunches to admire it. 'Have you found many more?' he asked. 'How many?' But she would not say.

Agnes, who like her charge had become less shy with him, came forward with a basket half-filled with eggs and Betsy added hers to it. Will tried to persuade the child to count them, but she knew her limitations. *One-two-three-four-five*, she said boldy, and then lost interest.

'But you have learned a rhyme to say to your father,' prompted Agnes. 'You remember it: 'What is the . . . ?' '

Betsy waved the prompt crossly aside. She stood at her father's crouched knee, her hands behind her back, her eyes closed tight in concentration.

'What is the way to London Town?
One foot up and one foot down,
That is the way to London Town.'

Her eyes flew open on the last line and she beamed with pleasure at having remembered it to the end. Will chuckled proudly. 'Well said, my sweeting! So it is the way, and a long one, for all those who must walk. But my horse will carry me there in two and a half days, and back again to see you at Christmas.'

As he stood up to thank Agnes for her care of his daughter, the dogs began to bark and there came a clattering of hooves across the bridge. Three horses were approaching through the gatehouse. Two of them carried attendants, one man and one woman. At their head, beautifully erect on her side-saddle, rode Julian Corbyn.

Astonishment made Will unmannerly. He hurried to meet her, but it was only the lack of something to do with his hands that reminded him to doff his cap. As before, her hair glowed chestnut brown against the green velvet hood of her riding cloak, making him catch his breath in admiration.

'Mistress Julian — pray dismount and enter the house,' he stammered.

It seemed that her discomfiture matched his own, for her cheeks had coloured and she kept her eyes down. Her words came tumbling out almost as Betsy's had done, as though she had rehearsed them.

'I thank you, Master Will, but I must not stay. I am riding to Lynn with my aunt and uncle, and they are waiting for me in the market place. I am here solely to bring a lace collar for your sister to copy. I promised it to Dame Meg when I was here before, and she showed me the fine lace you brought her from Flanders . . .'

Julian ran out of words. Emboldened by her pink-cheeked breathlessness, Will went forward to take the small package she held out to him.

'I will give it to Meg later,' he said, aware that his sister might well be watching but confident that she would not emerge from the house. Agnes, he noticed, had taken Betsy away on another egg hunt.

He stood boldly at Julian's stirrup, so close that she could not avoid looking at him. 'When we last met, you said — '

'I know what I said. Truly, I have regretted it ever since. Forgive me, Will, I was foolishly hot-headed.'

He breathed his relief. 'Then you'll take my advice?'

'No, I shall not!' Julian coloured again, this time with pride. 'I shall not change my beliefs, nor my affections. But I have need of you as a friend, and I would not cast you aside for all the world.'

It was small consolation, Will reflected wryly; but better than nothing. 'My friend-ship for you is assured,' he said. 'But as a friend, I must ask you to be guarded in what you do and say — especially when you are in Norwich.'

'Well, you need have no fear of that,' she said with vexation. 'My father will not allow me to spend this winter in Norwich. My mother and I are to accompany him to London instead.'

'To London?' His hopes took a great leap.

'Then I may see you there?'

'That was what I thought,' she agreed, 'as soon as my father told me. We shall be at our house in Whitefriars — is that far from Gray's Inn?'

'No distance at all!'

'Good.' Preparing to leave, Julian gathered her reins. 'You must call on us there — I know my father will be glad to see you.'

'And you?'

She made no direct reply. But the smile she gave him before she turned her horse and rode out of the castle yard left him in no doubt.

24

The bell of the parish church was ringing the noonday hour when Will rode out, in high spirits and his saint's-day-and-Sunday doublet, to go to dinner at the prior's lodging.

He went first to Northgate, where his godfather was about to leave his house attended by a groom. Lawrence Throssell sat his placid horse stiffly and rode with care, unwilling to jolt his frail bones more than necessary. As they paced across the corner of the market place and along Priorygate, Will told him what he had discovered concerning the bailiff's murder; or rather, a part of what he had discovered.

Though he revealed Sibbel Bostock's influence over Jankin Kett, he did not mention Gilbert's adultery with her, nor yet the constable's. His main purpose was to convince the justice of the peace that Gilbert was not guilty of the murder of the prior's bailiff, and so he related what he knew of poor Jankin's undoubted guilt.

The old gentleman listened and nodded and tugged his sparse white beard in thought. 'Does Mistress Bostock confess to having procured the death of her husband at the hand of Jankin Kett?'

'She denies that she procured it, sir, but I have reason to think she lies. I believe the truth of this matter is to be found within the priory. We may hear it at dinner if we ask the right questions.'

Lawrence Throssell *hmm'd* and *haw'd* with unease. 'It is not fitting for such questions to be asked by guests of the prior.'

'Two of the priory's servants have been murdered, sir. Surely that is even less fitting?'

His godfather sighed. 'Well, well. But as to your brother Gilbert, there is no longer a case for him to answer. Bring him to my house before supper, and I will withdraw the charge and release you from your bond.'

They had reached the priory gatehouse, from the grandeur of which was emerging a foul-smelling rabble of the poor, clutching their midday dole of food. With his groom riding ahead of him through the gates to clear the way, the justice of the peace looked them over sternly.

'Their numbers increase weekly,' he observed with a frown, 'and I have no doubt that many of them are merely idle. They're vagabonds and sturdy beggars, who could earn their living if they would. I' faith, I know not whether to be thankful to the priory for feeding them and keeping them from begging at our doors, or to be vexed with the priory for encouraging them to come to Castleacre.'

Burdened as he was by the duty of maintaining public order, Master Justice Throssell sighed and shook his head. Then, as the rabble passed by, his face cleared. 'But let us go to our own dinner. No doubt Prior Nicholas will have something better to offer us than half a loaf and a piece of cheese.'

★　★　★

At the prior's lodging, everything was of the finest quality. The building had been greatly enlarged by Nicholas de la Pole to make a fitting house for a nobleman. Though it was smaller than Sir Ralph Corbyn's mansion at Oxmead, the hospitality the prior provided for his guests was even more splendid.

On this occasion, when Master Justice Throssell, Will Ackland and the reluctant sub-prior were the only guests, dinner was served in the prior's own chamber on the upper floor of the lodging. It was a handsome room lit by two oriel windows, its walls lined with linenfold panelling and a tapestry depicting scenes of hawking, a sport of which the prior was very fond. The wooden roof, supported by moulded beams, was painted all over with Tudor roses complete with stems and leaves. Sculpted on either side of the great stone chimney place, and painted in the same colours, were musicians with angels' wings.

The table was covered with the finest damask cloth, in the centre of which was a handsome silver salt in the shape of a galleon in full sail. Every dish and charger was of silver or silver-gilt, all worn smooth from daily use. Noble guests would no doubt dine from better silver. Royal guests such as Queen Katherine, who stayed there on her way to and from the shrine at Walsingham, would use the gold plate that stood on the side board in gleaming array.

At each guest's place was a silver-handled knife, a silver spoon, fine drinking glasses and a damask napkin. The prior's own servants, dressed in his livery, brought towels and silver basins of warmed rose-water for the guests to wash their hands, not only before the meal but during the course of it whenever there was need. And as soon as the prior had finished calling down God's blessing, rolling the Latin as richly round his tongue as he would shortly roll the food, an unseen lutenist began to play for their entertainment during dinner.

Prior Nicholas was an affable host, evidently glad of the company of Lawrence Throssell with whom he had been at the priory school and later at university, though at a much grander college. The two of them — one portly, one bird-like — carried their years and white hairs well, despite the dimming eyesight they shared.

They spoke first, over oysters with vinegar and pepper, of their years at Cambridge. Will, who had travelled through the university town the previous week, told them that it had begun to resemble a great builder's yard; with so much new construction being done at so many of the colleges, the air was filled with the noise and dust of a host of stone-cutters, scaffolders, carpenters, smiths and masons.

'But the stonework of King's College chapel,' he reported to the prior, who was a Kingsman, 'is now complete. The glaziers are working to insert the windows, and they're wondrously coloured. With those and its fan-vaulted roof, it will be without equal in Europe for size and beauty.'

He offered this as a compliment to the prior, who accepted it graciously. Lawrence Throssell, concealing his annoyance that the buildings of his own college were now completely outshone by those of King's, added his own compliments. Then he turned eagerly to Will.

'You visited Queens', of course? Did you meet anyone you knew?'

'Yes, the professor of Greek — but his reason for remembering me,' admitted Will ruefully, 'was not to my credit. True, the porter claimed to know me — but I think he'd be willing to remember anyone for a groat.'

The sub-prior, Father Arnold, who came from a humble family and had been educated entirely within the church, sat silent during this conversation. Austere and aloof, his hooded eyelids lowered, he made it clear that he was present at such a gluttonous meal only as an act of obedience to the prior. He would eat nothing but a little of the fine brown bread that was served with the oysters, and drink nothing but water.

As the different wines flowed and fresh dishes were brought in for the company to taste — broiled carp with a high Dutch sauce, a salad of fennel, rosemary and borage, griddled larks nesting on a bed of watercress, a roast goose with oranges, baked artichokes, a haunch of venison with sugared mustard — the prior's heavy jowls became moist and darkly red. And all the while the sub-prior sat with his hands folded within his sleeves, disapproval encircling his tonsured head like a halo.

Will sought to draw him into the conversation. 'I am partly indebted to you, Father Arnold, for the good fortune of being invited to dinner by my lord prior. It was you who introduced me the other day, if you remember — on the occasion when you found me trying to speak with Jankin Kett.'

'Jankin Kett?' The prior paused in the act of crunching a griddled lark, and fastidiously removed some tiny bones from his mouth. 'The name is familiar.'

The sub-prior broke his silence, though without lifting his eyes. 'One of the lay-brothers, Father Prior. The simpleton.'

'He was the son of our old nurse at the castle,' said Will, 'My father put him in the care of the priory when he was a boy.'

'Ah yes, now I remember him. Jankin Kett — he serves as your messenger, Father Arnold, I believe?'

The sub-prior inclined his head in acknowledgement, then gave his attention to the crumbs that had fallen from his bread, using one long finger to arrange them in a meticulously straight line across his silver plate. It was clear that he would say no more of his own volition.

'Then you have not heard, Prior Nicholas,'

said Will, 'that Jankin Kett is dead? He was found drowned in the river on Saturday morning.'

The prior paused again, the tiny body of a second lark poised on his silver fork. He frowned. 'Why did you not tell me of this, Father Arnold?'

Obliged to explain, the sub-prior reluctantly raised his deepset eyes. 'It was not a matter to trouble you with, Father Prior. Jankin Kett's death was an accident. He spent much of his time by the river, and he must have fallen in.' He gave Will a sidelong glance. 'Sadly, he could not swim — as Master Will Ackland can tell you.'

'True, he could not,' Will agreed. 'But Jankin was tall, and the river within the priory precinct is barely waist deep, as I have cause to know. Had he fallen in by accident, he could have stood up and floundered back to the bank.

'This was no accident, though. The laundress who laid out his body found bruising on the back of his neck. I have reason to believe that someone held Jankin's head under water, to ensure that he drowned.'

The prior stared at Will, his dark red jowls quivering with unease. 'You are saying he was murdered? But it was only a few days ago that our bailiff was murdered, by vagabonds at the ford.'

'Not by vagabonds, Prior Nicholas. I fear that it was Jankin Kett who killed your bailiff, on the instructions of another. And the same person, I believe, killed Jankin because he knew too much.'

25

'Enough, Will!' advised his godfather sternly. 'You are unmannerly to trouble our host with such matters.'

Prior Nicholas sat in silent dismay, his breathing heavy, his brow furrowed as he tried to digest what he had heard. The sub-prior leaned forward across the table to offer him an explanation.

'I have these matters in hand, Father Prior,' he said with intensity. 'Responsibility for discipline within the priory is mine, and I am making enquiries as to Jankin Kett's death. When I reach a conclusion, I shall of course inform you.'

The prior's face cleared. 'Ah,' he agreed with relief. 'Then we need trouble my guests with our concerns no longer. Now, friend Lawrence, you must taste this roasted goose — the orange sauce gives it a delectable flavour.'

Will's hopes of uncovering the truth, so strong a few minutes ago, were suddenly slipping away. Worse, Father Arnold now put aside his napkin and half-rose from his chair.

'My duties are pressing, Father Prior. Will

you permit me to thank you for your hospitality and take my leave?'

Will held his breath. The prior wavered. But then his eye fell on the sub-prior's plate, containing nothing but the meticulously straight line of breadcrumbs. Piqued that his subordinate should set this example of frugality, Prior Nicholas refused his request.

'No, you may not leave us, Father Arnold. To do so would be an insult to my guests. You shall remain while we continue our meal — and if the sight and smell of our food offends you, you must think of it as a penance.'

His good humour regained, and his plate newly filled with roast goose, Prior Nicholas turned to his younger guest.

'Now, Master Will Ackland — I long to hear of your travels. What news from Rome?'

Will could guess what the prior hoped to hear. Having entertained Queen Katherine at the priory on several occasions, he was no doubt seeking assurance that the Pope would refuse to allow the King to divorce her. But Will's concern was to find the truth about Jankin Kett's death, and he decided to approach the subject by speaking plainly, first about the church.

'The authority of His Holiness the Pope is by no means secure,' he warned, disregarding his food so as to give all his attention to what he was saying. 'There are many in northern Germany and the Netherlands who speak and write against the power of the church, and deny the supremacy of the Pope.'

'Heretics!' asserted the prior with lofty scorn. 'Led by that pestiferous priest Martin Luther. Ha! There have been heretics before, but they have been rooted out and put to the flames like noxious weeds. It will be so again.'

'No doubt,' said Will, reminded of the danger Julian Corbyn's friend was in, and thankful for more than one reason that she would be spending the winter in London rather than Norwich.

'But as you know, Prior Nicholas,' he continued, 'it is not only the power of the church that is attacked by Luther. He condemns the practices that have brought it so much wealth over the centuries. He has denounced indulgences, and pilgrimages, and the veneration of relics — and supposed miracles, such as those of the renewal of blood on St Matthew's bones on which the fame of your priory rests.'

Will paused. Prior Nicholas, unaccustomed to such plain speaking, was clearly astonished by his temerity. The prior's jaws were stilled, but his mouth was so full of goose that a dribble of its juices ran unheeded down the side of his chin.

'For myself,' Will offered quickly, by way of apology to his host, 'I often witnessed this miracle in my youth, and learned from my father to venerate it. I have seen how pilgrims flock to the shrine and make offerings, in the hope that through the intercession of the saint their petitions will be granted, or their ills cured. I know they believe that what they witness is a springing out of St Matthew's own blood from St Matthew's own bones.'

Prior Nicholas wiped his chin, and a servant immediately removed his soiled napkin and replaced it.

'The bones are indeed those of St Matthew,' said the prior firmly, but he took the precaution of dismissing all the servants with a gesture.

'I shall not dispute it, my lord prior. But you will agree that there is no miracle about the blood that appears on the bones. Where else should it come from, every year without fail, but the priory slaughter-house? Jankin Kett went there as usual on St Matthew's Eve and brought away a jug of pig's blood — no doubt on the instructions of the sub-prior, to whom he gave his obedience.'

'*William*! Such mysteries should not be

spoken of!' hissed Lawrence Throssell in dismay.

Father Arnold raised his head. He spoke coldly, but an angry red blotched his gaunt cheekbones. 'The practice is time-honoured. The simplest of the lay brethren has always, by tradition, been sent to fetch blood on St Matthew's Eve.'

Lawrence Throssell began to make apologies to the prior for his godson's outspokenness, but Nicholas de la Pole was too wise to take offence.

'And why should we not be allowed to enhance the pilgrims' faith, Master Will Ackland?' he enquired, his voice reproachful. 'They come in hope — and have you not seen the joy on their faces as they leave the priory church after the Festal High Mass? Would they still flock here, after all these centuries, if what we offer does not supply their spiritual needs?'

'True, true,' said Lawrence Throssell with uncomfortable haste. 'Enough, Will.'

'Prior Nicholas asked me for news from Europe, godfather. I have one more thing to tell, and I believe he will want to hear it, for it has a bearing on the fortunes of Castleacre priory.'

The prior hesitated, then graciously nodded his assent. The sub-prior remained aloof, head bent. Will drew breath.

'What I have learned is that things are not as they were in northern Europe. Books are being read, ideas are being exchanged. The old certainties, given to us by the church, are being questioned. There is change in the wind.

'Here in England, we are just beginning to feel the breath of it from across the north sea. It may take some time to reach us in strength. But when it does, my lord prior, I fear it will blow cold through your cloisters.'

There was an uneasy silence in the room. But when the prior spoke, it was with complete confidence.

'These changes will never take place in England. Our people are too devout, and King Henry will never deny the supremacy of the Pope. Why, the King was so incensed by Luther's arguments that he wrote a counter-blast demolishing them! It was in return that His Holiness granted him the title of Defender of the Faith.'

'But that,' Will reminded the prior, 'was nearly ten years ago. Since then, King Henry himself has changed. He is a man so in love with a bewitching mistress that he can refuse her nothing.'

Will paused. Thinking of his sweet Anne, dead these four years, he shook his head.

'No: 'in love' is too tender an expression to describe the hold that Anne Boleyn has over our king. He is in thrall to her — bogged inextricably, as though in a mire. A man in that state of helplessness will do whatever his mistress urges, whether or not it accords with his own conscience.'

Will turned to the sub-prior.

'Would you not say so, Father Arnold? For I believe you yourself are in thrall, to Mistress Sibbel Bostock.'

★ ★ ★

The sub-prior rose slowly to his feet, pushing back his heavy chair. His white face had taken on a greenish tinge and his thin lips began to move soundlessly. When his voice emerged, it was cracked as though with exhaustion.

'Father Prior, this is a foul lie! I have never broken my vow of chastity.'

Will rose too. 'Not in your deeds, perhaps, Father Arnold. But I believe you have broken it in your thoughts and in your heart.'

Master Justice Throssell had also risen, distressed by Will's behaviour as a guest at the prior's dinner table, but at the same time anxious to discover the truth. The prior himself could only sit back in his great carved chair and stare in dismay at his subordinate.

'I regret the necessity of telling you this, my lord prior,' said Will. 'I learned of it yesterday from Mistress Bostock, when I accused her of having procured the murder of her husband the bailiff. She denied it. She told me that Father Arnold was enamoured of her, and that he was jealous of her husband.'

'Untrue, Father Prior, untrue!' The sub-prior turned to Will with a look of deep-burned hatred. 'How should I be acquainted with the bailiff's wife — or with any other woman?'

'Mistress Bostock tells me that you sought her out and spoke to her whenever she went to pray at the priory church. She tells me that it was you who wanted the bailiff dead, and you who planned his murder in the madness of your lust for her.'

'Then she lies! She lies!' The sub-prior's face was suffused with anger. 'It was Sibbel Bostock herself who — '

Too late, he snapped his thin mouth shut. A tense silence pervaded the room, heightened by the buzzing of a bee trapped against a window pane.

'Sibbel Bostock does indeed lie,' agreed Will. 'I believe it was she who urged you to procure the death of her husband. You could not refuse because you were in thrall to her. But if it's of any comfort to you, Father

Arnold, you are not the only man to fall under her spell. I know two of the priory's tenants who have had the misfortune to do so, Thomas Gosnold and my brother Gilbert Ackland.'

The sub-prior raised his head for a resentful moment, then looked down again.

'And so of course did poor Jankin Kett,' Will continued. 'What with being under obedience to you, and in thrall to Sibbel Bostock, he had no choice but to carry out your instructions for murdering the bailiff. But you made a mistake in telling him to return the Bromholm rent rolls to the cellarer. That was the action of a responsible man, a holder of high office in the priory. When I heard of it, I knew that Sibbel Bostock had not planned the murder on her own.'

'What of Jankin Kett's death?' demanded the justice of the peace, forgetting for a moment that he was not in his own court. 'Is there any evidence against the sub-prior?'

'None that I can provide, sir,' admitted Will. 'I believe the sub-prior drowned Jankin, perhaps at the prompting of Sibbel Bostock, when my questioning became too persistent. I can offer no proof. But if Father Arnold did indeed commit that murder, the guilt must weigh heavily upon him. No doubt he will want to confess to it.'

Thinking only in legal terms, Will wanted to hear the sub-prior's reply. But his godfather seized his arm and motioned him towards the door. 'Come, we have long outstayed our welcome. I ask your pardon most humbly, Prior Nicholas, for the hurt we have caused you . . . '

The prior seemed not to hear. His eyes on the sub-prior, he pushed himself up wearily from his great chair and stood with his fingertips splayed on the damask tablecloth, presiding over the array of silver dishes and the congealing remains of lark and goose. He looked old, shrunken within the space of five minutes. His white hair had become disordered and his red jowls drooped sadly, lengthening his long Plantagenet face.

'Arnold . . . ?' he said, his voice low. 'My son, do you wish to make your confession?'

Will was not clear what happened next. He was at the doorway, standing back to allow his godfather to precede him, when there came from the room behind him the crash of an overturned chair. He and Lawrence Throssell were both pushed vigorously aside. With a swirl of his habit and a wild look in his eyes, the sub-prior leaped out of the doorway and down the winding stair.

It was not the action of a sinner about to

confess. Will glanced from the prior to his godfather, saw their expressions of alarm and plunged after the sub-prior, his boots clattering on the stone stairway.

Behind the fine rooms of the prior's lodging was a centuries' old rabbit warren of passages and spiral stairs and doorways and dark entries, leading Will knew not where. Father Arnold sped on ahead, seemingly unhampered by the length of his tunic, out of sight except for an occasional glimpse of blackness in motion against the background of stone. Every now and then Will lost him, and had to pause and listen. And then the slap of sandalled feet, from some unlikely direction, would draw him on.

A glimpse of the monk silhouetted against sunlight at the far end of a passage made Will quicken his pace. By now, though, the spiral stairs had taken their toll on his weaker leg, and he was forced, angrily, to limp rather than run.

When he emerged from the passage he found himself in the priory cloister, where a square of vaulted arcades surrounded a sunlit garth. Here, the assembled black-garbed monks were taking their recreation while they waited for the early afternoon service, some walking and talking, some playing chequers on the stone seats of the cloister.

All of them had stopped and stared as their sub-prior ran past. They stared even more, their faces an indistinguishable white blur against the darkness of their cowls, as Will came hurrying after him.

It was clear that Father Arnold was making for the door that led from the cloister into the south transept of the priory church. As he neared it, the bell began to ring for Nones. By the time Will had followed him through the doorway, the monks had begun to form their procession in the cloister, two by two, eyes lowered and hands folded in obedience.

The church was empty of all but the carved and painted host of saints and angels. The sub-prior had disappeared. If he were still on the move, his footsteps were covered by the sound of the bell. Will hunted for him up and down the transepts and the nave, round the great stone piers that supported the massive central tower, and in and out of the side chapels. But reverence for the image of the crucified Christ, high on the candlelit rood loft that separated the people's nave from the monks' Quire, made him hesitate to go beyond it.

The procession entered the church, led by the preceptor. Will paused in the shadow of a pier beside the great open space immediately under the tower, watching as the monks moved beyond the rood screen and out of sight into the Quire. The bell stopped ringing. There was the murmured Latin of a prayer, and then the unseen voices were raised in plainchant, the cadences now spiralling up, now dipping, like candle flames lighting the darkness.

From somewhere high above, rising over the plainchant, Will heard a distant shout. He thought it sounded like *In Manus Tuas, Domine* —

It was followed by a long thin scream, fading as it neared. Looking up, Will saw a figure falling from the topmost gallery of the tower, his black tunic and scapular spread like a bat's wings as he tumbled through the incense-laden air.

The monks' voices wavered uncertainly as they heard the muffled crash of the body striking the marble floor. Then they resumed, continuing their calming benediction.

Will ran to the crumpled body of the sub-prior. Father Arnold had fallen face-down in front of the rood screen, his arms outflung, as though submitting himself to the mercy of God.

26

The following morning was bright with sunshine and the downward drift of yellowing leaves, though a coolness in the air hinted at chill winds to come. It was a good day for saddling up and galloping off towards London.

Will felt glad to be leaving Castleacre. As Meg had said, there was no occupation for him here — least of all in winter, when days were dark and roads were foul. Whereas London, he thought eagerly as he prepared to set off, held never-ending interests and pleasures; not least the prospect of seeing Julian there.

But he was leaving with the satisfaction of knowing that he had been of assistance to his family, and also to his godfather, the justice of the peace. As soon as they had returned from the priory the previous day, Master Justice Throssell had dealt promptly with those matters that came within his jurisdiction.

The Justice's first act had been to send his own servants to arrest Sibbel Bostock and bring her before him on a charge of conspiring to procure the death of her husband. Mistress Bostock, still defiantly protesting her innocence, was now being held in the town gaol to await trial.

'In truth,' the justice of the peace had confided to Will, 'there's little evidence we can bring against her without implicating the sub-prior in the deaths of the bailiff and Jankin Kett. Prior Nicholas has asked me to let her go free, for a trial at the county Assize court would cause scandal and harm to the priory; but I have my duty to do. However, I intend to leave her to languish in the town gaol until the time of the Assizes, and then free her on condition that she leaves the parish of Castleacre and never returns within ten miles, on pain of further imprisonment.'

Next, Master Justice Throssell had summoned Gilbert Ackland, withdrawn the charge of murder against him and released Will from his bond. He had also taken it upon himself, in the interest of good order within the town, to give stern advice to the two offenders against church law, Gilbert Ackland and Thomas Gosnold the constable. Telling them that he was aware of their adultery, he had advised them to go immediately to the parish priest and confess, before the archdeacon got to hear of their offences.

Later that evening, Will had heard that

Thomas Gosnold had paid a large sum to the parish church by way of penance. As for Gilbert, he said nothing about his penance. But he was undoubtedly relieved to be a free man again, and he had given Will an unprecedented embrace last night and again before breakfast this morning.

It pleased Will to know that he was leaving his family in good heart. Meg was glad that he was at last returning to his studies. Betsy had sat happily on his knee yesterday evening, too young to understand that he was going away. Only poor Alice was woebegone; but her sad condition was reason enough for that.

The entire household — outdoor as well as indoor servants, all of them glad of any diversion — turned out in the castle yard to see the travellers depart. Old Jacob held the two horses, while Ned Pye busied himself with strapping on the laden saddlebags.

Ned, it seemed, had done much to enliven the servants during his short stay at the castle, and there was a parting exchange of ribald jokes and laughter. As usual, Agnes stood apart from this, holding Betsy's hand. But Will noticed that this morning there was a becoming flush on her homely face, and she did not take her eyes off Ned Pye. For his part, Ned seemed to ignore her; but once or twice his master saw him give her a great wink from under his fringe of yellow thatch.

'Where's Gib?' asked Will, eager to make his final farewells, mount up and go. 'I haven't seen him since breakfast.'

There came a shuffling and an astonished muttering from the servants standing nearest the house. 'Why — Master Ackland's here, sir,' spoke up Lambert the gangling boy.

The crowd parted like the waters of the Red Sea, staring at the near-stranger who was advancing through their midst. Gilbert Ackland was dressed in the gabardine smock of a beadsman, with strong walking boots and a broad-brimmed leather hat that had belonged to their grandfather. He carried a small pack on his back, and walked with an ash-plant in his fist.

'Friends,' he announced, his eyes shining out from the tangle of his hair: 'you see me as I now am — a pilgrim.

'Two days ago, I was falsely accused of murder. I vowed then that if my innocence were proved with my brother's help, I would make a pilgrimage in thanksgiving. Last night I confessed my sins to the parish priest, and he has given me his blessing. The time has now come for me to make good my vow.'

'Well said, Gib!' applauded his sister. 'You are right to do so. Shall you go to Walsingham, or Bromholm?'

'Neither.' Gilbert struck the ground impressively with his staff. 'My pilgrimage is to the shrine of St James at Compostella.'

The servants gasped in astonishment. Alice, who had been resting on the mounting block, gasped with unhoped-for relief. Ned gave a suppressed snigger, and Will and Meg, knowing that their brother had never travelled further than Swaffham, were hard put not to laugh.

'Gib,' said Will, struggling to keep his face straight, 'have you any idea where Compostella is?'

'No — but I shall find it,' said Gib stoutly. 'The priest tells me that if I walk to London, and cross the river there, I shall come to Dover. And in Dover I shall find many other pilgrims to companion me on my way.'

Will scratched his ear. 'True. But Compostella is in Spain, hundreds of miles away. It would take you many months to walk there. Besides, this is the wrong season to begin a pilgrimage. With winter coming on, you'd be beset with difficulties and privations.'

'It will test my faith,' agreed Gib. 'But I have bought from the priest a medal of the blessed St Christopher, who will guard and guide me on my journeyings.'

'Aye, aye!' cried one of the servants devoutly, before his fellows — agog to hear more of the family argument — could clap their hands over his mouth to hold his noise.

Reminded that they had an audience, Dame Meg immediately dispersed it. She scolded the servants back to work, shooed away Agnes and Betsy, glared at Ned Pye until he took the horses off to the gatehouse, and then addressed the elder of her brothers with exasperation.

'Gilbert Ackland!' she said. 'Walk anywhere you will in England, and you'll come to the shrine of a saint. Surely St Edmund at Bury, or St Thomas at Canterbury, would be pilgrimage enough for you? You cannot think of going so far as Compostella — what of your farm while you're away?'

'I leave my farm, and my wife Alice,' said Gib solemnly, 'in the care of my brother William. I know he will manage the one, and protect the other, until such time as I return. And if it should please God to take my life while I am on pilgrimage . . .'

Will was dumbfounded. He had never known his brother to make a jest, but he could not believe that he meant what he said.

'Don't play the fool, Gib! I know nothing about farming. And besides — '

'I showed you the management of the land,

331

yesterday,' Gib reminded him. 'And my foreman, Mat Fielding, knows what work the men must do.'

Meg confronted him, her handsome face flushed with anger. 'Enough, Gib! You cannot unload your duties on to Will — he must return to his studies at Gray's Inn. *I* will look after Alice, and manage the farm, while you make a pilgrimage in England. Compostella is too far. It's out of the question.'

Gilbert sighed, aggravating them further by his new-found patience. 'I am truly sorry to vex you, sister,' he said, 'and to inconvenience you, brother. But the oath I swore was by the Holy Cross of Bromholm, and I cannot choose but honour it.'

Silenced, Will and Meg looked at each other in dismay. *By the Holy Cross of Bromholm* was the solemn oath Gib had used to convince Will that he was not guilty of the bailiff's murder. It was one of the most binding of all oaths. Gilbert could not break it without committing a grievous sin, nor could they ask it of him.

Gib shouted to a servant to bring him provisions, and Alice eagerly offered to help. Meg took Will's arm and drew him aside.

'You are to go back to Gray's Inn, as you planned,' she insisted. 'I can manage

332

everything here — better than Gib, if the truth be told.'

'I don't doubt it,' said Will. He tried to speak lightly, though disappointment weighed him down. 'But I cannot in all conscience leave you burdened with Alice, in her condition, and with my daughter, as well as the farm. Especially not at this time of year, with winter coming on. No — I will stay for a few months, until Alice has recovered and the worst of the weather is over. Ned can fetch some of my law books, and I'll spend a virtuous winter reading them.'

Meg tried to argue, but he took her sternly by the shoulders. 'Enough!' he said. 'I am master here now!' And they both laughed, though in truth he found little enough to laugh at.

★ ★ ★

Ned Pye was holding the horses under the gatehouse arch, and looking glum.

'No doubt you heard?' said Will.

'Aye — you're staying here.'

'It won't be so bad, with my brother gone. And we sha'n't be imprisoned — we can ride over to Lynn, or to Norwich . . .'

'Ha! And to Swaffham on market day, I suppose?'

Will ignored the gibe. 'We always keep a good Christmas here, as you'll find,' he went on, hoping fervently that Julian's family would return to Oxmead for the festival. 'And as soon as spring comes — '

'Save your breath to cool your porridge, Master Will,' Ned advised him. 'This is where we part company. I'm off to London whether you come or no. I shall die of dullness if I stay in your poor little town an hour longer.'

Will was dismayed, but tried to hide it. 'Castleacre, dull? How can you say that, when we've had two murders within the space of a week! Aye, and discovered the culprits, between us.'

Ned shrugged. 'I've had small thanks from your brother for that. But there — servants are always disregarded.'

'Not so, for he's given me a purse for you!' It wasn't true, but Will acknowledged the justice of it; and if it would appease Ned, he was willing to make good Gib's omission.

The horses had begun to toss their heads restlessly, their bridles jangling. Ned, somewhat mollified, busied himself quietening them. More hopeful now, Will set about persuading him to change his mind.

'Come, Ned — you cannot leave me so suddenly, after all we've been through together! Think how I took you into my service, when you were looking for wages as well as adventure. Think how you saved my life. Think of our travels — the excitements we've shared — '

'Aye, and think of the good horse you were too miserly to buy me!'

'Ah! As to that,' said Will recklessly, 'I'll make you a promise. We'll go to Lynn horse fair, and I'll buy you whichever mount you choose, up to the quality of my own. But first — '

'First, Ha! I might have known there'd be something in the way.'

'First, you must ride to London and bring me back some of my law books. I'll give you a letter to take to Gray's Inn. And as an earnest of my pledge, you shall borrow my own horse for the journey. How say you?'

Ned looked at his master suspiciously. 'How do I know you won't trick me over my new mount?'

'How do I know you'll ever return from London?'

They were still arguing when the great bell of the priory began a solemn tolling, as preface to the Requiem Mass for Dom Arnold, sub-prior of Castleacre. The sub-prior — news of whose death had spread the previous evening from the priory to the precinct and from the precinct to the town — had died, it was said, by accident, as a result of a fall while going about his duties. And no-one who knew the truth would speak of it, for in 1530 the church was still the greatest power in the land, as King Henry and his mistress Anne Boleyn had cause to know.

THE END

STRANGER IN THE PLACE

Anne Doughty

Elizabeth Stewart, a Belfast student and only daughter of hardline Protestant parents, sets out on a study visit to the remote west coast of Ireland. Delighted as she is by the beauty of her new surroundings and the small community which welcomes her, she soon discovers she has more to learn than the details of the old country way of life. She comes to reappraise so much that is slighted and dismissed by her family — not least in regard to herself. But it is her relationship with a much older, Catholic man, Patrick Delargy, which compels her to decide what kind of life she really wants.

PAINTED LADY

Delia Ellis

Miss Eleanor Needwood was about to be married to a most unsuitable suitor when Philip Markham came to her rescue. He arranged for Eleanor to be in London for the Season, a guest of his sister, who decided that everyone would benefit if Markham married Eleanor. And thus the rumour started. The surprised couple decided to play along with the mistaken impression until a scandal-free way to end the betrothal could be found. But when Eleanor agreed to pose for a daring artist, the result was far more scandalous than any broken engagement.

IF HE LIVED

Jon Stephen Fink

Lillian is a woman who feels too much. As a psychiatric nurse, she empathizes with her patients; as a mother, she mourns for her lost, runaway daughter. Now suddenly she has a new feeling, that her house, one of the oldest in the small Massachusetts town where she lives with her husband Freddy, has been invaded, violated by some past evil. And then Lillian sees the boy . . .

A GOOD MAN'S LOVE

Elizabeth Harris

Hal Dillon and Ben MacAllister had been deeply affected by the appalling death of their university friend Laurie. Hal journeyed to Mexico to continue his anthropological studies, and there found distraction in his passionate affair with Magdalena. But was he inviting even more heartache? Ben became a wanderer. While working in Cyprus he had met English girl Jo Daniel, and, after a nomadic summer together, they travelled to England to embark on what promised to be a lifetime of marital bliss. But Jo discovers that promises don't always come true.

BLACKBERRY SUMMER

Phyllis Hastings

Debbie converted a wing of the old farmhouse into an Academy for Young Ladies. She hoped this would enable her to make provision for her children's future careers. But she could not foresee the disastrous fire or the regret and guilt she would feel for giving her youngest son to be reared by her twin sister Dolly. Next to the farm, Dolly's wealthy husband Christopher built an imposing mansion in the Gothic style, and planned to run a racing stable, but his schemes were doomed to end in tragedy.